Forever Moore

Frankie Page

With ♡ + steam,
xoxo
Frankie Page

Copyright © 2020 Frankie Page

The characters and events portrayed in this book are fictitious. Any similarity to real persons, living or dead, is coincidental and not intended by the author.

No part of this book may be reproduced, or stored in a retrieval system, or transmitted in any form or by any means, electronic, mechanical, photocopying, recording, or otherwise, without express written permission of the publisher.

The design was created with the use of a licensed stock images and fonts from:
https://www.stock.adobe.com
https://www.canva.com

Editor: Kat Pagan, Pagan Proofreading
Cover Image: 154519495, majdansky

This is for my husband and daughter...

Contents

Title Page
Copyright
Dedication
Introduction

Chapter 1	1
Chapter 2	7
Chapter 3	13
Chapter 4	22
Chapter 5	26
Chapter 6	31
Chapter 7	39
Chapter 8	45
Chapter 9	54
Chapter 10	58
Chapter 11	62
Chapter 12	68
Chapter 13	77
Chapter 14	84
Chapter 15	91
Chapter 16	97

Chapter 17	104
Chapter 18	109
Chapter 19	117
Chapter 20	123
Chapter 21	131
Chapter 22	137
Chapter 23	143
Chapter 24	149
Chapter 25	154
Chapter 26	163
Chapter 27	170
Chapter 28	174
Chapter 29	180
Chapter 30	187
Chapter 31	192
Chapter 32	202
Chapter 33	209
Chapter 34	213
Chapter 35	219
Chapter 36	226
Chapter 37	231
Epilogue	237
Works Cited	243
TBD Moore Family	245
Robbie	247
Cassie	255
Acknowledgement	261
About The Author	263

Follow Frankie	265
Frankie Page Book List	267

Introduction

Jax Harris has been in love with Tilly Moore for as long as he can remember. But timing has never been on their side. A dream career opportunity sent Jax traveling around the world but after a decade apart, tragedy has brought him home. Now that he has returned, he is not sure if he has the strength to leave Tilly all over again. But faced with life-altering choices, will he fight to stay?

Forever Moore is a full-length romance complete with a HEA, no cliffhanger, and no cheating. Note: this story is not suitable for persons under the age of 18. Potential triggers lie within this book.

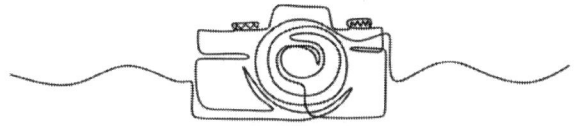

Chapter 1

Jackson

Standing on the beach, feeling the softest sand in between my toes, I stare out into the sunset. The shades of pink, purple, and gold bleed into the blue sky and reflect onto the crystal-clear water. The sound of my shutter clicking is nearly rhythmic as I capture images of the waves crashing—the sun setting in the background. All I can think at this moment is how much I love my job. I am visiting Oahu, not for the first time, to help take images for a resort that will be opening next month.

The last time I was here my best buddy and childhood friend, Scott Moore, was with me. It was pretty epic—we spent the entire week surfing, drinking, and going to amazing luaus. Working for a premiere travel magazine comes with many advantages; one of the best perks is the travel vouchers I get, which allow me to stay at luxury resorts and hotels for free. When my editor finally forces me to use up vacation time, since I rarely take any, Scott and I travel the world in style.

My phone begins to vibrate in my pocket; speaking of Scott and as if he had just heard me reminiscing, his name lights up the screen of my phone. Although it is great to hear from my best friend, it is pretty late for him to be calling. Back in Minnesota, it is past eleven at night. Granted that might not be super late to the average adult, Scott tends to get up for work at four in the morning.

"Hey, Scott. I was just thinking about you. Guess what? I am back in Oahu. Do you remember the last time we were here? Damn, we got into some shenanigans that week. What's going on? How have you been?" I don't get to talk to people too often and tend to talk a little too much sometimes. But I cannot help but get excited when Scott calls me. He is like the PB to my J.

"Hey, Jax." Something seems off; he sounds sullen. Usually Scott is hyper and on a permanent caffeine high.

"What's up, man? You sound a little off. Did you have too much to drink at Harper's again? You know how dangerous those buy-one-get-one Long Islands can be for you." For his twenty first birthday, we went to Harper's Bar and Grill to celebrate, and he found his love for Long Islands. Unfortunately, they do not love him back. The guy was a mess for like a week.

"Fuck, man, I don't know how to say this." I can hear the strain in his voice. This doesn't sound like off-the-wall-drunk Scott. Something is truly wrong.

"Hey, what's going on, Scott? You are starting to worry me." I stay on the phone waiting. There is a pregnant silence. I look down to see if Scott is still on the line—yep, his name is still there, flashing on the screen. "Seriously, man, you are scaring me."

"It's mom and dad," Scott finally states. I can feel my heart plummeting into my chest and shattering into a million pieces.

"I'm on my way," is all I say before I hang up the phone. Nothing more needs to be said between us. Like I mentioned, we have this weird link. I already know he needs me to come home.

∞∞∞

    Thirty hours, four planes, and an hour and a half cab ride later, I am finally home. It's been at least a decade since I've been back to Tral Lake. Staring at the two-story farmhouse that I used to call home, I feel like an asshole for staying gone for so long.

    I'm not sure how much time has passed as I stand outside the front door. But when the screen finally swings open, Scott is clutching the brass knob, stoic as ever. His six-foot-two frame fills the doorway—all of the Moore men are built like linebackers. Fortunately for me, it is a trait I inherited from my family as well. Scott and I could almost pass as twins. The only significant difference between us is he has green eyes while I have blue, and his hair is a shade or two darker.

    "Are you going to stand out there all night like a creeper, or are you going to man-up and come in the house?" Fuck, I've missed Scott. One of the things I love about him the most is his no BS attitude—he has no filter.

    I slowly climb the steps to the porch, taking in Scott's appearance up close. His eyes lack their usual brightness. Normally, they are a shade of emerald, both glowing and vibrant. But now the color has dulled to an almost gray, and dark bags underline each, as though he hasn't slept in days. I've never seen him so broken. We stare at each other for a few moments before I drop my luggage on the porch and give him a big hug.

    After a few moments, we finally break apart and enter the home I haven't seen in so long. Nothing has really changed—maybe a few new pictures on the wall, a bigger TV and newer recliners. But otherwise, it is still all the same. It even smells the same—ambered fig—Mrs. Moore's favorite scent for the fall.

    Robbie and Jake are slumped in the recliners, each with a serving (of what I assume) is whiskey in their hands—based off of the amber liquid in their glasses and the near empty bottle sitting on the coffee table. Fuck, this is bad. I knew it wasn't good, but I guess I didn't think about how bad it might actually be.

"Where's Tilly?" I can't help but notice that the petite Moore is missing.

As I ask, in unison, the Moore brothers each rub a hand over their faces. It would be funny, if it wasn't for the situation. After a few minutes, Robbie finally speaks up, one hand now massaging the back of his neck. "Upstairs, in her room."

I raise an eyebrow; this doesn't sound like Tilly. I would have assumed she would be downstairs with her brothers. Especially if there is some sort of family emergency. It isn't like Tilly to be away from her family. When Robbie broke his knee in high school playing football, Tilly refused to leave his side and took care of him the whole time, making sure he had everything he needed. She was only eleven.

Jake, realizing the look on my face, speaks up. "She hasn't left her room since we came back from the hospital." I notice how distraught Jake appears, and not just because of his parents, but because of Tilly. While I joke that Scott and I have this strange twin-link going on, Jake and Tilly are actual twins. It is almost scary how in tune they both are to each other. When Scott, Jake, and I went bike riding one day, he ended up falling and skinning his knee pretty good and was crying. Without calling her, Tilly came running down the street sobbing for her brother. We were over a mile down the road. There was no way she could have known that he had fallen and gotten hurt.

"What exactly happened?" Despite the gnawing feeling in my gut, I have been too afraid to ask for the details—it would make this all too real. I already knew based off of Scott's tone when he called, that whatever happened was going to be bad. I just really hoped, that for once, that bad feeling I had was wrong.

The brothers all glance between each other, using their brotherly telepathy to decide who is drawing the short stick, and has to explain what the hell is going on. Robbie is the unfortunate loser in that draw. "They were driving back from some sort of convention in Minneapolis. And a drunk asshole running a red-light T-boned them." Taking a seat on the couch next to Scott, I grabbed the bottle of whiskey on the table to chug down the remnants. The sting of the liquor is not enough to numb the pain I feel in my heart. The flames of fury burn within Robbie's amber eyes. His fists keep clenching and unclenching as he tries to continue. "Dad... he died instantly on the scene. Mom and Tilly were rushed to the hospital—"

I feel the blood rush from my face. I must be as pale as a ghost. Tilly was involved in the accident... Panic over that realization quickly settles in. "Wait, Scott, you didn't mention anything about Tilly? Fuck, she was in the car? Is she okay? How bad is it?"

"You didn't give me much of a chance to explain," Scott states matter-of-factly, shrugging his shoulders before taking another sip of his whiskey.

Robbie swirls the amber liquid in his glass before continuing, "Mom made it to the hospital, but was gone by the time we got there. Tilly needed surgery; her arm got broken during the accident. She is pretty banged up, but it will all heal, at least physically."

"We were able to take her home this morning," Scott adds. "Emotionally, she is a wreck—she has barely said a word to us. We have tried to go to her a few times, make sure she eats and what not. But she just lays in bed, not saying a word."

"I've tried everything. Letty was even over not too long ago. But she just won't talk to us," Jake says, sounding dejected. "She won't talk to me." I can't imagine what he must be feeling. Not only losing his parents... but his sister being practically catatonic and he, of all people, not being able to reach her. If Jake cannot connect with Tilly, it is bad. I stand up from the couch and make my way to the stairs.

"Where are you going?" Scott asks.

"I'm going to check on Tilly." I don't wait for a reply. I continue climbing the familiar stairs I haven't walked up in so long. Making my way to Tilly's room, I pass numerous pictures of the Moore family and myself, most of which were taken by me. I can't help but smile. She still has the sign I gave her on her fourteenth birthday hung up on the door. It was nothing fancy, just a simple sign I had made in shop class that said "Tilly".

Opening the door slowly, I slip inside her room before gently shutting it behind me. Tilly is lying on her side, curled up and looking smaller than usual. Not physically, Tilly has always been petite just like her mom. But even at five foot four, she was never small. Her personality stood tall and her presence was big. In spirit, Tilly has always towered over us.

It is difficult to see her well in the dark, but I notice the large cast on her right arm. Her long blonde hair is piled on top of her head. I see the hints of some sort of tank top, while the rest of her is covered by her blankets.

Carefully, I lift up her covers and crawl into bed, snuggling in behind her. I wrap my arm around her waist and pull her close, being mindful of her injury. I take in the smell of her hair—mangos and coconuts. Tilly startles for a moment as she feels me at her back. She must have been asleep or she didn't notice me enter the room. I shush her. "It's okay, Tilly. I'm home."

Tilly immediately starts sobbing, sinking into me. I just hold her, attempting to pass any strength I have into her. I don't bother with trying to talk to her. I know Tilly will talk when she is ready. Right now, she needs me to anchor her so she can fall apart. After she is done, I will help her put herself back together again.

Chapter 2

Matilda

I wake in my familiar room. I do not remember how I got here, nor do I know how much time has passed. Everything feels like a blur. A terrible nightmare that I am only able to recall bits and pieces of. I can still hear the sound of metal crunching. The feeling of spinning like on a tilt-a-whirl. The blood-curdling screams. All things that I would honestly prefer to forget.

The feel of a warm, hard body shifting alongside my back causes me to panic for a moment. I know it is a male based off of the sound of his breathing. As best I can, I slowly turn to see who has invaded my bed. It is difficult to do with this stupid cast on my arm, but I finally manage. And oh my god, I cannot believe who I am looking at… Jackson Harris.

I haven't seen him in forever, not since I was eighteen—the summer before I went off to college. He looks so handsome, not that he wasn't always attractive. But age and maturity have been good to him. His brown hair has sun-kissed highlights, the sides are short while the top is long enough to run my fingers through and push back, and he is sporting two-day-old stubble. I notice the hint of laugh lines; at least I know he has been happy in his travels.

As I stare at him, the memories of last night come back to me. I remember him startling me awake when he pulled me into his hard chest. His warm breath tickled my ear when he whispered that he was home. The second that I heard his voice I broke down. All the tears I had been holding in, finally forced themselves from my eyes. God, the first time we see each other in a decade and he has to witness me fall apart.

Maybe he is not really here? Perhaps this is all just part of that horrible nightmare? And any moment, mom will storm in here wondering why I am still in bed. I'll walk downstairs and see dad sipping his coffee while reading the paper. Because, honestly, my life is too average to have anything this tragic happen. Things like this don't happen to normal people.

I turn my body more towards him and caress his face with my good hand. He feels real enough though. I know it is weird, but I cannot help but lie here, lightly running my fingertips up and down his face like a total creeper. I haven't seen him in so long. But I shouldn't be surprised. I am guessing that as soon as he heard, Jax dropped everything to come home. I just wish he was here under better circumstances. I wish he was here visiting because he missed us, missed me. But no, he is here because everything is falling apart.

His eyes slowly open, the cerulean blue reflecting back at me. He has always had the prettiest eyes I have ever seen. I could lie in this very spot and look into them for hours.

"Hey," he says lightly. All I do is continue to stare and get lost in his mere presence, because anywhere is better than here right now. There is so much I want to say to him, but the words seem caught in my throat.

We don't move, choosing to gaze into each other's eyes instead. I wonder what mine are showing him? I continue to run my fingertips over his face, learning all the new lines and features he possesses, while he lightly strokes my arm. It would tickle... if I could feel anything. His hand raises to tuck loose strands of my hair behind my ear.

"Tilly," he whispers as he leans forward and kisses my nose lightly, nothing sexual just familiar. "You know I love you, right?"

I nod in response, giving him a curious look.

"And because I love you, I need to tell you... that you stink." I stare back at him, completely caught off guard. Only Jax would think to say such a thing to me right now. I am not sure how it happened. But all of a sudden, I cannot hold it in and I burst out both laughing and crying at the same time.

Laughing hurts, and I end up wincing from the pain. Jax notices this. "Shit, sorry, are you okay?"

I wipe the tears from my eyes. God, I must look like a total psychopath right now. I finally calm down and stop laughing. I still cannot find the words to respond to him, so I just nod letting him know that I am okay.

He gives me one more kiss on the nose, before getting out of bed and stretching his arms above his head. God, he is tall... I shouldn't be so amazed by his height, given that my father and my brothers are all over six-feet tall. His black T-shirt lifts a little bit, and I notice the V that points down to his low-hanging sweatpants. He definitely has been staying in shape. I start to feel that familiar ache in my lower belly.

I turn away from him—*what the fuck is wrong with me*? My father isn't anything anymore... because my father is gone. Both my parents just died, and here I am getting all lusty over Jax. Jax, who I haven't spoken to in ten years. I quickly get out of bed and rush to my bathroom, slamming the door behind me. The mixture of guilt and anger I'm feeling is starting to bring back the tears, and he cannot see me breakdown again.

"Tilly, are you all right?" Jax asks from the other side of the door. I can tell he is standing there, waiting for my reply. "Please, talk to me. Let me help you," he pleads.

I shouldn't have looked at myself in the mirror. I expected that I would look like shit, but I had no idea it would be this bad. My hair is a total rat's nest, and my face is covered in varying shades of purple with some specks of dry blood. All, while my eyes are red and puffy from crying—*god, I can't believe Jax saw me like this*. And this god-awful cast feels like it weighs a hundred pounds. Removing my shirt, I notice more bruising on my shoulder, above my broken arm, and down lower on my ribs.

Jax gently knocks on the door again. "Tilly, are you okay?" I turn on the shower. Luckily, it seems like he finally gets the hint when he says, "I will be downstairs when you are ready."

I strip down, and I am about to enter the shower when I remember this stupid cast. I've never needed one before, but I recall something about not getting it wet. I look under my bathroom sink and find the stockpile of small trash bags I keep there. Quickly covering my bandaged arm as best I can, I close the curtain and enter. Hopefully the scalding water can help wash away some of this dread.

After cleaning up and putting on fresh clothing, I debate whether or not I should just go back to bed. But the sudden audible growl of my stomach tells me I need to go downstairs and eat something.

Standing in the kitchen doorway, I look in at my brothers and Jax. Robbie, Jake, and Jax are sitting at the counter drinking coffee and eating; while Scott is at the stove making pancakes. It reminds me of when we were younger. Although mom was an excellent cook, weekend breakfast became Scott's thing. He would always whip us up a giant feast every Sunday morning.

As I think back on those times, I find myself smiling, but then the reality of the situation hits me like a ton of bricks. The guilt and grief begin to wash over me again, as I grasp the door frame for support. Jake notices me first. Likely sensing my breakdown, he rushes over to help steady me.

"Hey, Tilly, are you okay? Come on, you need to sit down." He pulls me over to his chair at the counter where a fresh stack of pancakes sits. They smell divine, but I don't think I have it in me to eat. "Why don't you take my pancakes and I will get the next batch."

I start to shake my head when he replies, "Please, Tilly, you need to put something in your stomach." I can see the desperation in his eyes. Jake is a firefighter, a first responder. It is in his nature to care and nurture. Seeing me so broken must be killing him.

While I do not feel like I deserve to eat—it isn't like mom or dad will ever get to have pancakes again—I do it for him. I cannot stand hurting him more than I already have.

The guys remain quiet as I slowly pick at my plate. I feel like the giant elephant in the room. I just don't know how to act around everyone. The silence is finally broken by Robbie when his phone rings.

"Hello...Thank you, Mr. Jenkins. I will stop by later today to finalize the details." Robbie puts his phone back in his pocket and rubs a hand over his face.

"What was that about?" Scott inquires while making a new stack for Jake.

"It was Mr. Jenkins from the parlor. He was letting me know everything was all set for the funeral this Friday. I just need to go in and sign a few things today."

"Oh," Scott replies. Everyone continues to sit in silence.

I can't sit here anymore; being around everyone is like a lead blanket suffocating me. I quickly stand, leaving my partially eaten breakfast on the counter. The once sweet golden rounds now taste like ash in my mouth.

"Hey, Tilly, where are you going?" Jax asks as I stand. I can see the sadness and concern on his face. I look around the room and everyone is staring at me—all with equally distraught expressions.

I know everyone is hurting right now, and that they are all worried about me. But it is not helping the situation. I want to smile at them, and tell them I will be fine. But I've never been able to lie to my family.

"I'm sorry," is all I can manage before I rush out of the kitchen and back upstairs to my bedroom.

    I lie back down and stare up at the plastic glow-in-the-dark stars my dad had hung on my ceiling. When I was little, I used to obsess about the stars. Whenever it was nice outside, we would always grab our gear in order to camp out in the backyard and sleep under the twinkling night sky.

    One morning before school, I mentioned to my dad how it sucked that we couldn't sleep under the stars every night. He gave me a big old smile and promised that if his princess wanted to sleep under the stars every night, she would. Later that evening when it started to get dark, my dad asked me if I was ready to sleep under the stars again. It was gloomy and raining out, so I didn't understand how that was possible. He just gave me a wink and asked me to follow him. As we approached and then entered my room, I became even more confused, until he turned off the lights. That is when I looked up and saw my ceiling covered in glowing stars.

    The dam breaks, and tears spill down my cheeks once again. It sucks how some of my happiest memories—those that I could look back and smile at—now, only cause me pain and sadness. Curling into a ball, I cry myself to sleep.

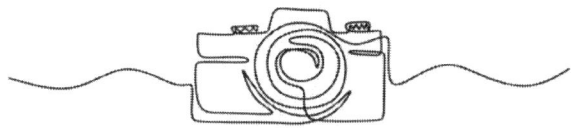

Chapter 3

Jackson

It's been almost a week since I've returned home. While I notice that Robbie, Scott, and Jake are still grieving (just as I am). I can also tell that the grief is starting to become more manageable for them. We have spent the last few days preparing for the funeral today, going through old photo albums and laughing at old memories. I know there were some tears as well, but we each did the manly thing, and excused ourselves to do some menial task to avoid crying in front of the others.

However, I do not think the grief has lessened for Tilly. Since I've been here, she has mostly confined herself to her room. She comes out at least once or twice a day to pick at her food. Then, the only thing she will say to anyone is "I'm sorry", which I still do not understand. What exactly is she apologizing for? My assumption is she is either sorry for being sad, or it is some sort of survivor's guilt, or both. All I want to do is wrap her in my arms and absorb every bit of her grief and guilt. But she has shut everyone out now. After that first night I slept in her room, she keeps her door locked.

While it sucks to see her so dejected, we have all agreed to give her some more time. Scott has the shop covered with Jake and Letty helping to watch over everything, so that Tilly can continue to mourn.

Tilly descends the stairs, looking thin and frail. The bruising from the accident has lessened, and I assume she has used some makeup as well (in order to minimize the appearance of the wounds). Regrettably though, her cast isn't anything that she can cover up, and it stands out.

As I look at her, I kind of hate myself. Even though she is frail and broken right now, she is still the most breathtakingly beautiful woman I have ever seen. I feel ashamed that my dick rises to attention whenever she is near me. That is probably the only good thing about her locking herself in her room. But it has made for some awkward moments while going through the family pictures, especially the beach photos.

The awkwardness is not because Tilly is "off-limits", or whatever bro-code nonsense people think. It is awkward because everyone is grieving, and it is not a good time to lust after a girl who is clearly heartsick right now. I've been attracted to Tilly, probably since forever, but I didn't really notice or acknowledge it until I was nineteen. But even then, it was a little weird because she was only fifteen. While four years isn't that much of an age gap as an adult, when you are young, it feels like a whole lot more.

Scott noticed the second I started looking at Tilly differently. I remember him calling me out on it when we came home to visit after our first year in college. He actually brought my feelings to light. It was confusing at first. I mean, I had known her since she was born and then lived with the Moores since I was twelve. I thought of Scott, Jake, and Robbie as my brothers, and they never treated me any differently. But with Tilly, no matter what I did or how hard I tried, I could never think of her as my sister.

Even though I knew how I felt, I never revealed it to her. I was away at college and only visited during the summer. It never seemed fair to tell her how much I cared about her, and then to turn around and be gone for so long. It wasn't until my senior year in college and her senior year in high school that those feelings came out into the open.

∞∞∞

Ten Years Ago
This is the first spring break I have been able to come home and visit. Usually I am stuck working and covering for everyone else. But since this is my senior year, I was given priority for some time off. As I stand at the kitchen counter bullshitting with Scott, I cannot help but glance over at Tilly. She is sitting at the dining room table wearing black leggings, a pink long-sleeve Henley shirt, and pink fuzzy socks pulled up to her calf. Her blonde hair is piled on top of her head in a messy bun, her face is void of makeup, and she is absolutely stunning. If it wouldn't be creepy, I would take a picture of her right now.

Tilly and Letty are giggling while going through some girly magazines. I have no idea what they are talking about. But all I know is she is glowing, radiating pure happiness. She must sense me staring because those giant whiskey-colored eyes look up at me. The sight alone leaves me breathless; because while she hasn't said a word, I know that whatever I am feeling, she is feeling it too.

∞∞∞

Present
"Is everyone ready?" Robbie asks, pulling me back to reality. We all nod in agreement and head out to Robbie's car. I'm not sure why we decided to pile into his car instead of taking multiple vehicles. But being cramped in the backseat with Tilly sitting in the middle, her leg pressed against mine, it was totally

worth it. I know... I know... It is wrong for me to be looking at her the way I am right now. But I cannot help it. Matilda Moore is my kryptonite, especially when her black dress rides up her thigh as she shifts in the back seat.

Tilly must sense me staring, since she looks up at me. I cannot see her beautiful whiskey-colored eyes behind the giant black sunglasses she is wearing, so I cannot get a good read on her. But I guess my staring isn't appreciated, because she sighs, looks down and pulls her dress back to where it should be. Then she doesn't look in my direction for the rest of the car ride.

The funeral is beautiful; most of the town is here today. Tral Lake isn't a very big town and the Moores were very well-liked people. During the service, the story of Robert Moore Sr. and Samantha Moore is told as a way to celebrate their life together. They had a very classic small-town love story—high school sweethearts, who got married right after graduation. Samantha was pregnant not too long after their nuptials. Instead of going to college or taking over his dad's junkyard, Robert opened the book store. Shortly afterwards, Samantha purchased the space next door and opened the cafe. They ended up connecting the two and developed Moore Books and Coffee. They had the perfect life... filled with a lot of love, joy and happiness. And they will be missed in this small town.

Following the service and the burial, the immediate family and friends gather at the shop. Townsfolk come to give their condolences to the Moore siblings. Well, most of them anyway. Keith McCalester is here, but his intentions are not so wholesome. This prick has been after Tilly since high school. It has always pissed him off that she wouldn't give him the time of day. He might be considered attractive—classically tall and muscular, dark hair, and blue eyes. But anyone who talks to him for more than five minutes realizes he is nothing more than a douche who relies on his looks (and mommy and daddy's money) to get what he wants.

When he approaches Tilly, it takes all my willpower to not punch the asshole in his pretty-boy face. Everything looks copacetic to the casual observer; it appears he is just there to offer his condolences. But when he leans in and hugs Tilly, he lingers too long and one of his hands travels too low to be decent. If Tilly was herself right now, she would have dodged the hug. He is absolutely taking advantage of her current mental state. Luckily, Letty notices the grabby asshole and politely shoos him off and avoids causing the scene I was about to make.

The remainder of the recession is uneventful, and fortunately it doesn't last very long. After it is all over and everything is cleaned up, Scott suggests heading over to Harper's—which seems like the best idea ever. I am amazed that even Tilly wanted to join.

At the bar, a few of the patrons give us their condolences but are respectful enough to understand that we just want to be left alone. Letty comes over and hugs Tilly for the hundredth time today. I think she is feeling withdrawals from barely seeing her best friend this past week. Those two are always attached at the hip, and it makes Jake jealous sometimes, which is absolutely hilarious.

While Letty makes sure to keep the drinks and appetizers coming all night, Scott, Robbie, Jake, and I all continue to reminisce at the table. After a few drinks, Tilly finally starts to loosen up a little bit. She still hasn't talked or added any stories of her own, but she has at least smiled and laughed at a few of ours.

I'm not sure how many rounds of drinks we have, but I know we are all pretty wasted, especially Tilly. She has barely eaten and likely has drank as much as any of us. Towards the end of the night, she is resting her head on my shoulder and holding my hand under the table. It feels so good to touch her again. Jake has smirked at me a few times, but hasn't teased either of us yet… like he typically would. He is probably too happy that his sister seems to be coming back to life right now, even if it is just a little bit.

It is finally closing time. Letty is kind enough to offer us a ride home, since none of us are in any sort of condition to drive.

"Can we walk?" Tilly asks me, catching me completely off guard. Everyone stops and stares at us, while Tilly just looks up at me, still holding my hand.

I glance back to her brothers, trying to decide what to do. Robbie nods at me in approval. I guess he is hoping the same thing that I am—maybe she will finally open up about her grief so she can start to process it, just as we all have been.

Tilly gives Letty another hug before we continue wandering down the main street towards home, hand in hand. It isn't an extremely far stroll, maybe a few miles. But when you are drunk, it seems like fifty. Tilly doesn't say anything as we make our way, but this time the silence feels comfortable. When we get to the driveway of the house, Tilly stops and I look down at her.

"I'm not ready to go inside yet," she says, looking at me and then upwards. It is a beautiful night tonight and the sky is clear. I know what she wants to do. I smile in return, kiss the top of her head and tell her I will meet her out back.

I run inside and see Scott sitting on the couch watching TV, presumably waiting for us. "Where's Tilly?"

"She is out back. She didn't want to come inside yet," I admit, kicking off my dress shoes and putting on my slippers.

"Oh." He seems confused. "What are you doing?" he asks, as I walk towards the basement door.

"I'm going to go get the gear." I smile back at him. Scott nods and resumes watching TV—he knows exactly what I have planned.

Tilly loves nothing more than sleeping under the stars. Growing up, whenever it was nice out and the skies were clear, Tilly would always sleep outside. For her tenth birthday, her parents got her this awesome pop-up tent, where the top can be removed and it is just netting which allows you to see the stars.

I grab the tent and bedding, then rush outside to meet Tilly. She is lounging in one of the chairs and looking up at the sky. I was always amazed she never wanted to be an astronomer or something, given her fascination with the stars. No, just like her dad, her true passion is books. I swear she has read almost every book in the shop. She reads everything too—she does not discriminate. I remember her even stealing Scott's and my comics to read at one point in time.

I quickly get the tent set up with a couple of sleeping bags. Tilly then joins me lying down. She surprises me when she snuggles up next to me, draping her casted arm over my chest. We lie there in comfortable silence, staring up at the starry sky. It is a little cool tonight; fall has officially started. But I guess growing up with Minnesota winters, forty degrees does not seem so bad.

"I missed you," Tilly whispers. I turn my head to look at her and notice her staring up at me.

"I missed you too." She gives me a faint smile. Though it is faint, it is genuine.

"Do you remember the last time we camped out in the backyard?" she asks, blushing.

Of course, I remember. It is something I will never forget... even after all of these years and being away from home, being away from her. How could I forget leaving behind the only woman I ever loved? Or the fact that she practically packed my bags and pushed me out of the door? Or the feel of her warm embrace, or how my lips traced lines across her soft glistening skin memorizing every curve and divot?

Ten Years Ago
Tilly and I are lying in the tent in the backyard, staring up at the starry sky. It is what we have done practically every night this summer, weather permitting. We are both naked and sticky with sweat. The sex tonight was different, more intense—likely because this is our last night together. Tomorrow morning, she is off to college, and then I am off to start my new job. As much as this job is everything I have ever wanted, having Tilly in my arms is so much more. I am not sure I can give this up.

"Maybe I can stay... look for work around here, even if I have to commute to the Twin Cities. There are a lot of marketing opportunities there," I bring up again. This has been a frequent argument as our departure dates approach.

"Jax," Tilly sighs. "Marketing would have been a good fallback career for you. But you managed to get your dream job. All you have ever talked about since you were a kid was how much you wanted to travel and photograph the world. That is exactly what you will get paid to do. It would be silly to give up that opportunity."

"I don't think I can leave you." That is the truth. A life without Tilly in my arms seems dull and without joy.

Tilly sighs and moves to straddle me. Her gorgeous breasts are shining in the moonlight. I proudly notice the love bites I left on her. "Jackson, I love you. And because I love you, I cannot ask you to stay here and give up your dream. This is a once in a lifetime opportunity. Besides, I am off to college tomorrow. For the next four years, you will barely see me."

I pull her down so her chest rests against mine, and kiss her deeply. As we pull apart, she keeps us together—forehead to forehead. "I know. It's just that I am going to miss you so damn much."

"I am going to miss you too, Jackson. But knowing you are out there living your dream—it will help lessen the sadness I'll feel. We will have our time together later. Right now, you need to do this."

We spend the whole night making love, memorizing each other's bodies. It is the best and worst night of my life. The sex is incredible and intense, but knowing it is my last night with her breaks my heart.

Present

Tilly leans up on her uninjured arm and looks down at me. Even with all the sadness, she is still just as breathtaking as I remember. Heck, maybe even more so now. Her features are defined, and her golden hair is long and flowing. She looks like a goddess with the stars behind her.

Tilly presses a tentative kiss to my lips. It catches me off guard a little, but I quickly return and deepen it, as I hold the back of her head. I feel her mouth open, granting my tongue entry. I have missed kissing Tilly. No one has ever come close to comparing to her.

Tilly starts to grind against my leg, looking to get friction. I want nothing more than to let my animal instincts take over, to throw her on her back and start ravishing her. But I know she is still grieving and injured. I need to be gentle, which is hard to do as she rocks against me. I carefully shift her so that I am on top and in between her legs.

"Are you sure?" I need to ask. While she has been drinking, I'm aware that she isn't drunk anymore, especially after our long walk home. But her mental state recently has had me worried. I don't want to push too far, or take advantage of her.

"Yes, Jax, please. I need you. I need you to help me forget, even if it is just for a moment. I need to feel anything other than the emptiness I feel now," Tilly pleads with me.

Chapter 4

Matilda

Jax is looking down at me, but I can't tell what he is thinking. I know I have been lost recently—heck, I am still lost. While it may be selfish and I don't deserve it, I just need to feel him inside me again… at least one more time. I need this connection. I know it is temporary, nothing with Jackson Harris can ever be permanent, but I will always take what I can get. Besides, it isn't like I can get any more broken than I am now anyway.

After a moment, and when I think he is going to get up and leave, he finally smiles at me. Whatever internal battle he was fighting must be over, because he resumes kissing me like I am giving him oxygen. God, no one has ever felt as good as Jax.

"I need you too, Tilly," he whispers between kissing me. "I'll always need you."

As he kisses my neck, his hands trail down my body and underneath my dress. He lightly caresses my skin with his fingertips, grazing past my underwear, up to my stomach and then to my chest. He massages my breasts over the cups of my bra. While this feels good, I need to feel his skin touch mine.

I try to reach down and unbutton his pants, but it is a struggle with this stupid cast on my right hand. He notices my predicament and smiles at me. "Sit up," he demands in a deep gravelly voice.

I do as he requests. He reaches behind me and unzips my dress, quickly pulling it over my head and leaving me in just my bra and underwear. Kneeling above me, he begins unbuttoning the black dress shirt he wore for the funeral today. After removing his top, he pulls his white under shirt over his head. I watch his hands travel down to undo and remove his pants, leaving him in just his delectable black briefs.

Jax has definitely gotten sexier over the years. Traveling has done him well. He has a deliciously lean and muscular body (like a swimmer) with those almost photoshopped-looking abs that lead to the perfect V, all the way down to his briefs, which contain a sizable bulge.

Laying himself back down, he resumes kissing me like a lustful teen. It is almost as if we are making up for a decade of missed kisses. I arch my back to allow his hands access in order to unclasp my bra. Finally, with it removed and my bare breast rubbing against his toned chest, the friction on my hard-as-diamond nipples is almost enough to push me over the edge as the aching in my core grows.

Seeming to notice how excited I am, Jax presses kisses to my neck, working his way down to my exposed breast. He takes one of my nipples into his mouth, while pinching and rolling the other between his fingers. He coordinates amongst both of my breasts, ensuring they each get the necessary attention they deserve. The sensation is overwhelming, and I come undone. My whole body tightens and vibrates, releasing its orgasmic buildup.

I am so lost while gently moaning his name that I don't notice him work his way along my stomach, before pressing his mouth to my mound through my underwear. Still coming down from my last orgasm, the light gentle kisses he is giving me now are going to set me off quickly.

I feel his fingers delicately roll my underwear down my legs, leaving me bare for him as I kick them off. His face drops to the apex of my thighs, as his fingers softly caress my lips. Slowly sliding one between my folds, he groans, "Fuck, Tilly. You are so wet." His comment only makes me wetter. "I'm barely holding on by a thread here, but I cannot survive the night if I don't properly taste you first."

The next thing I know, he is spreading me open and sucking on my clit. The experience is absolutely divine. I try to hold off the next orgasm, wanting to enjoy this as long as I can. But as he starts to pump—one, then two fingers inside me, rubbing my G-spot as he goes—I unravel again, whispering his name to the stars.

While riding out my orgasm, Jax rids himself of his briefs. I only catch a slight glimpse of his beautiful cock before he is on top of me, lining up with my entrance. It appears time has been generous in that department as well. It wasn't that he was ever small, but I do not remember him being so long or thick.

Jax enters me slowly, filling me inch by delicious inch. This is exactly what I needed, just a moment to feel alive and loved, even if it will all be over in the morning. "Damn, you are so tight, hot, and wet. I told myself I need to be gentle with you, that I don't want to hurt you. But, fuck, Tilly. I don't think I will be able to hold back."

I use my inner muscles to squeeze his cock inside me. He groans in reply. I know it must be complete agony for him and I cannot help but giggle. Then, he gives me the sexy, smoldering look that comes with a warning not to push him.

"Then don't hold back. If I feel any pain, I will warn you. Please, I need you. I need all of you Jax," I plead.

This must have been the right thing to say because next thing I know, he lifts my legs to rest over his shoulders before thrusting deep inside of me. The pain from the pressure is absolutely intoxicating. I love every second of it. It doesn't take long for another orgasm to hit me. I can feel myself convulse around his cock, which makes him groan more and continue thrusting.

He keeps fucking me hard through my release, dragging it out and making it the longest one I have ever had. I am not sure I can take much more. Sensing my exhaustion, Jax looks at me and smiles. Then he leans down and kisses me deeply while he thrusts, nearly bending me in half. It hurts my ribs a little, but the pleasure is enough to block it all out. I am sure my body will regret my choices tomorrow. But it isn't like I have anywhere I need to be.

"I need you to give me one more, sweetheart," Jax whispers against my mouth.

"I can't," I pant; the stimulation is almost too much.

"Yes, you can." Jax reaches between us as he continues thrusting hard and kissing me deeply. I feel his thumb as it starts rubbing circles on my overly-sensitive clit. Damn him, he coerces one more major orgasm from me, which triggers his own. I can feel his cock pump warm liquid inside of me, and it only continues to fuel the flames of my climax.

At this point, we are both exhausted and can barely move. Jax pulls out of me, slowly and carefully. The sensation causes him to shutter slightly. I forgot that his cock becomes almost ticklish after he comes. I always hated how he was never ticklish. But when I learned this little tidbit, let's just say, I got my revenge for all the times he held me down and tickled me when we were younger.

We lie there facing each other, both completely spent. He gives me one more kiss, before pulling me in close. I find myself nestling into his chest. For the first time since the accident, I am starting to feel a little better. The guilt and grief are still there, but for the first time in days, I honestly think I might be able to survive this.

"Thank you, Jax," is the last thing I remember saying before falling asleep in his embrace.

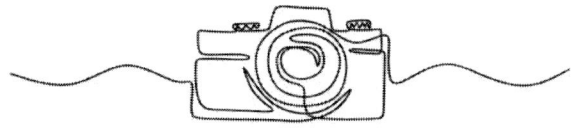

Chapter 5

Jackson

The sounds of birds chirping and the sun shining brightly wake me up. It seems to be the start of the perfect day, especially as I remember each sordid detail of last night. It appears my dick has started to remember as well, as he salutes the morning. I roll over trying not to groan. My back is stiff from sleeping on the hard ground. I guess spending all my time in luxury resorts has softened me up a bit. That, or I am getting old—I hope it is just the former.

As I stretch my arms, I notice Tilly is missing. My dick loses some of his height in disappointment. I don't blame him. I am disappointed as well. I didn't expect morning sex, given that we are in the back yard in broad daylight. But I wouldn't have been opposed to morning snuggles and some light fooling around.

Quickly getting dressed, I slip out of the tent and make my way inside the house. The sight before me almost stops me dead in my tracks. Tilly is sitting at the counter, wearing a t-shirt and sleep shorts. She has a full plate of breakfast that she is eating

—not just nibbling on, but full-blown eating. On top of all that, she is smiling and talking to Scott and Jake.

While I can still see a hint of grief in her eyes, it is almost like slowly, the real Tilly is coming back. I must have a big grin on my face because Robbie comes up to me and whispers, "I don't want to know the details of what you two did last night." He looks over at Tilly. "But whatever it was, keep doing it." He gives me a quick pat on the back, before returning to his stool to resume drinking coffee and reading the paper, and reminding me so much of his dad right now.

I make my way to Tilly, giving her a hug from behind and a light kiss on the cheek. She turns and smiles at me. "I'm sorry for leaving you alone this morning. I didn't have the heart to wake you."

Although I would have loved waking up with Tilly in my arms, I can't be upset with her right now. She looks so happy and at peace for the first time since I came back. I just smile at her, remarking, "No worries." I give her one more kiss on the cheek, before sitting on the stool beside her.

Jake gives me a knowing smirk and, when Tilly isn't looking, a celebratory thumbs up. I look over at Scott, and I am a little surprised when he doesn't give some sort of nod of approval. It isn't that he is giving me any indication of his *disapproval*. Instead, it appears as though he is conflicted over the matter—which, to me, is surprising. Scott is the one who was my cheerleader when Tilly and I finally got together way back when. Maybe I am just reading into things. I need coffee—*that is probably it.* Coincidentally, our "twin-link" must be working because all of a sudden, Scott is passing me a cup of delicious nectar.

"So… any plans for today?" Scott asks Tilly.

Tilly looks up at Scott with her mouth full of food. She almost looks like a chipmunk with her cheeks puffed out—she is too damn adorable. Tilly quickly finishes chewing then swallows, before smiling at Scott. "Actually, I think I might go into the shop today. I dread seeing what condition it is in."

"Hey," Jake quickly adds, pretending to be offended by the

comment. "The store has been doing great under my care. Honestly, I might quit the station and take over the shop. I think it might be my true calling."

Tilly and Jake both burst out laughing. For as much as they are alike, they are also very different. Jake cannot stand reading. He is more of a movie and TV kind of guy. Whereas Tilly's ideal vacation involves a tropical beach and an unlimited supply of books. Hmm, maybe I should take Tilly away somewhere. I have a shit ton of time off saved up, and not to mention, multiple vouchers for resorts.

"Sure, Jake. Can you recommend a new book to me? How about a good nonfiction book?" Tilly challenges.

"Umm..." Jake sits, holding his jaw in his hand and pondering, as he taps his index finger. "How about *Lord of the Flies*? That is a pretty good one."

Everyone bursts out in hysterics, except for Jake. Tilly laughs so hard that she almost falls off the stool. "Do you even know what nonfiction means?"

"Yeah, duh, it means real," Jake scoffs.

"So, you mean to tell me, you thought *Lord of the Flies* was based on a true story?" Robbie adds, raising his eyebrow at his youngest brother.

"Well, of course. Fiction is all that fantasy made-up stuff. People crashing in planes and being stranded really happens. Remember *Alive* and those guys who got stuck in the mountains?" Jake defends his suggestion.

Realizing that he is serious, Tilly finally stops chuckling. "Jake, sometimes a fiction story can be plausible. Just because it doesn't have witches and fairies, it doesn't mean that they are all based on true events."

Jake seems baffled by this. "Hmm, that's not good."

Tilly looks concerned. "Why? What is not good?"

"Well, a couple of days ago, some kids came in from the middle school looking for a book suggestion." Tilly starts shaking her head knowing exactly how this story will go. "They needed to do a book report on a nonfiction novel. I remembered how good that book was, even though the movie was better. Anyway, I suggested that title to them and also let them know about the movie—in case they wanted to watch it and pretend that they read the book."

I can practically see the steam shooting from Tilly's ears. "First off, the book is way better than the movie. Second, almost no movie or show is made in a direct replica of the word version. So, if some poor kid chooses to write about the movie they watched, instead of reading, they are going to fail. Third, they are going to fail anyway, because the book is fiction." Tilly pauses for a moment, considering her next words wisely. "Jake, I appreciate all the help you have provided this week. I cannot imagine that it was easy, given your shifts at the station. But please, never ever work at the bookshop again."

Jake scoffs, crossing his arms over his chest and mocking that he is offended. "Fine."

Tilly lets out a deep breath. "Besides, I was thinking we should expand the shop anyway. Or cut down on those old dusty books and add a video section. We will make more money that way," Jake says, trying to add fuel to the fire.

"Are you kidding me? Video stores are totally extinct because of streaming media." Tilly immediately dismisses the idea.

"Yea, but streaming doesn't have everything. And you can only have so many subscriptions. Also, we live out in the middle of nowhere, and our internet is far from reliable. The wind blows or it's a cloudy day and everything shuts off. The box thing is nice for new movies, but what happens when you want to binge on old stuff? Remember back in the day? Going to the Movie Gallery: five movies, five nights, five dollars. We would binge those old horror and action flicks. Also, I hate to break it to you, sis. But with all these e-books, no one wants to buy dirty old books anymore. They take up too much precious space."

"How dare you?" Tilly seethes, now truly insulted by her brother. "Books are a precious commodity. The printed word will never die. Your video stores died out because the consumers moved on to something better. While people enjoy e-books, there is something special about owning an actual book. Especially when it comes to collectors, first editions, and author-signed copies."

"Okay, nerds. Quit your bitching," Scott interjects. "Jake, the bookstore is not going anywhere or changing."

"See?" Tilly smugly interrupts, then sticks her tongue out at Jake. Scott holds up his hands, stopping her.

"But, Jake, you do have a good point. We do live out in a rural area with poor bandwidth for streaming media at a decent quality. I miss the rental place, and I think enough people in town could be interested in that business." Scott states diplomatically; he is usually the one to break up fights between the twins.

"See?" Jake looks at Tilly, mimicking her by sticking his own tongue out.

Tilly huffs, "Fine." Before she concedes, "It isn't the worst idea, Jake. But you are not touching the books."

Sitting here, and watching the Moore siblings bicker, makes me realize just how much I have missed home. I love my traveling and I love my job. But honestly, it is starting to get old. I realize how alone I have been, especially now that I am in the same room with everyone again. A majority of my relationships are via email or phone calls. Girlfriends are not an option. Though truthfully, there is only one girl that I have ever wanted to tie myself to, and she is right here in the-middle-of-nowhere, Minnesota. I'm not saying that I've been celibate this past decade. But they were nothing more than the casual vacation hookups, used to satisfy a craving for the one thing I couldn't have.

I don't know. Maybe it is time I started looking to put my roots down somewhere. Life is short. Mr. and Mrs. Moore have been a grim reminder of that. Also, right now, I am starting to worry that one day I will wake up and be old and alone... with nothing but the memories of all the traveling I did by myself... and filled with regret over the life I could have had with Tilly. But didn't.

Chapter 6

Matilda

As I open the doors to Moore Books and Coffee, it feels as though I haven't been here in ages. I know it has only been a week, but it seems like a lifetime ago. I guess, in some ways, it was. The last time I was here, dad and I were working together on inventory. Although dad still worked at the shop, he ultimately passed it down to me years ago. He knew that out of the four of us, this was my dream.

As a little girl, I used these books to travel the world, explore different time periods, and visit different planets and universes. I have lived many lives, have had many loves and many heartaches within the pages of this store. Jax and I always had that in common. Except he wanted to escape and see this world, while I wanted to escape and live within the ones these pages offered.

I have lived hundreds maybe even a thousand different lives. And yet, when the book shuts, I am ultimately alone. I had my parents. I have my brothers and Letty. But it really isn't the same. While I love my fantasy worlds, I understand they are just that—fantasies. They are not real. I've had a few boyfriends over the years, but not as intense as Jackson. Then again, can anything ever truly be as intense as your first love? Or should I say— my *only* love, besides reading, that is.

The bell chimes overhead, signaling the front door has opened. I can smell her Victoria Secret Love Spell body spray before she is even near me. Not that it is a bad smell, but Letty has been wearing the same body spray since junior high. I remember she bought a bottle on our first trip to the Mall of America, and has not worn anything different since. The next time we went to a mall that had the store, she ended up buying eight more to ensure she would never run out.

I feel her arms wrap around me. "Oh my god, Tilly, I have missed you sooooo much."

I turn around and embrace her as well. "You know I saw you yesterday, right?" I sigh, "I missed you too, Letty. Thank you for helping at the shop while I was… well, you know."

"Absolutely, I would do anything for you. Even tolerate Jake for a whole week," she says, winking at me. Those two have always had a love-hate relationship. I think they are both jealous of each other.

"Anything interesting happen while I was gone?" I ask as I start walking around the store, tidying up.

"No, not really. The sales were pretty good. We sold a couple of the higher priced collector books to some tourists passing through," Letty mentions, while taking a sip from her tumbler.

"Oh, that is good. Those rarely sell," I reply while adjusting a few books on an endcap.

"Yea, so how are things with you?" Letty inquires, her voice laced with concern.

"I don't know." I pause and think about how to explain this. "I am still grieving and stuff but, I guess, today feels like the first day I have truly taken a breath since everything happened."

"Oh, hun. No one expects you to be one-hundred precent right now. Grief takes time. How much time—well, it is unique to each person. But just know I will be with you, and do everything I can to help you along the way."

I give Letty another big hug. "Thank you, Letty. I love you so much."

"I love you too, Tilly. Now, speaking of love, how was last night? I noticed you and Jax seemed pretty cozy." Letty waggles her eyebrows at me.

I can't help but blush, thinking of last night. It was absolutely amazing and exactly what I needed. Letty and I have never shied away from sharing our sex lives with each other. So, we sit down behind the counter drinking coffee as I recall each dirty detail.

"He must have a magical cock," Letty announces, a little too loudly for the shop.

I can't help but laugh and shake my head at her. "What do you mean magical cock?"

She pauses thinking about how to explain her thought process, something Letty and I both do. "How do I explain this without hurting your feelings?"

"It's okay, Letty. You won't hurt my feelings." Growing up with three brothers who teased and tormented me relentlessly and, not to mention, my dad who was always joking with me—well, let's just say, I have developed Kevlar skin.

She sighs, but then resumes. "Well, Tilly, since the hospital... you have been almost catatonic. That first day we brought you home, I was scared because you shut down, and I feared I would never see you again. Then, at the funeral, it was like you were not even there. For fuck's sake, you didn't even notice Keith's grubby hands on you. So many people tried to talk to you, but you shut everyone out. I was surprised to see you at the bar, but then I noticed you slowly coming back to us. I figured the alcohol was allowing you to lower your guard a bit and let us back in. When you asked Jax to walk home, I was so happy for you. You were finally reaching out to someone—even if that someone wasn't me. Then, hearing about your awesome sex last night and seeing you this morning, it is almost like his cock gave you CPR or something. He breathed some life force back into you."

I cannot help but smile, and I burst out laughing at her explanation. I fold over, holding in my stomach. It hurts to laugh, but I can't help it. Letty starts laughing hysterically as well.

"Whose cock can give CPR? I think this is a specialty I might want to get certified in. You know I am all about saving lives." Jake casually stands in the archway that connects the bookstore to the cafe.

"Sorry, Jakey. I am not sure you have the proper equipment for this type of life-saving. But don't worry, saving kittens from a tree is honorable too." Letty dismisses Jake, which she tends to do whenever she can.

"Jakey" (clearly offended by Letty's comment) starts unbuckling his pants. "I can show you just how proper my equipment is. Probably the most proper equipment within the county. Heck, the state even. If any cock is capable of life-saving, it is mine."

"Oh. My. God. Jake, stop undoing your pants. I do not want to see your ding-a-ling." I shiver in disgust.

"Fine, sis." Jake re-buttons his pants, walks over to the counter and leans in before whispering in Letty's ear, "Just so you know, Letty, I have seen Jax's *equipment* and I can assure you that mine is bigger and better." Jake steps back with a shit-eating grin.

"Jake, get out of here before I throw up. You have now given me too much of a visual when it comes to your *equipment*." I pretend to dry-heave at the comment.

"Well, this makes up for listening to my sister have, what was it? Three? Oh no, I am pretty sure that it was four orgasms last night." Jake counts on his fingers.

I sit there in complete and utter embarrassment at the thought of my brother, or brothers, hearing Jax and me.

Jake walks over and pats me on the back. "No worries, sis. I will make sure to give Jackie-boy a few pointers. Four orgasms is little league. If someone is going to bone my baby sis, he should at least be playing in the majors and offering her six per go."

"Jake. Get. Out. Now," I seethe.

Jake holds his hands up, as if he is innocent and not sure what he did wrong. "What? It isn't a big deal, Tilly. Siblings talk about orgasms all of the time. Not to mention, we are twins. Our minds are linked. So, when you get some, you send wavelengths to my brain telling me all about it."

"I think I am going to be sick," I say as I put my head between my knees.

"Seriously, Jacob, what is wrong with you?" Letty asks, completely offended on my behalf.

"Oh, come on, you guys. It is not fair to discriminate against me."

Letty starts laughing, "Are you joking?"

"No," Jake says, puffing out his chest. "Tilly, you only don't talk about your sex life with me because I am a boy. If I was your twin sister, I am sure you would talk to me about sex, no different than how you talk to Letty. And just like Scott, Robbie and I talk about our sex lives."

"Damn, Tilly. I hate to admit it, but Jakey-poo here, does have a good point. I am sure if he was your sister, you two would talk about sex all of the time."

I cannot believe these two. I look at both of them in shock and horror.

"Okay, you both need to leave. I have work to do." I'm over this conversation.

"Oh, come on, Tilly. Don't be such a sourpuss because I am right and you are wrong. Like always," Jake mocks.

"You are not right, Jacob." I cannot help but lash out now. "The fact that you are my brother and related to me *at all* makes thoughts of *you*, in any sexual manner, disgusting to *me*. Just like my sex life should be disgusting to you. I do not have a sister, but envisioning any of my siblings and sex is simply nauseating, and I doubt I would talk to a sister about it either."

"Well, that's not true considering you fucked Jax," Jake proposes.

"What. The. Fuck. Are you talking about, Jacob?" I say with venom dripping from my voice. But Jake was never the smarter twin—because he doesn't know when to back down.

"Well, dear sister of mine, Jax is our brother. He has been with our family since we were both born. I am sure, at one point in time, he has likely even assisted Scott or Robbie in changing our diapers, while helping out mom. Then, and not to mention, our parents took him in as legal guardians when he was what, twelve? And we were eight? So, for all intents and purposes, Jax is our brother. We might not share the same DNA, but he was raised alongside you, and no differently than Scott, Robbie, or I."

My anger has me too stunned to respond. I cannot believe my brother would put this shit into my head. Then, he decides to take my silence as agreement and adds the cherry to this shit-covered sundae.

"Also, Jax and Scott are practically identical twins. Even though he might not be your flesh and blood, you are still essentially fucking Scott." I want to incinerate the shit-eating grin he is sporting right now.

I grab the first thing within my arm's reach, which happens to be a stapler. Then, I chuck it at his big stupid head. It smacks him right in the cheekbone, and he stumbles backwards, holding onto his face.

"What in the actual fuck, Tilly?" Jake asks, looking down at his hand to see if he was bleeding.

"Leave. Now. I do not want to ever see you again," I demand.

"Come on, Tilly, you don't mean that. I am your favorite brother." Then, the fucking bastard grins that evil grin. "Well, I guess besides Jax, that is. I guess, technically, he is your *favorite brother.*"

For the next few moments, I must have blacked out. Because the next thing I know, I am sitting on top of Jake, punching him repeatedly in the face as he cries—just like the kid in that Christmas movie.

Suddenly, I feel strong arms wrap around me, pulling me off of Jake.

"What the hell, Matilda?" Scott asks, while helping Jake off the floor, Jax still holding me back.

"You are dead to me, Jake." I give him my ultimate death stare. "Dead. To. Me." The words feel like ash in my mouth as the weight of what I said sinks in. I consider apologizing or taking them back, but as I look from Jake's stupid face back to Jax's—the rage bubbles up.

Scott, realizing this is a serious matter, asks if Letty can walk Jake out.

"Sure thing." Letty takes Jake by the arm. "Come on, you big duffus. I gotta go start prepping the bar for opening. Why don't you come with me and I can get you some ice for that pretty face of yours?"

"Can I have a beer too?" Jake asks innocently, allowing her to lead him out of the shop.

"See you later, hun." Letty waves as she exits.

"What the fuck, Tilly? Why were you beating Jake into a bloody pulp in the middle of the store? Customers could see you from the cafe. Everyone came running when they heard the sounds of a small child wailing." Scott was obviously disgusted with the level of sibling rivalry that was displayed in our place of business.

Jax turns me in his arms and lifts my chin with his hand, forcing me to look at him. Fucking Jake. Now, as I stare at Jax (with the exception of his cerulean eyes and some other minimal features) all I can see is Scott. Did Jake seriously ruin Jax for me? The one and only man I have ever loved? *Just like you love your brothers,* my internal bitch adds. I cannot even look at him anymore... without feeling the need to vomit.

I push out of his arms. I notice the hurt and confusion on his face. But I cannot deal with this right now. I know this is just all of my emotions going haywire, because of grief—Jax is not Scott. He is not my brother. But Jake's ridiculous comments are too fresh.

Also, what future do I even have with Jax? He is going to leave me again. He will never stay. So, maybe Jake just did me a favor. Maybe, by opening my eyes to this non-incestual-incest, I can finally move on from Jax and find someone who will actually stick around to love me.

"I think you should go, Jax," I say pulling away from him.

"What? What happened? What did I do?" Jax's tone is laced with hurt.

"I'm sorry." I give him my catchphrase of the week, before walking to the backroom.

I hear him try to follow me, but Scott stops him—telling Jax to give me some time and to let me cool off.

But when it comes to Jax and me, there is no time, because it is always running out.

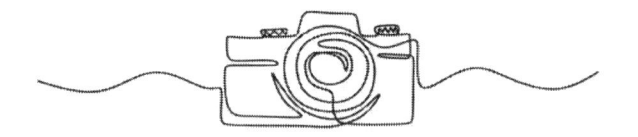

Chapter 7

Jackson

What the hell just happened? What did Jake do? Last night (even just this morning) I had my Tilly back again. She was looking at me—happy and in love—like she always used to. Then, I come into the shop to see her and offer to take her out to lunch (or at least bring something in) and I find her on the floor assaulting Jacob. It wasn't the play fighting they used to do as kids. She was absolutely fuming. She almost looked rabid as she foamed at the mouth. I have never seen so much fury inside of her before.

I realize her emotions have been all over the place this week. But rage like that was never Tilly's style. I know Scott said to give her some time, but I need to know what the hell Jake said to enrage her like that. Especially because (whatever he said) it had her looking at me with shame and disgust. A sudden shift, which makes no sense to me. Jake was literally giving me the thumbs up this morning. I mean, did things change so much over this decade that now they don't even want me with Tilly anymore?

No, that can't be it. I know Scott had a weird look on his face this morning. But Jake and Robbie were practically giving me high-fives. I need to find Jake and make him tell me what he did to piss off Tilly like that—then maybe beat him up a little more. Because I am certain he deserves it.

"Hey, man, where are you going?" Scott asks as I start to leave.

"Going to find Jake, and make him tell me what the hell he did to Tilly," I respond.

Scott starts to say something, but I don't hear it—I am already out the door and walking to the bar. I must look as furious as I feel, because as I stomp my way up Main Street, everyone parts for me like the Red Sea.

I reach my destination and violently push open the doors. The few patrons in here all look at me. It feels like the Wild West right now and everyone is waiting for the showdown. I spot Jake sitting at the bar with one hand holding ice and a towel to his face, while the other holds his beer.

I take a seat next to him. Letty offers me something cold from the tap. She seems to know that I am going to need it. "Don't go too hard on him, okay?" I raise my eyebrow at Letty, so she elaborates. "Jakey here, was being a dumbass and took it too far. I am pretty sure he knows that he fucked up and is now feeling the sting of regret."

I turn to Jake. "What did you do?"

Jake tries brushing it off with a shrug of his shoulders. "It was nothing really, just a misunderstanding. I forgot Tilly is a little touchy right now. She will calm down in a few minutes and come begging me for forgiveness."

"Ouch!" Jake yelps after Letty hits him over the back of the head. "What the fuck, Letty? Come on, you are supposed to be taking care of me. Not causing more damage," he wails, rubbing the back of his head.

"Don't you dare, Jacob Andrew Moore. I know you and Tilly like to joke around. But this time, you took it way too far. The only one in this scenario who should be doing any groveling or begging for forgiveness is you. Not only to poor Tilly, who we both know is going through a lot right now. But you also owe Jax one hell of an apology as well."

Oh no. "Jake, what did you do? Why do I deserve an apology *as well*?"

Jake finally looks guilty, as if his actions are now starting to settle in. He refuses to make any eye contact with me.

"Jacob, you tell him now. Or I will not only tell him myself, but I will cut you off from this bar indefinitely, *and* hold you down while Jax kicks you in the balls," Letty threatens.

Jake lets out a huff. "Fine, but I'm serious. This is all just a simple misunderstanding. I was only joking with Tilly... I thought joking around with her, like normal, would help her with her grieving."

"Jake, stop making excuses, tell me what you did?" I'm done with his attempts at beating around the bush.

"Okay, so I came into the shop to get my morning coffee order for the guys at the station. I like to bring them some even on my days off, because I am a good guy and all," Jake says, brushing non-existent lint from his shoulder.

"Get on with it, Jake," Letty scolds.

"Fine. Anyway, I walked in and those two were sitting there talking about how magical your CPR penis is. Then, Letty went on to tell me how my cock wasn't sufficient *equipment* to give CPR. So, I told her how I have seen your *equipment* and mine is much, much bigger and better," Jake says matter-of-factly.

"Okay, so? I am not sure why this would make Tilly punch you, or make you owe me an apology. I am comfortable with the size of my dick. My dick is a fucking champion, and there is such a thing as too big." I glance down at my groin and shake my head. Yea, no way will I ever feel insecure in that department.

Jake chuckles, and Letty just shakes her head. "Come on, Jake, get on with it. You know that is not why Tilly is so mad at you."

"I am trying to explain it all to him, so he sees how this is just an innocent misunderstanding." Jake holds up his hands in self-defense.

"There is nothing innocent about what you did," Letty scolds Jake.

"Fine, whatever. Anyway, Tilly got her feathers ruffled over it. Saying she doesn't need to hear about how wonderful my cock is. I told her she was discriminating against me because I was a boy and her brother." Jake rolls his eyes. "And that if I was a girl and her sister, she would talk to me about sex, just like she talks to Letty. Also, that it is only fair I mention how wonderful my cock is, since I had to listen to you give her four orgasms last night. Good job by the way, but I know you can do better." Jake leans over and gives me a congratulatory pat on the shoulder.

At this point, I am stunned, my mouth gaping open. Have I been gone for too long? Jake has clearly gotten dumber since I left. Only an idiot would say something like this to his sister. Unfortunately, I have a sneaking suspicion his story isn't finished yet.

Jake continues, "So, that made her get angry. She told me that it has nothing to do with my gender. That even if I was her sister, she would likely never talk to me about sex. Because talking about or thinking about sex with your sibling is wrong."

I can feel my face go pale as Letty slips another beer in my hand. I start chugging, because I know I am going to need a lot of alcohol. I can already tell how this story is going to end.

"I told her that can't be right, since she seems to have no problem fucking her brother—considering she fucked you *again*." Jake shrugs his shoulders. "Well, you *are* basically our brother. I get not by blood, but for fuck's sake, my parents treated you no differently than they treated any of us. They even grounded your ass, alongside Scott, when you two snuck out for that party. Anyway, she didn't seem to like me calling her out on her hypocrisy."

"Ouch!" Letty slaps him upside the head again. I'm still chugging my beer and trying to process what this idiot said. "What the fuck, Letty? I told him, just like you asked. Now get me another beer. I need to wash this pain away," Jake whines, begging Letty with his best puppy-dog eyes.

"Jacob, you know that is not all of it." Letty stands with her arms crossed, tapping her fingers on her elbow.

"Oh god, there is more?" I cry to the heavens.

Letty looks somber. I know she knows that whatever he is about to say, it is really bad. But I honestly cannot imagine anything worse than what he has already admitted. "Numb-nuts here, forgot the small detail of his story that officially sent Tilly into a state of pure rage and fury." I set my beer down as Letty takes a deep breath. "This fucktard here, decided to point out to Tilly that you and Scott are basically twins. So essentially, when she is fucking you, she is fucking Scott—who *is* her biological brother."

All I see is red now. It is the only color in the world that currently makes sense. I feel Jake pat me on the back, trying to calm me down. I hear him mention an apology and a comment about how she will get over it… that he was just messing around.

I turn to see Jake getting up, coming in to give me a makeup hug or some shit. I am not sure what comes over me, but I stand up and knee Jake as hard as I can in the nuts. I know the man-code states you should never hurt another man's balls, unless he is a sick pedophile or rapist or something. But in this case, I think any man would look past my indiscretion.

He literally planted the worst thing in Tilly's head he could have ever planted. I know Tilly… Right now, when she looks at me, she is only going to see Scott. And once Tilly sees something, she cannot unsee it. Like the time when she was a kid and she refused to eat brussels sprouts after watching *Earnest Scared Stupid* (just because Earnest made a comment about the "pods" looking like the gooey green vegetables).

"Fuck, Jax. What the hell, man? You don't ever kick another guy in the nuts," Jake wails on the floor.

Letty hands me another beer that I quickly chug. I am definitely getting tipsy now. I squat down next to him, and grab him by the shirt. I can feel this rage, a kind I have never felt before. I now understand why Tilly had the sudden urge to kick his ass.

"You fucking reject. Do you understand what you just did?

You know Tilly. You planted the most disturbing image and scenario you could in her head. She will not just forget this." I can see things clicking into place for Jake as his guilt finally presents itself.

"I'm sorry. I wasn't thinking, man." Jake tries to apologize, but I already know it is too little too late.

"Do you know how she looked at me before I came over here? She didn't look at me like she used to—she looked at me with shame and disgust. Also, I could see her heart was broken. I am not sure if she will ever look at me the same again. Not to mention, she was just starting to act like Tilly again, finally moving past her grief. I was helping her, and now she won't talk to me. Fuck, she won't even look at me."

I sink down to sit on the sticky bar floor, holding my head in my hands. Panic is starting to settle in. Jake scoots closer and puts his arm around me, trying to offer some comfort. "I am sorry. I was just joking around and I took it too far. Tilly loves you. She will get over it. I will apologize and also point out how different you and Scott actually look."

"Jake, please—*for the love of god*—do not try and repair things with Tilly and me. I'm already certain that you have done irreparable damage. I cannot afford for you to do any more than you already have."

"Come on. You are being dramatic, dude. I am her twin. We share a special bond. If anyone can make it better, it is me." Jake pats me on the back.

Letty comes over and sits on the floor next to us. She leans her head on my shoulder. "I am sure she will get past it, Jax. When she calms down, I will try and talk to her."

Chapter 8

Matilda

It has been a week since the "incident" at the shop. I still haven't talked to Jake. I cannot even look at Scott or Jax now. All that keeps going through my head is that I practically have been fucking my brother. Surprisingly, Jax is still here… though I am not sure why. He has been here for almost two weeks. I figured he would have gone to some far away tropical place by now.

I feel bad for shutting him out. I am sure this is something we could work past. But what is the point? He is just going to leave me. He doesn't belong in Tral Lake anymore. He belongs in tropical and exotic places that I will never see… and only ever read about. If I am being honest with myself, it doesn't matter anyway. I don't deserve him… or anyone really. Not after what happened with mom and dad.

"Okay, I cannot take this shit anymore. What the hell is going on?" Robbie finally speaks up, setting down his paper.

"Nothing," I deadpan.

"Bullshit, something is going on." Robbie motions to Jake. "No one is talking to Jake, and he looks guilty as fuck." Robbie gestures between Jax and I. "You and Jax look heartbroken." Robbie points to Scott. "Scott looks annoyed. You won't look at either of them. What the hell is going on? A week ago, everything was starting to get better. Then, almost immediately, you guys started acting like this," Robbie growls.

"Ask Jake," Scott comments. I know he is annoyed with all three of us at the moment. He tried talking to me about it, asking me to be an adult, but I just cannot look at him right now.

"Jake, what happened?" Robbie asks.

"Look, Robbie, I am sorry you feel left out. But it has nothing to do with you, okay?" I am too dead inside to relive all of the awful things Jake said. Besides, as soon as Jax leaves, everything will go back to normal. Well, whatever that means now.

"Excuse me, Matilda? It absolutely has something to do with me. This is my family, and right now, all I see is my brothers and sister sitting around angry with each other." Robbie crosses his arms over his chest. "Alright now, someone, speak up."

Scott, Jake, and Jax all take in a deep breath, knowing *brothers* was not the greatest statement to use right now—especially, in regards to Jax.

"Okay, what was that? I know there is something. If you don't start talking, I will make one of you talk," Robbie states, staring at Jake, knowing he is the easiest to break.

"Fine," Jake says, knowing he will be the first one tortured. "I might have accidentally implied that Tilly fucking Jax, is like her basically fucking her brother. Especially since Jax and Scott are practically twins." Jake points at Jax and Scott, as if doing so makes his stance obvious.

Robbie sits and stares for a moment, glancing at each one of us, before he bursts out laughing. "Are you fucking kidding me, right now?"

We all just stare back at him. It is crazy. I can't think of the last time I heard Robbie laugh like this.

"Are you all that big of idiots? Grow the hell up. Jax, *brother*, I may love you like I love Scott, Tilly... and I guess, even Jake. You may have even grown up with me like the rest of my annoying ass siblings. And you basically are one too. But when it comes to Tilly, you have never been *that* to her. You two have never treated each other like siblings. You have been making googly eyes at one another ever since you were both old enough to make googly eyes."

I go to say something but Robbie holds up his hands, stopping me and pulling the big-brother-in-charge card right now.

"Let me finish," Robbie states. "As far as Scott and Jax being twins—although you both look similar, you are not twins and you two do not actually look anything alike. You might share similar mannerisms because you have been best friends for as long as you can remember. But you, Tilly—you fucking Jax..." Robbie shudders momentarily at the image. "...is not you subconsciously fucking Scott. So please, you all need to get over yourselves, be fucking adults, and move past this. We are a family, and we need each other more now than ever."

We all sit for another minute. Jax is looking at me with pleading eyes.

"I'm sorry, Tilly. It was a shit thing for me to say. I honestly didn't mean it. I was just trying to mess with you and get you to talk to me like we used to," Jake says, like a wounded animal and while giving me puppy-dog eyes.

"I forgive you, Jake," I reply. Because I do forgive him. Robbie is right. We are just being stupid.

"Good. Let's not bring this up again. *Ever again*. I have filled my lifetime quota of discussing who my baby sister is fucking—I really don't want to think about it anymore." Robbie ends the argument.

The rest of dinner continues with light conversation. After everything is cleaned up, I sneak out to the patio. It is another clear night tonight and the stars always help calm me. It is getting too cold to sleep outside, but I still enjoy bundling up and gazing at them all the same. Part of me likes to hope, or believe, that mom and dad are up there amongst the stars and staring back down at me.

I hear the door slide open and shut. I don't need to turn around to know that Jackson is behind me. I can always sense where he is. Jax walks over to me. He sits on the end of the lounger, pulls my legs towards his lap, and begins rubbing my feet. I want to embrace his touch but, even if I let the whole brother thing go, Jax is still Jax. He can never really be mine.

"Are we okay?" Jax asks. I can tell he is nervous.

"I was never angry at you, Jax." I wasn't. If anything, I've been angry at myself.

"Okay. Well then, why do you feel so distant from me? I feel like you are pushing me away." Jax pleads for me to let him in.

This is going to be difficult. But I should probably just be honest. "Because I am."

I feel Jax stiffen, as he stops massaging my feet. But he hasn't dropped them yet. It is almost as if he is frozen in place, while he processes what I am telling him. "Why?"

"Because we both know what this is, Jax." He is only here because of what happened.

"Clearly, we are not on the same page. So, if you could catch me up, I would greatly appreciate it." Jax sounds offended by my accusation.

I pull my feet away and sit on my knees, facing him. He turns and takes my hands into his own, and almost subconsciously, he begins to trace circles on my wrist. It is too easy to melt into his touch.

"I am not naïve. We both know this is temporary and at any minute, you will be off somewhere exotic and I will still be here." I rationalize with him.

"Maybe I don't want to leave again," Jax says, shrugging his shoulders.

"I can't ask you to stay, Jax. I know how much you love your career. I am not trying to make you feel guilty. I am just being honest."

"I don't need you to ask me, Tilly. I am telling you I want to stay." He sounds vulnerable right now.

"I don't understand, Jax. I know how much you love what you do. I can tell based off of the pictures you take." I blush, realizing I have admitted to keeping track of his work.

"You read the magazine?" he asks with a knowing smirk.

"Yea, mom and dad subscribed when you got hired on. We used to sit together every month, read it and look at where you had been. It was nice. Sometimes it made me feel like I was with you," I admit.

"Which one was your favorite?" he inquires.

"I think the resort in Greece. The photographs you took there were so beautiful. But then, I saw all your personal images on your Instagram. The food, the clothes, the culture—it was amazing. Seeing all of that, I knew you were never coming back here." I feel a tear running down my face at that sudden realization.

Jax reaches over and brushes it from my cheek. "I thought you didn't do social media? How did you follow my Instagram?"

"Letty. We used to get together sometimes and scroll through your page. We decided to start planning a trip based off of your account. We figured who better to inspire our vacation than someone who vacations professionally."

He seems to ponder my statement for a moment. "Do you remember what you told me, when I asked you why you don't do social media?"

"Yea, because it is all fake. People only show you what they want you to see." I remember Jax and Scott leaving for college. They tried to convince me to open a Facebook account so we could easily keep in touch. I told them that if they wanted to keep in touch, they could call or text. The idea of taking time out of my day to snap a picture of myself or post something about what I was thinking or feeling—it just seemed ridiculous to me. I also noticed how everyone on there only posts half-truths. Trying to show everyone else how perfect they were. When in reality, they were just as much of a train wreck as the rest of us.

"Then you should understand that those photos were not telling the whole story."

"I know. I am sure that, while Greece was beautiful, there are still seedy back alleys and crime." I chuckle. I can't imagine an evil underbelly in Greece.

Jax reaches towards me and grabs the back of my head. He pulls my face closer to his, so we are nose to nose. "No, Matilda. Those pictures didn't show what I was missing... *how lonely I am.* Though I enjoyed going to all those beautiful places, I have realized how meaningless it all is... when I don't have anyone to share those experiences with."

I close the distance and begin kissing Jax. He pulls me into his lap and deepens it. As we continue kissing, I rub myself against his hard cock. I know it may seem juvenile, but I definitely enjoy making out and dry humping Jax like we are teenagers again. As his hands move down and start grabbing my ass, I know he enjoys it too.

"Fuck, Tilly," Jax whispers as he starts kissing and biting my neck. His right hand moves up and under my shirt, grabbing my breast over my lounge bra. Because there is no padding, he can easily feel how hard my nipples are.

"We should go upstairs, before one of my brothers comes out here," I say, noticing we are out in the open.

Jax reluctantly pauses his targeted ministrations. He then moves his hand back to my ass. He quickly stands, pulling me up with him and instinctively, I wrap my legs around his waist. While still carrying me, he walks us upstairs to my room. I don't pay attention to see if any of my brothers have witnessed us, because honestly, I do not care.

Once we make it to the room, I hear Jax fumble with the door before locking it behind us. As he sets me down on my bed, I stare back up at him. He is definitely the most handsome man I have ever seen. And at least, for right now and in this moment, he is mine—for however long it might be... Because, as I have recently learned the hard way, time is precious and not a second of it can be wasted.

Jax quickly removes my clothes and then his. Obviously, this last week has left him pretty pent up. He kneels on the floor in front of me—positioned between my legs—as he pulls each ankle over his shoulders, so that I am now straddling his neck.

"Lie back, Tilly." I do exactly as he demands.

Lying back, I glance down to where two mesmerizing cerulean eyes stare at me, Jax's mouth upturned into a small grin. I know he is about to torment me. Turning his head but still trying to maintain eye contact, he begins kissing my inner thigh. After a dozen or so kisses on one side, he turns and starts the process over again on the other. At this point, I am shaking with anticipation.

"Please, Jax," I beg.

He lifts an eyebrow at me. "Please what, Tilly?"

"I'm dying over here, Jax. Come on!"

He gives me a soft chuckle. "Is this not what you wanted?"

"You know damn well what I want. If you don't do it, I—" I am cut off by Jax giving me one long lick from bottom to top. I cannot help but moan. Once again, he has me so worked up that I know my orgasm is not far off.

He continues with these long, slow and agonizing licks from bottom to top, only occasionally stopping and pressing a light kiss to my clit. His intention is to build this orgasm, but not give me the pressure that I need to release it. I cannot take it anymore. I reach down and grab his head, as best I can with my good hand, and hold him against my clit.

"Someone seems a little greedy?" Jax muses.

"If you don't make me come in the next five seconds, I will make sure to give you blue balls for the next week," I threaten through clenched teeth.

Jax sits up a little and looks at me with a stern brow. "Tilly, you already gave me blue balls for the last week."

"Jax, please." At this point, I am legitimately begging him, something I typically do not do.

He finally grants me mercy as he begins sucking and lightly biting my clit. I am just at the tipping point, when I feel two of his giant fingers pumping into me.

"Oh. My. God. Jax." Finally, my orgasm breaks free in all of its glory. I can feel my body shaking and convulsing around his fingers, still pumping inside of me, as he continues to press soft kisses onto my clit. I am so worked up that this orgasm rolls into a second one.

I must black out for a minute while in the throes of ecstasy. Because now I am lying on my bed with Jax on top of me as he presses kisses into my neck, his cock nudging at my entrance.

"Tilly, that was probably one of the hottest things I have ever witnessed," he praises in between breaths.

Jax then moves into a deep passionate kiss. I am able to taste myself on him, and it only turns me on more. It makes me possessive, as if I am marking him with my scent. I am not sure why, but sex always seems to turn me into a cave woman.

While our tongues continue to interlock, Jax pushes inside me with one hard, deep thrust. It causes me to squeal… in a mixture of pleasure and pain. The feel of him fully sheathed is pure bliss. It is what I imagine heaven feeling like. This is my taste, reminding me to be good on this plane, so I can enjoy the same sensation for eternity in the next.

Jax begins thrusting in and out of me, slowly almost pulling all the way out, before slamming back in. He is still being mindful of my injuries, though they are more healed this time around. It is nice, that even in the throes of passion, he still is thinking of my well-being.

I feel the familiar build and push of my orgasm approaching. Jax seems to sense it as well, because he reaches between us to rub circles onto my clit. "Tilly, come now."

It is as if his command breaks my dam. I fall apart, attempting to strangle his cock inside of me. Jax continues thrusting deep and hard, like he is rendering little punches to my cervix. It hurts but the pressure feels good at the same time.

As my orgasm starts to calm down, Jax gives one more giant thrust and finally, I feel the warmth of his liquid exploding inside of me. Being that I am already so sensitive from my previous orgasms, this additional stimulation sets off another mini one. It is almost a spiritual feeling—us coming together. It is like my body is sucking the orgasm out of him, and then breathing it back out of me.

Tired and spent, we both collapse into the bed. Jax pulls me to his side, wrapping himself around me and lightly caressing the spot just above my cast.

"When does this come off?" he inquires.

"I go for a check-up in a few weeks. They said it was a clean break... that they were able to reset with screws. It could be five to eight weeks maybe."

"Does it still hurt?" he asks, continuing to lightly stroke his fingertips along my skin. My body feels so relaxed right now.

"No, not really. I mean, sometimes... after I've been working all day, I get exhausted and it causes the little aches and pains to hurt more."

He kisses the top of the shoulder he has been caressing. "Well then, let's get you some rest now, Tilly."

"Good night, Jax."

"Good night, Tilly," he replies, as we both drift off into post-orgasm rest.

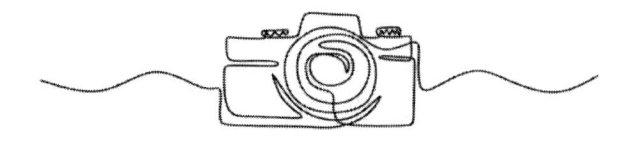

Chapter 9

Jackson

As the sun shines through the windows waking me, I glance around Tilly's room. It hasn't changed much since high school. Tilly still has a picture collage on the wall. She started it with the photographs I took with my first DSLR that her parents bought me for Christmas. It was the best gift I had ever received, and that camera was always attached at my hip. I captured still images of everyone and everything in town. But Tilly was always my favorite subject. Not in some creepy-perv way; she was still too young when I got that camera. But even as a dweeby little pre-teen, she was the most beautiful person I had ever seen.

Tilly is not only beautiful on the outside, she is also drop-dead gorgeous on the inside as well. This internal beauty radiates from within, causing her to have this soft glow about her. No matter what she was doing—painting her nails, reading, doing homework, curled up on the lounger and staring at the stars—she always looked like some sort of untouchable goddess.

I feel Tilly stirring awake, as she rubs her ass against my groin. If my dick wasn't alive a minute ago, he sure is now. I lean down and press a kiss to her cheek, before whispering in her ear, "Tilly, unless you are ready for morning sex, please stop."

A wicked grin spreads across her face. Maybe she is not a goddess. Maybe she is a succubus instead. She appears ethereal, but as soon as you are close, she sinks her talons in you and sucks you dry. Regardless, it doesn't matter to me. I will always gravitate towards her.

Tilly gets out of bed naked and stands before me. She stretches her arms above her head, looking delectable as fuck at the break of dawn. Not to mention, she has the kind of hair that says she was royally fucked last night. Knowing I did that to her sets me off inside.

I scoot off the bed and stand in front of her, showing her all of my morning glory. Her eyes go wide, looking down at how hard I am for her already.

"I think I am too sore to do much this morning," Tilly says, gulping a little bit.

I try not to look as disappointed as I feel. I am not upset. I know I was a little rough with her last night. And, well, I am a gentleman. I would never guilt her into taking care of my hard-on if she wasn't into it. Only a douche would do that. I can take care of myself in the shower—which has become a frequent routine for me since returning to the Moore household.

I lean forward and give her an affectionate morning kiss. "While having sex with you is always fun, hearing that you are still recovering from me last night… well, that is about the best compliment you could ever give a guy."

She smiles at me. Then, I look down as I feel her hand grabbing and rubbing my length. "I might be too sore to handle *this* right now. But I am not too sore to make sure you get what you need this morning."

Before I have a moment to reply, Tilly drops to her knees. She presses a soft kiss to my head as she strokes up and down my shaft. Tilly continues delivering those same feather-light kisses and soft licks to my cock. She is definitely teasing me this morning. I guess, I deserve a little payback for last night. But being on the receiving end of mischievous foreplay... it isn't as enjoyable as giving it.

I hear Tilly hum as she licks me from the base to the head. "I can still taste myself on you this morning." She practically purrs as she says it.

"Does tasting yourself on me, turn you on?" God, I am so close to coming and she hasn't even put me in her mouth yet.

"Yes, it is like marking you as mine."

"Fuck. Tilly, I am yours."

Apparently, that was the magic phrase because I am quickly rewarded with Tilly taking me into her mouth as far down as she can go. I can feel my head tickling the back of her throat. Tilly bobs up and down a few times and my balls tighten, ready to explode.

I reach and grab Tilly's head as a courtesy, letting her know I am about to finish at any moment. She seems to know exactly what I mean, because the next thing I know, she is taking me down her throat and squeezing my balls. I am a goner. As soon as she squeezes, I can feel myself emptying into her esophagus.

As Tilly sucks me dry, I enjoy the sensation of her swallowing down my load. The moment she slowly pulls her mouth off my shaft—releasing me with a popping "p", Tilly starts to lick me clean, causing me to shiver and nearly collapse to the floor. She knows how ticklish I am after I come, and she is purposely fucking with me.

I glance down at her. She is still kneeling, looking up at me and trying to appear innocent. "Oh, I am sorry. Are you ticklish?"

Before she knows what is happening, I bend and pick her up, tossing her lightly and unceremoniously onto the bed. I hover over her, pinning her down so she cannot escape. "I think you remember very well that's where I am ticklish. But if I recall correctly, so are you? And unfortunately for you, you are ticklish in a lot more places than I am."

"Jackson Lee Harris, no, you don't." She gives me her no-bullshit expression.

I lightly graze my fingertips along her side, causing her to shiver. "Please, Jax, no. I hate being tickled."

I continue softly tickling her side, getting closer to her armpit, fully aware that it will send her off. I know she hates being tickled. We used to torture her with it when we were younger. I remember this one time, Jake had chased her down the hallway as she was trying to crawl away, only to capture her and tickle her more. I thought she was going to pass out from exhaustion or something from him tickling her so much.

"Fine, Tilly. I will not tickle you." I see the look of relief on her face. *"Right now."*

Ha! She will be paranoid for at least a week, wondering when her time will come. Though, honestly, the only reason I am saving her from the tickling she deserves is because of that damn cast. When you tickle Tilly, she goes wild, thrashing her whole body. Knowing my luck, she will end up breaking my nose with that thing, and consequently hurting herself. So, she is safe, *for now.*

I give her a quick kiss on the nose, before getting up. If I lie on her naked any longer, my greedy dick will come back to life. "Come on, let's take a shower and get downstairs. It smells like Scott is making something delicious down there."

Tilly stands up, giving me a brief peck on the cheek, before shaking her ass seductively on her way to the bathroom. That little cock-tease. She looks back at me over her shoulder. "Are you *coming*?"

"In about two minutes, *you* will be."

She laughs, walking further into the bathroom and turning the water on. I follow her in. As we shower, I do make sure she comes at least two more times this morning. If this is what life with Tilly could be like, I am not sure I ever want to leave again.

Chapter 10

Matilda

Jax and I walk into the kitchen, hand in hand. Robbie, looking more like our father every day, sits at the counter drinking his coffee and reading the paper. Jake is seated at the end, shoveling food in his mouth. And (as always) Scott is at the stove, frying up some delectable-smelling omelets.

Scott is such an amazing cook. I hope we can expand the cafe soon and offer a full-service option. He already prepares baked goods at a commercial kitchen in town, which he stocks inside the cafe. But if we could get one of our own in the shop and offer a full breakfast menu, I know we would always be packed. With the exception of the diner, we don't have any breakfast eateries in town.

Scott is the first to notice Jax and I enter the kitchen. Glancing up, he smiles at me. But then, as he looks down at our joined hands, he scowls. Instinctively, this causes me to untwine our fingers. Jax doesn't appear to be aware of the weird look Scott is giving us.

"Morning, Tilly, would you like an omelet?" Scott inquires. He seems a little guarded right now. I will make sure to talk to him about this later.

"Yes, please. The usual." This at least gets Scott to smile. He proceeds to make me the best mushroom, spinach, bacon, and feta omelet.

Robbie clears his throat still reading the paper, or at least I think he's still reading it. For some reason, he is not making eye contact with me. "I think I am going to start staying back at my place," he announces unexpectedly.

I guess this shouldn't surprise me. I mean, he does have his own place. Not to mention, staying in mom and dad's old room must be weird. I know I wouldn't be able to sleep in there. I honestly don't think I could even step foot in there right now. I still remember when he first moved out to this little apartment above his garage. He said that Jake and I were annoying as fuck, and that he needed to get the hell away from us. Honestly though, I think he just said that to cover up the fact he was moving so that I could have my own room (when Jake took over his). I was fourteen, and it was a little weird still sharing a bedroom with my brother.

"Yea, I think I need to go back to my place as well. While bunking with Jax like old times has been fun..." Scott turns and gives Jax a pointed look. "...we are too old to keep sharing a room," Scott adds, rubbing the back of his neck and seemingly just as uncomfortable as Robbie.

The sadness and disappointment on my face must be evident. I know Scott and Robbie have their own places, and their own lives. And it's not like they are that far away. I see both of them almost daily, between Moore Books and Coffee and helping Robbie at the shop, balancing his books. But the thought of them leaving and knowing Jax will be gone soon enough, all while Jake is frequently sleeping at the station—I am just not prepared for how quiet and empty this house is about to become.

"Hey, Tilly, don't cry. What's wrong?" Robbie asks, taking on his role of a concerned big brother. Wiping a tear from my face, I look down at it. I didn't even realize I was crying.

Jax pulls me into his embrace. Though it is comforting, I know I need to hold back a little from sinking into him. It wouldn't be fair of me to depend on him, and then to make it a habit. When he leaves, it will end up shattering me. I'm broken enough as it is. I don't need to add another heartbreak to the situation.

"Sorry, you guys." I quickly brush the tears away from my eyes. "I don't mean to be all emotional. It's just... I am not sure I am ready to be alone here yet."

"Don't apologize, Tilly," Robbie says, rubbing my shoulder. "We aren't going to leave you alone. I will stay if you want me to. It is just that..." He rubs his hand over his face. "...I don't want you to take this the wrong way Tilly, but it is a little awkward staying here with you and... Jax."

This immediately makes me stop crying. I can feel myself turn beet red as I glance at each one of my brothers, getting the message *loud and clear*. Only Jake seems completely unfazed by the concept of Jax and I bumping uglies. But Jake has always been a weirdo, I guess.

Now completely mortified, I put my face in the palm of my hands. I cannot look at any one of them. "Oh. My. God."

"You sure do like to say that a lot?" Jake adds, chuckling and fueling my humiliation all the more.

"Look, Tilly, don't be embarrassed. It is just a little awkward." Scott tries to comfort me. I look up at him. "But hey, my lease is almost up. I know Jake is hardly here, and pretty soon Jax will be back doing his thing," Scott says, glaring at Jax. "So, I can move back in. I know you will need help around here, and I don't want you to be alone."

I feel Jax stiffen next to me as I glance at him. I notice he is giving Scott a pointed stare I have never seen before. It appears as though he is angry or annoyed with Scott, which is weird. Why would he care if Scott moved in with me? It makes sense. I will need the help. The house is big and we have a few acres of land that need to be maintained.

"Thank you, Scott, but I would hate for you to give up your privacy and freedom to come live with your baby sister and brother," I offer. As much as I would love the help, I don't want to put my brother out.

"Hey, no way. It would be awesome. Not to mention, I could save on rent and look into expanding the cafe. Honestly, you would be doing me a favor," Scott says, giving me a giant smile as though I am doing him a larger kindness than he is doing for me.

"Well, in that case, I think that sounds like a good idea. I know I will need the help." Jax's gaze turns back to me. Now, he looks almost sad or disappointed. I am not sure what his deal is? But we will talk about it later. Right now… really isn't the time.

"Don't worry. You and Jax getting jiggy with it doesn't scare me away." Jake pats Jax on the shoulder. "Besides, I still need to give you some pointers, man. Four orgasms is for the minor leagues, dude, but I'm here to help you make it pro."

Everyone collectively groans at Jake. "Seriously, dude, stop talking about our baby sister's orgasms. It is creepy," Scott wails, throwing a dirty dish towel at Jake. While what he says is absolutely disgusting, I am happy he breaks the tension in the room. We are all able to continue eating our breakfast and making small talk. I can sense something is still bothering Jax. But he doesn't seem angry anymore, just a little withdrawn.

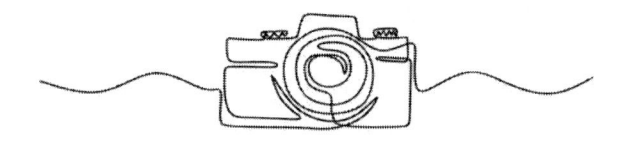

Chapter 11

Jackson

After breakfast was over, Tilly went out with Letty. I think they are planning to get their nails done, or something? As much as I miss Tilly right now, I am happy that she is spending time with Letty. I know she is still grieving, but keeping that in mind, it is nice seeing her start to find her new normal.

Robbie took off shortly after breakfast. He already had his bag packed. I will admit I was excited to hear that he and Scott were going back to their places. I am sure it has been weird staying in his parents' room. Then Scott and I, with the exception of a few nights I've been with Tilly, have been sleeping in our old bunk beds. Now that I think about it, I still cannot understand how we made it through high school in those things.

I knew Jake wasn't going anywhere but honestly, he is barely even here. He sleeps at the station and is on call a lot. As weird as I think it is, I know he could care less about hearing Tilly and me have sex. I've tried to keep it quiet—because I am not a monster and I know that it is awkward for Scott and Robbie. But Jake, he has always been a sex fiend. Not in a bad way. We have talked about it in the past. He almost views sex as like a hobby. He is all about physical pleasure, and with the exception of his family, he does not discriminate. I have seen him hook up with girls of all shapes, colors, and sizes.

I know he sounds like an awful man-whore, but he treats the girls that he hooks up with well. This is also a small town and his reputation is known. So, women do not tend to get emotionally involved. If anything, they want to sleep with him to learn new tricks or experience a few different things. He really doesn't judge. He has told me stories of the weird stuff girls want to try with him just to see if they like it. He is like their sexual safe space.

Regardless though, I am currently sitting in the living room, pissed off at Scott. This is a new feeling. I have never been mad at Scott before and Scott has never been mad at me. But what he said at breakfast—about Tilly being alone and me leaving—it infuriated me. It took all my willpower not to slug him. But the real gut punch was the fact that Tilly had agreed.

It was as if they both already decided that I am leaving. I know Tilly and I didn't talk about it much last night. We got a little distracted. But I told her how lonely I've been, and how empty the traveling has felt (having no one to share it with). And I also told her that I *wanted* to stay. In typical Tilly fashion, she brushed it off (just like she did ten years ago) by telling me she isn't going to hold me back.

She doesn't seem to understand, that to me, it doesn't feel like she is holding me back. If anything, I feel like she is pushing me away. We have been intimate a few times, but she is still keeping part of herself from me. I *want* to stay with her. I am not sure what this means for my career. There isn't much I can do with photography in this town. But I would be willing to find a new career for her and let photography just become a hobby. However, before I give everything up, I need to know that she is all in.

Scott comes down the stairs, duffle bag in hand. I can tell he is unhappy with me also. I am not sure how to handle this, considering we have never been upset with each other before. I guess I should approach it the same way Scott does, by barreling in headfirst.

"What's your issue, dude?" Scott stiffens. *Good*—clearly, we are both holding shit back and a fight is what we need.

Scott sets down his bag. "Do I really need to explain the issue?"

I stand; this seems like a standing situation. "Yes, you never had an issue with Tilly and I before. Fuck, I remember you telling me to dive in… to give it everything I got. But now, you are practically pushing me out of the door."

"Yea, back then it was no issue, Jax. I loved seeing you and Tilly together. But you didn't see Tilly after you left," Scott replies defensively, crossing his arms over his chest.

Fuck, Scott knows how to throw verbal punches like an MMA fighter. I guess, I never really thought about it. Tilly was practically packing my bag for me. I recall the first few months being tough. I almost came home several times. I remember Mr. Moore called to check in, and I confessed to him how much I wanted to come home. He told me it was okay to be homesick, and it was also okay to come home. But then he cautioned me. He said that I had better make sure I was certain and that I wouldn't have any regrets. He didn't want me to grow up old and bitter, and thinking about the opportunity I gave up… just because it was difficult right now.

I gave it a few more months, and the trips started to get better. I started finding new happiness and comfort in my travels and career. By that same token, throwing myself in my work left me little time to think about how much I missed home. Mr. and Mrs. Moore used to check in on me (almost monthly) after that for a while. They told me how well everything was going at the shop, how good the boys were doing… and finally, how happy Tilly was. As much as I still missed her, I knew that at least right then, it wasn't time for me to come home.

"How was Tilly after I left?" I can hear how broken my own voice is, realizing that the happiness I thought she had experienced all this time might have never been true.

Scott seems to notice, and cools down a bit. He takes a seat in the recliner across from me. "She was devastated. I ended up staying down at the college with her for the first week to make sure she was okay and not alone."

"She told me to go… I wanted to stay… But she said that with school, there was no point."

"You seem to forget who Tilly is. She is selfless, she would break every bone in her body to make someone she loves happy. You had been talking about leaving Tral Lake since we were kids, about how much you wanted to see the world. As much as Tilly loves you, she would never ask you to stay."

Dammit, I know he is right. I even told Tilly I wanted to stay again, and she told me how much I love my career. "I told her I want to stay."

"Yea—well, based on the conversation at breakfast this morning, it doesn't sound like she really believed you," Scott states, pointing out the obvious.

"No, she told me she couldn't ask me to stay. I told her I wanted to. Then, she kind of changed the *subject*. The conversation was dropped."

Scott smirks. He knows exactly what I mean. "Look, I would love it if you stayed. But, with the exception of Tilly and us, what do you have here? You never wanted to be tied down to this town. I know that right now, you are sad about my parents. And probably feel guilty for not seeing them or visiting. Also, I am sure seeing Tilly again after all this time has your hormones all over the place. But when the guilt wears off, when you have given up your dream career, when the "new relationship" vibes wear down and you are sitting here drinking iced tea with Tilly in this small boring-ass town—are you still going to be happy with your choice? Or will you end up resenting Tilly *and us* because you stayed?"

I pause to think about it. I know he is speaking some truth. I don't think I could ever resent Tilly. But, at the same time, is he right? Does my desire to stay here have more to do with guilt than what I actually want?

Scott sighs. "Jax, all these years you *chose* to be gone. Your work sends you all over the world. You *chose* to have an apartment in New York, when you could have come back here during your off time. Then even if you didn't live here, you have vacation time, and still you never once thought about coming back home and visiting. While it has been awesome to travel to some cool-ass places with you, I've only gotten to see you because work forced you to take time off. Tilly would never admit it... but the fact that you wouldn't come here, or even invite her to go on vacation with you, broke her heart even more. It was hard for her to hear the stories about our trips or look at the pictures we had taken. But she suffered through because she is the best sister in the world, and took whatever chance she could to get some sort of glimpse into your life —a life that *you* shut her out of."

Fuck, he is right. And I hate that he is right. I can make all the excuses I want, but at the end of the day, I made no effort to keep in touch with Tilly. I can blame it on her lack of social media presence, but I know the real reason was because thinking about her made me homesick. And that wasn't fair to her. If she only knew how many times I had picked up the phone to call her... Or how many unsent emails I wrote her... Or that I wanted to beg her to come with me and forget this town...

"I'm guessing by the dumbfounded look on your face, you understand where I am coming from? So, then you know while I love you, it is my job to protect and look out for Tilly? When you leave again, especially after what she is going through with our parents, someone will need to be here to pick up the shattered pieces."

Scott stands and heads back to the door, grabbing his bag again. "I am not telling you to go, Jax. I miss the fuck out of having my best friend here. But I am also not telling you to stay either. The choice has always been yours. And because we all love you, we will always support whatever you choose. But Tilly deserves someone who is here, not just passing through. I know you say you want to stay, and I believe that this is what you want right now. What I don't know, and it seems you don't either, is how long that will last."

As Scott opens the door, the only thing I can think to say is, "I love her."

Scott sighs. "I know you do. But is it enough?"

That is all Scott says before he is gone, leaving me alone in the house.

I love Tilly. And getting to spend every moment with her these past couple of weeks (even the hard and sad ones) has felt like being home. But Scott is right—is this just my grief talking? Or is this what I really want? In a couple of months, or years, will I suddenly wake up one morning with an itch to explore the world? If I stay, I need to know that I am staying permanently, and so does Tilly.

So, I do the only thing I can think to do... I pick up the phone and call my boss.

Chapter 12

Matilda

"So, how are things going with Jax?" Letty asks as we sit in the comfy massage chairs, getting our toes done.

"Umm, they are going good." I cannot help but blush thinking about last night.

"That look on your face tells me you got over the whole 'brother' thing?" Letty grins at me.

"Please, let's never bring that up again, Letty." I sigh, mulling over the personal hell I was in for the last week.

She laughs. "Sure, no problem. We will pretend the *incident* never happened. But seriously, how are you?"

"I don't know. Robbie and Scott decided to go back home this morning. It has been nice having all of my brothers at home. With them gone... I don't know... it will just feel so empty in that house."

"Well, isn't Jax there?" Letty inquires, flipping through the color wheel and still looking for a gel color for her fingers.

"Yea, that is kind of why they are leaving," I admit bashfully, "but when he is gone, it'll be like I'm living there alone. Granted, Scott did offer to move back in when his lease is up. But I feel bad having him give up his private space."

"Has Jax mentioned when he was leaving?" Letty inquires.

"No, not yet. Actually… he kind of mentioned the idea of staying last night," I offer nonchalantly. While I would love nothing more than for Jax to stay, I know better than to get my hopes up.

"Oh yea, what did he say?" Letty asks, her tone becoming profoundly serious.

"Not much really… we didn't talk about it long. Just that he has been lonely while traveling. But I cannot ask him to stay here. Jax could never be happy here." I attempt to school my own tone and hide that glimmer of hope that lives deep within me. The one that thinks it might finally be time for our happily ever after.

"Well, I think that is up to Jax. Who knows, maybe he has gotten all of the traveling out of his system?" Letty points out matter-of-factly.

"I don't know, maybe? But what if he isn't done? What if he wakes up one morning and realizes this isn't good enough? That I am not good enough? I don't think I could handle that." The thought of giving myself fully to Jax (and having him toss it back at me) is almost too much. Not to mention, do I really even deserve him? What kind of person would I be for keeping him tied down here with me?

"I know, babe, but it isn't fair to push Jax away if he is finally ready to commit." Letty thinks for a moment. "I mean, if he isn't what you want, then by all means push him away. But if you are doing that thing where you deprive yourself because you think it is in his best interest…" Letty pauses to ponder. "…well, that just isn't your choice to make. How would you feel if he did the same to you?"

∞∞∞

Letty and I parted ways following our afternoon together. She is closing at the bar tonight and needed to get ready for her shift. I thought about meeting her there, but I am just feeling so exhausted, and I am not sure it is really my scene right now.

When I finally get home, Jax is the only one there. I know Robbie and Scott packed up and left this morning, and that tonight, Jake is at the station. But it is still weird—just Jax and me being here. I will try not to be too sad about it, and attempt to enjoy this time we get together.

Especially since Jax is trying to cook. It is almost comical. He is clearly lost in the kitchen right now.

"I guess cooking is not something you learned with all of your travels?" I muse, taking in his appearance.

Jax peeks up at me—he is a total mess. Whatever sauce he is making has stained his shirt, and I see at least three burn marks on his hands and arms. It also appears as if he cut himself, since I notice two new bandages on his finger. Even though he looks like the ultimate disaster waiting to happen, I cannot help but smile. Domesticated Jax is absolutely adorable.

"Yea, I eat a lot of takeout. But I got bored while sitting here and turned on the TV. I was watching some cooking show that talked about easy 30-minute dinners. Well, the lady on the TV made it look super simple, like even I could do it. So, I ran out to the store, bought some ingredients, and now here I am." It is obvious he is immensely proud of himself.

I love seeing him like this. But it is also a stark reminder that he is bored. Which means he will likely be getting back to his life soon. I always knew what this was, and I refuse to waste another moment being sad over it. I want to enjoy my time with Jax, for however long it may be. He might be only a tiny Band-Aid on this enormous wound I need to take care of, but I will accept the small fix now and worry about the full recovery later.

I give him the biggest, most genuine smile I can muster. "Do you need help with anything?"

"Actually, no. Everything is about finished. I thought maybe we could eat in the dining room tonight. I have everything all set. So why don't you go take a seat? I will dish everything up and meet you in there."

I walk into the kitchen and give him a quick kiss on the cheek. "Thank you, Jax."

I go to the dining room. He has the fine china set out, the candles lit, and bread and olive oil sitting on the table along with a bottle of red wine. He has really gone all-out this evening. This is one of the most romantic things anyone has ever done for me. Granted, this isn't the first time Jax has surprised me with such a thoughtful gesture.

I take a seat at the table. Jax is not far behind me, carrying in two plates of what appears to be Chicken Parmesan and asparagus. "Wow, this looks and smells really good, Jax."

"Thanks. It doesn't look as pretty as the dish she made on the TV. But everything seemed to taste good as I was cooking it. I also made sure the chicken was done. She reminded me like five times during the episode... about how dangerous undercooked chicken can be."

I can only smile at him. Jax cooking me dinner is downright sexy. I can tell he is totally out of his comfort zone. But I can also see that he is actually enjoying this experience.

We eat dinner, which as it turns out, is actually really delicious. I've never had authentic Italian food before, but I am guessing this is relatively close. He explains to me how he made the sauce from scratch. It is really impressive. I do a little cooking, but it is pretty basic stuff. Cooking was always my mom's and Scott's thing. I was better as a taste-tester or salad-tosser.

Jax clears our plates and comes back with two servings of some sort of layered pastry. "It is tiramisu," he says. "I didn't make it. I bought it. But I saw it was a good dessert to go with our Italian meal."

"Wow, you really thought of everything. I haven't had it before, but it looks good." And it was good. I've never been that big on sweets or cakes. I was always more of a fresh-fruit pie sort of gal. My favorite indulgence, however, was when my mom and I would go pick fresh strawberries and rhubarb. We would then combine the two distinctly tart flavors. The end result was one of the best made-from-scratch pies I have ever tasted.

"Thank you, Jax. Everything was absolutely delicious." He takes my hand and kisses the top of it.

"Anything for you, Tilly." He gives me his big panty-melting smile. "Why don't you pour us a couple of glasses of wine and we can sit outside. The sky is clear tonight, and I heard that there should be a meteor shower we could see. I will get the last of the dishes in the washer and meet you out there."

Jax goes back to the kitchen. I pour one glass of wine and grab some water for myself. I'm not sure why, but wine just doesn't sound appealing right now. I get out to the patio and see he already has it set up with two loungers pushed side-by-side and our sleeping bags zipped together, making one larger bag. I place our drinks on the end table and get cozy.

Jax comes out a few minutes later to join me. He looks down at my glass and his brows furrow. "Do you not like the wine?"

"Oh, no. I am sure it is fine. I'm just... I am not sure. I've been a little tired lately and I don't want the wine to make me sleepy," I say, fighting off a yawn.

Jax wraps his arm around me and pulls me close. "Oh, I'm sorry, babe. If you are tired, we can go lie down inside—maybe watch a movie? I know things have been stressful for you and that has to be exhausting. Hell, even I've been exhausted recently. Grief can do that to you."

"Thank you. I think you are right. But I do not want to go lie down. Everything tonight has been really thoughtful and wonderful. And I am not ready for it to end."

Jax kisses the top of my head as we lie there, looking out at the night sky. It isn't dark enough yet to see much, but it is still nice regardless. At least the moon is out and the sun is almost gone. It is something I love about Minnesota. Usually in early

September, sunset starts at 7pm. But then, come winter, the sun starts to set around 5 or 6pm instead—meaning more time for my stargazing.

"I had a talk with Scott today," Jax says abruptly.

"Oh." I am not sure why, but all of a sudden, my blood runs cold. I had already gathered that Scott was upset about something earlier; however, I had yet to discover its root cause. That being said, I can't imagine that any conversation he had with Jax, was a good one.

"Yea, we had some stuff to air out." As if he feels the tension in my body, he kisses the top of my head again and pulls me in close. "Please listen, before you stress yourself out more, okay?"

I take a deep breath and nod. I now understand the intent behind the nice dinner and evening. He is likely buttering me up to leave again. I knew he was going soon, but I am just not ready yet. *Will I ever be ready for him to go?* This last week, I've avoided him like he was the plague... and... well, I just want some more time with him, I guess.

"The discussion with Scott was a tough one. But unfortunately, I needed to hear what it was that he had to say. I won't get into all the specifics, but essentially, he is worried about you and me. I meant what I said last night. I *want* to stay here. My job, I do love it, but it has become so lonely. Being back home with all of you... it has made me realize just how alone I have been. Except for stalking friends on social media, or talking to Scott on the phone, I am by myself. The past couple of weeks, being here with you—even when you would barely speak to me..." he chuckles. "Well, it is the happiest I have been in a very long time."

"If you are lonely, Jackson, get a fucking cat. Not wanting to be alone doesn't mean the same thing as wanting to be with me," I seethe. I don't typically have outbursts like this. But what Jax said pisses me the hell off.

"Whoa, Tilly, hold-up that isn't—" Jax starts pleading, but I cut him off.

"No, Jax. I understand a consequence of your job is loneliness.

But you made the choice to be alone. You shut everyone out —you shut me out." I feel the tears burning behind my eyes. "I won't lie. I love having you back home. But... I mean... you never really wanted to be *here* in the first place. Tral Lake was always too small for you. I just don't want you to risk ruining your career on a whim." *Then blaming me and breaking us in the process*, I say to myself.

"This isn't a whim, Tilly. I want to stay. I want to give us a chance. Scott had similar concerns as well. He said that I am making a big life-altering decision fueled by grief and regret. But this change in me, it isn't all just me trying to cope with what happened. Being home has only highlighted feelings I've had for a long time. Not to mention, seeing how easily I could have lost you... I don't want to take that risk again."

I sit up and pull away to look at Jax. "You are not the only one with regrets, Jackson. I have a ton as well." If only he could understand the sheer level of regret that I carry with me. "But it really hurt that throughout all these years, you never reached out. You never attempted once to see me or even talk to me. You called and spoke to Scott and my parents, but never to me. It hurt... feeling like you shut me out."

"I am sorry," Jax says, taking my hand. "It was too difficult. Any time I let my thoughts wander to you, the pain was agonizing. Remembering what we had started, how much I loved you, and how you pushed me away—kind of like you are doing right now." He holds his hand up in defense, knowing I am about to counter. "I get it. It is no excuse. I understand that I hurt you, and I regret that is how I handled the situation. But I don't want to just sit here with an acknowledgement and my unending list of regrets. I don't want any more missed moments... or any more missed opportunities with you. I love my career, Matilda, but I love *you* more. I am still not exactly certain what that all means or how it will work. But I know I want to make changes in my life. Scott had a lot of good points today... about me staying and about what I could have done differently over the years. It was the reality check that I needed."

"What does this mean?" I am so nervous right now that I'm vibrating. I cannot tell if I should be happy or sad yet. Jax squeezes my hand tighter.

"Well, for starters, I called my boss today. I have a lot of time-off saved that I almost never use... unless I am forced to. I decided to take a brief hiatus from work. I haven't quit, but I want to spend at least two or three more weeks here with you—to try and figure things out, to try and figure *us* out." He pauses taking a deep breath. "We have been apart for a long time, Tilly. While I feel like certain parts of us have rekindled easily, I want to take some time to get to know you again. I feel like I have missed so much of your life. I also want to look at Tral Lake with fresh adult eyes and see what opportunities there are here for me."

"I don't know, Jax. I am not sure I could handle potentially getting attached, and then having you take off again." I would love a couple more weeks with Jax, but I don't think I could survive the subsequent heartache... after he leaves.

"Please, Tilly. I know that I am asking a lot of you. I have plenty of decisions, wait no, we have plenty of decisions to make. I understand that you are going through so much right now, and I don't want to cause you any more pain. But please, give me a chance?" Jax pleads. And it just about breaks my heart —seeing how desperate he is for this to work, while knowing that it didn't matter—because I could never give him what he wants.

"I'm sorry, Jax." I let go of his hand and move to stand up. "This..." I gesture between the two of us. "...is a lot right now. I am trying really hard to move past my grief, to figure out what my life is like without my parents in it. If I give us this chance... if it doesn't work out... I am just not sure I will be able to survive that."

I look down at Jax. He is still pleading with his eyes, hoping that I'll reconsider my decision. As much as I want to throw myself at Jax and get lost in his embrace, my heart is too fragile right now. And I am not brave enough to face the devastation he might cause it. "Good night, Jackson." I give him a quick kiss on the forehead before going back inside, up to my room, and locking the door.

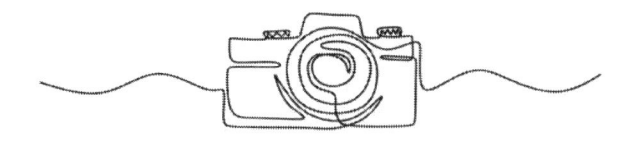

Chapter 13

Jackson

I can't believe she said no—is all I can think, as I stare down into my third glass of whiskey for the evening. Was I really that wrong about us? I know I messed up, and that I have a lot to make up for because of it. But honestly, I had assumed she would at least give us this chance. That we would finally try to be something more than a summer fling, or whatever the heck we have been doing? Maybe her feelings died for me a long time ago, and recently, all this has been is nothing more than grief sex?

"Seat taken?" I look to see Scott sliding onto the stool next to me. He quickly raises a hand to get Letty's attention. "What the hell happened to you tonight?"

"Fuck," I say, wiping my hand over my face. Frankly, I was still trying to figure that out for myself. What in the actual hell *did* just happen?

"That bad, huh?" Scott chuckles, taking a swig of the beer Letty had dropped off for him.

"I don't understand. I thought about what you said earlier and, as much as I didn't want to hear it, you were right. So tonight, I made—*I actually cooked*—Tilly a nice dinner and planned a romantic evening on the deck to watch a meteor shower. I told her that I wanted to stay, that I took time off from work, and that I want to give us and Tral Lake a shot… But Tilly didn't go for it."

"Shit, that sucks. Did she say why?" Scott inquires.

I recounted to Scott what Tilly had told me this evening. Then how, after she went back inside, I sat waiting—hoping that maybe… she would come back out to me and reconsider my offer. When she didn't, I went to her room in an attempt to talk to her again, but she locked her door on me.

"So, what now?" Scott asks, picking apart the burger he ordered.

"What do you mean? Tilly made it pretty damn clear she wants nothing to do with us." I quickly down the rest of my whiskey and slam my glass on the bar top. "I fucked up. I should have never stayed away from her. But it was the only way I could handle the distance… to just cut her out of my life. I feel like shit for doing it, but it was the best I could come up with at the time. I can't imagine going back to work now, and never seeing Tilly again."

"Then don't," Scott adds matter-of-factly.

"What am I supposed to do? Go to work and torture myself, try and call or visit as much as I can, and risk that Tilly will continue to shut me out?"

"So, that's it then. You are just giving up. Figured as much," Scott says, shrugging his shoulders.

I stand up and shove his arm. "What the hell, man?" I yell in the bar, gaining some attention.

Scott stands and faces me. While we are the same height, he feels taller right now. It's likely (that in my drunken state) I am not standing up fully. Scott shoves me back. "You heard me."

"That isn't fair, Scott. Tilly made her point pretty fucking clear tonight. Shit, she even locked me out of her room."

"So what?" Scott seethes. "You say you love Tilly... you say you want to stay here with her. That you are taking time off to explore this relationship and where it might lead. The first obstacle in your way, and you are already bailing. You are a coward, Jackson..."

I am not sure what comes over me, but Scott has fucking pissed me off. I don't let him finish. Without realizing I am even doing it, my fist collides with the side of his face. *What the hell is wrong with me?* In the span of a week, I have hit two guys I've grown up with like family.

Scott wipes the small amount of blood dripping from his lip. He looks down at the red smear on his hand before looking back at me. The Cheshire grin that spreads across his face is my only warning. It happens so fast... In my drunken state, I barely have a chance to defend myself. Scott pulls me by the collar of my shirt and returns the face punch I gave him. White hot agony burns in my jaw, and I collapse on the ground as he lets go of me.

Lying on the bar floor I groan, but Scott isn't finished. Kneeling down, he picks me up by the collar for a second time and throws another blow. "As I was saying, Jax, you are a fucking coward. The first sign of trouble, and you are already packing your bags... ready to leave Tilly behind again. She deserves someone who will fight for her. Not some asshole who is going to break her heart before galivanting across the world. What? You think maybe you'll come back in ten more years, and Tilly will be here sitting and waiting for you?"

The flood of rage from Scott's words (and the pain radiating from my jaw) sobers me up enough to fight back. I shove Scott off of me, and we both stand—each of us eyeing up our opponent. I am about ready to take my shot when Letty comes between us. "What the fuck, you guys? What the hell is wrong with you?"

"He started it," Scott and I both say in unison.

"I don't give a rat's ass who started it. I am ending it." Letty looks sternly between the two of us. "And you..." Letty points at me. "You need to stop fighting with your brothers in this bar. Do it again, and I will ban your ass."

"It doesn't matter. He is leaving anyway," Scott sneers at me.

Letty moves out of the way as I lunge at Scott. We are a mixture of grappling and blows as we take our fight outside. The cold air is shocking against my hot skin. I look at Scott's heaving chest and bloodied face, guessing mine must look similar. As I throw another hit, Scott sweeps my leg, knocking me down onto the concrete.

"So, is this it, then?" Scott asks, yelling in my face.

"What do you want from me?" I yell back. My head is swimming with whiskey and Scott's words.

"If you want to be with Tilly, it is time you start acting like it."

"What am I supposed to do if she is pushing me away?" I ask.

"You have what—two to three weeks you took off, right?" Scott recalls.

"Yea, but what's the point? Tilly was adamant that she's not interested in pursuing anything with me… anymore. The vacation seems a little unnecessary now."

"I don't see how the plan has changed?" Scott says, pulling me up from the ground to stand. "You wanted to take time off, to give you and Tilly a shot, and to figure out a career to keep you here? So what if Tilly turned you down at first? That doesn't mean you should pack your bags and take off. If you want Tilly and you want to stay here with her, then prove it," Scott retorted, shrugging his shoulders. "I'm out of here," Scott says before walking away.

"Prove it?" I let the idea roll around in my mind. Quickly coming up with a plan, I smile and yell to Scott, "Fuck, man, you are brilliant!"

∞∞∞

The next morning, I wake with my head pounding. Partially from the hangover, but mostly because of the beating Scott gave me.

I could tell Tilly was giving me the cold shoulder. She woke up earlier than normal for work, and it seemed as if she was trying to be extra quiet in doing so. Looking at the kitchen, it appeared as though she had even skipped breakfast to avoid running into me. But that is fine. I know where she is going, and I will not let her keep me at a distance... *for long.*

I quickly get up, get dressed for the day, and make sure to grab my camera and a few lenses. I spend most of the morning walking around Main Street, taking some pictures, and enjoying the updates the shops have made to their outward appearances. I do not remember there being this much foliage on Main Street before—it looks as though a lot of new trees have been planted. They also installed some cobblestone and lined the sidewalk with those vintage-style lampposts. They are definitely going for that classic old town feel.

Around noon, I rush over to the diner to grab a couple of sandwiches to go. Entering the book store, I don't immediately see Tilly. She must be in the back. After a brief pause, I hear her call out. "One moment, please." I set the bags down on the counter and wait. Not long after, she comes rushing from the office. "I am so sorry to make you w—" She gives me a curious glance. "What are you doing here?" Tilly takes in my appearance, her brow furrows in concern. "What happened to you?"

I give her a giant smile, ignoring her inquiry, and hold up one of the bags. "I thought I would bring you lunch."

"Oh, thank you," she says, cautiously taking it from me. She doesn't press any further into my appearance. While I can tell she is concerned, her need to distance herself from me has overpowered her curiosity. I wonder if she has seen Scott, and if he looks as bad as I do. "Well, I better get back to work."

She turns, attempting to sneak away, but I stop her. "Sure, what do you need help with?"

"Oh, nothing." She waves her hand, dismissing my inquiry. "I'm going to eat real quick. I'll see ya later." Tilly doesn't give me a chance before she disappears again.

Quickly, I scarf down my sandwich. I won't lie, I am a little bummed that she wouldn't even eat lunch with me. But oh well, I am not giving up that easy. Scott (though maybe he was being an asshole about it) was right. If I want Tilly, then I need to start fighting to be with her and not give up at the first sign of trouble.

∞∞∞

The next morning, I am the one to sneak out early, and prior to Tilly waking up. Scott (surprisingly) agreed to help me by getting me into the shop before it opens. While I can tell things are tense between us, I think he is happy seeing me actually make an effort. I had noticed yesterday, while eating lunch there, that the place needed a good scrubbing. And with her injuries, I didn't want Tilly to get hurt trying to climb up the ladders to dust or something.

I have been dusting, mopping, and polishing the shop for about two hours already when I hear the front shop doorbell ring, indicating that Tilly is entering. Fortunately, I am just about finished. "Oh. My. God!" Tilly exclaims.

Coming to the front, I see Tilly admiring the freshly polished wood fixtures and overall clean appearance of the shop. She must have sensed me approaching, because quickly turning around, she asks, "Did you do all of this?"

"Yes," I admit coyly.

"How?" Tilly shakes her head. "I mean I know how, but how?"

Chuckling, I respond, "Scott let me in early this morning and showed me where all the supplies were."

"Thank you," she whispers. "I won't lie... This is probably the cleanest I have ever seen the shop before."

"I saw that it could use a good dusting yesterday, and well, I didn't want you to risk hurting yourself trying to crawl around or climb things with that cast on your arm." As she admires the store, I take this opportunity to get closer to her. "Also, while I was cleaning, I noticed a few things. Changing up the displays and moving a couple of shelves could really brighten up the space. I would love to help you."

"You don't need to do that, Jax. This..." She gestures around the room. "...is plenty. I can't ask you to do anything more."

"You aren't asking, Tilly. I am offering." I seize the opening and take her hand into mine. "Please, let me help out?"

Tilly looks at me for a long moment. I can't tell exactly what is running through her head. But I know she is thinking through all the pros and cons of allowing me to help around the shop.

"Okay," she sighs, as though signaling a sound of defeat—with whatever internal battle she had been fighting. "I could really use some assistance around here... if you are up for it."

"I am more than up for it." I smile back at her, knowing that I am slowly eating away at the wall she has built around this concept of "us". I don't care if I need to spend every waking moment for the next three weeks trying to convince her that I am serious. It will be worth every pain-staking second.

Chapter 14

Matilda

It has been weird having Jax at the shop. He has been here every day for the last week helping me out. And not just with cleaning, but with everything. He has helped me finish up the inventory project I started with my dad before the accident. He suggested we change almost the whole layout of the shop, and he is right—it makes it seem so much larger and more open. He even helped me create a few new endcaps to do more feature sections.

On top of all that, he has also been assisting me with taking over the shop's social media, which is the biggest burden I have to deal with. One—I am just not a social media person, so whatever I do on there feels like the cruelest chore imaginable. Two—most of my posts are flat and boring, and I get little to no interaction from people.

Since Jax has taken over, we have a ton more followers along with a crazy amount of engagements on our posts. Then, to top it off, my online sales have increased this week. And it is all thanks to Jax and his brilliance when it comes to this kind of stuff.

Having him here and helping (though I hate to admit it) has been a blast. He hasn't brought up "us" again. While I have noticed a few longing glances, there has been nothing physical between us. We have just been hanging out like two old friends. I so desperately want to let go of my reservations and give into this, give into us. But I am still terrified of all the "what if's".

I am not one hundred-precent certain what happened between him and Scott. After I saw Jax, and then saw Scott's matching face, I realized they must have gotten into some sort of fight. I have never known them to come to physical blows before, and I tried to ask Scott about it, but he blew me off... just like Jax had at the shop. Later, when talking with Letty, she mentioned them getting into a fight at the bar. She wasn't sure about all the specifics, but she had overheard my name a bit and Scott calling Jax a coward. While I don't have all the details, I don't doubt that Jax being here at the shop is a result of that physical encounter between them.

Still... While I have definitely noticed a difference in Jax's behavior (he seems so determined to prove to me that this is what he wants) I can't help but fear... what if he leaves and doesn't come back again? What if he leaves and never contacts me? What if he leaves and I am too broken to move on? What if all of this joy is temporary, and after a while, he is bored with me? What if I don't deserve this happiness? With all of these doubts and insecurities swimming in my brain, it is hard to even think straight.

"Hey, Jax?" Looking up from his laptop, he raises an eyebrow and offers a questioning stare. A glimmer of hope twinkles in his eyes. "Would you mind watching the shop for a bit? I need to go over to Robbie's?"

"Sure thing," he replies, lowering his gaze back down to the computer. "If you need me to close up, let me know."

"Okay, that would be great." My chest tightens at the sight. I wish I could go back to last week and give into what he wants, what *I* want. But it just isn't meant to be... The sooner we can both accept that, the better off we both are. Quickly I rush out of the shop, avoiding any more of the awkward exchange. Working with Jax all day and then hanging out with him at home—while it has been strictly platonic—it is hard to maintain my composure with him around me all of the time. I just need a break, and Robbie's is the perfect opportunity to do so.

∞∞∞

Robbie's back office is nothing like mine. The bookshop is clean, well-organized, and feels homey with plants and pictures. Robbie's is the exact opposite. It is bland and minimalistic. It isn't messy—fortunately, he is a neat freak. But it has an old metal desk that is cold and rusty, and the chair is hard steel that conforms to your butt. I think it used to be an old tractor seat or something. The only artwork he has is the stereotypical garage pin-up magazine with half-naked chicks on it. But at least these ones are done tastefully in a 50's retro style with awesome hotrods like our grandpa used to have.

After a couple of hours of going through Robbie's books and ensuring everything is in order for the month's end, I look up when I hear a knock at the entryway.

"How's it looking, sis?" Robbie inquires, his large frame fills the doorway. He has his jumpsuit half off and tied around the waist, while his white undershirt is covered in grease and other automotive fluids.

Cocking my head to the right, I raise an eyebrow at him. "Everything is great. With everyone coming in and getting their winter tires done, you should have enough profit to easily hire more help. Especially someone to manage your office full time."

Crossing his arms, Robbie jibes, "I am not interested, so drop it."

"Robbie, this is ridiculous. You need someone to help you manage all this back-office stuff full time. Especially, if you plan on opening another location," I fume. The tension in my head builds to an ache, knowing that we are about to have this same argument again (for what seems like the hundredth time).

"I don't like the idea of some stranger coming in here messin' with my business. Things are going smoothly. No point in fixin' something that ain't broken," Robbie replies, his tone as sharp as a razor blade.

Narrowing my eyes, I stare at him. "Just because it isn't broken, doesn't mean that it is efficient," I retort, knowing this argument is not going anywhere.

Robbie's shoulders lower, shrugging half-heartedly. "Look, I like everything how it is. I don't want to change it. I am not even sure I want to open another shop. I can't be in two places at once, and I don't like the idea of leaving one shop unattended."

"Robbie," I sigh, "you've got to learn to trust people. I can help you find someone. I still have contacts from school who I could reach out to. Friends of mine, people I know and trust."

"I'll think about it." Robbie pivots to walk away but hesitates. Turning back, he forms a slow smile across his grease-covered face. "I noticed that Jax is still around."

"Yea." Robbie doesn't want to talk about hiring someone, and I definitely do not want to talk about this.

Robbie's face softens as he enters the room and takes a seat on an old torn vinyl chair. "You know you can talk to me, right? About anything, the accident, mom and dad, even Jax."

I nod in reply, afraid to speak, and knowing that I will not be able to stop the waterworks once they start.

"You know Scott has told me about Jax taking vacation time to stay here, and how he has been helping around the shop. I've even taken a glance at the shop's Facebook and I'm impressed. I am considering having him come over here and help me a bit. I could use some extra business."

I snort in laughter. Robbie has business coming out of his ears. He can't handle anymore without hiring help and expanding.

"Ha, knew that one would get ya."

"Did he tell you about whatever fight they had?" I ask, curious if Scott confided in Robbie.

He shrugs his shoulders. "Yea, he told me that he needed to beat some sense into that dumbass," Robbie says (with no ill will towards Jax). The amusement I see in his expression makes me think if Scott hadn't done it, he would have. Robbie ponders for a moment; his expression becomes more serious. "Scott also told me why Jax is still around. I know it isn't really any of my business, but why are you pushing him away?"

"Seriously, mister 'all-work-no-play' Robbie? You, the guy who has made no time or room for a relationship in your life, wonder why I am not risking everything for a chance with Jax? The guy, who had to have his ass kicked by my brother?" It is my turn to look sullen and cross my arms. Out of all of my brothers, Robbie is the last one I ever imagined who would pry into my love, or lack of love, life.

"Scott did what was necessary. He loves Jax, but he was being a pussy and needed some sense beaten into him before he made a grave mistake. And I... well, I've never had anyone worth making that time for. You and Jax are different. I understand why you pushed him away before. He needed to go out and live that dream of his. But now, you are pushing him away for different reasons entirely. And unfortunately, I don't think you are doing it in his, *or your*, best interest."

Defeated, I drop my shoulders and let the tears start to fall. "I can't, Robbie."

"Can't or won't?" Robbie challenges.

"Both," I admit in surrender, lowering my face into my hands as the tears begin to fall. Moments later, I feel Robbie's warm comforting embrace behind me.

"Talk to me, Tilly, please. Why are you denying yourself this?" I can hear the concern laced in Robbie's tone.

"I am terrified of all the ways this can go wrong, and I'm not sure I will be able to come back from that..." I pause, thinking about how much I want to share with Robbie. We have never really had many heart-to-hearts growing up. "It also feels wrong."

"Wrong? Because of that shit Jake said? I thought we already talked about how that was bullshit and Jake is a dumbass?"

"No, it isn't that. I know Jax isn't my brother by blood or legally." My parents only took guardianship of him. He was never formally adopted by our family. I take a deep breath, hoping that it will help loosen the tight knot in my chest. "It's just... I can't. He is only here because of mom and dad... and they are only gone because..." I struggle to get the words out. "It is all my fault, Robbie. How can I be with Jax knowing the only reason he is with me, is because... because I killed my parents?"

"Fuck, seriously, Tilly?" Robbie squeezes me tighter. "Is this what has been going through your mind? Do you actually blame yourself for mom and dad?"

I shrug, not wanting to say much more. My stomach twists and turns. I feel a giant lump in the back of my throat, causing it to burn—the emotional dam is about to break.

"Tilly," Robbie says. Taking my face into his hands, he forces me to look right into his amber eyes—eyes that match mine. "Listen to me, okay? Because I never want to repeat this conversation again. You are not responsible for the accident. Mom and dad are not dead because of anything you did. The only reason they are dead is because some fucknuts didn't have enough common sense to call for a ride home. It is his fault he was drinking and driving, it was his fault he ran the red light, and it was his fault that mom and dad are dead and that you were injured. None of that, and I mean—None. Of. It. Is. Your. Fault. Do you understand me?"

I try to catch my breath, now labored from crying so hard. Robbie's face is nothing but a blur through my sticky eyelashes. I want to believe Robbie, but it hurts so much. "We only went to the convention because I didn't want to go alone. We only left when we did because I—"

"Stop. It. Tilly." Robbie raises his voice, not in anger but in concern. "I don't know much about fate, and you know I am not really religious, but there was nothing you could have done to prevent what happened. It could have happened here in town.

We both know Jake has been called to enough tragic drunk driving scenes." Robbie pulls me closer. I nuzzle into his chest, wiping my tears and snot on his stained shirt, which still reeks of gasoline. "Mom and dad would never want you to carry this burden. Fuck, mom probably would have slapped you upside the head for thinking like that. You need to let this guilt go, Tilly, and move on. It isn't fair to you or Jax."

I sniffle, thinking about Robbie's words for a moment. "Still, when he leaves—"

"Come on. He is still here, Tilly." I look up at Robbie. Grabbing some tissues, he helps wipe my face. "But if any of those 'what if' scenarios you got going through that little head of yours come true, your brothers will be here to help put back together the broken pieces and kick his ass... *again*." Robbie smiles at me and I can't help but laugh.

"Thank you, Robbie." Feeling as though a thousand-pound weight has lifted from my chest, I can actually take a full breath.

"No worries, kid. It is what big brothers do." Robbie thinks for a second. "But let's not mention this to the others. I don't need them knowing that I am wise, and then coming to me for advice and shit. This..." He gestures between us. "...is only for you and me, get it? Those dumbasses can fend for themselves."

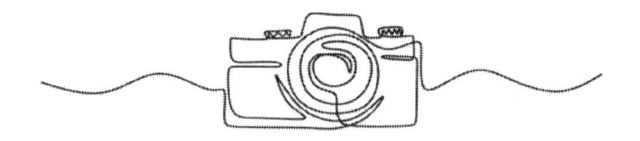

Chapter 15

Jackson

Tilly never returns to the shop. I wait around after closing, worried because I haven't heard from her. Shortly before I was about to call her and check in, Robbie sends me a quick text saying Tilly was just wrapping up and is on her way back home. Relieved, I quickly make my way back as well.

However, when I get home, Tilly still isn't here. I decide to try and whip up a quick dinner of pan-seared pork chops and roasted brussels sprouts—hopefully, she is over that ridiculous fear she has of them. It's nothing fancy, but it's way better than doing takeout. Noticing it has been over an hour since Robbie said Tilly was on her way, I start to get worried again—partially out of the sheer dread that something has happened to her, and partially out of concern that she is still avoiding me. We have been able to work with each other this week pretty decently, as long as we skirted around any deep conversations. Basically all we have talked about is the shop and food, and nothing more.

It has been nearly impossible to have her physically close to me all week, and at the same time have her so emotionally distant. This isn't the same sort of reticence as when I first arrived and her grief had consumed her. No, this emotional distance is cold and unsettling. Grabbing my phone, I decide to say *fuck it* and give her a call, which goes right to voicemail after two rings. Pissed, I am about to dial Robbie when I hear the front door open. Rushing to the living room, I am finally able to breathe a huge sigh of relief upon seeing Tilly hanging up her coat. That sensation of peace is quickly replaced by anger, as I remember how she didn't check in at all today and then how she (obviously) must have rejected my call just now.

I prepare to start grilling her about her behavior when she turns and looks at me. Her eyes are puffy and bloodshot. I can see streaks of dried tears staining her cheeks. My anger instinctually dissipates and I rush to Tilly, taking her into my arms. I don't care about the distance she has put between us. No force on this earth could stop me from trying to comfort her. "Tilly, what's wrong? Did something happen?"

She sniffles and wipes her face. "Sorry, I had a bit of a rough day today."

"Do you want to talk about it?" I offer, hoping she will open up to me like she has always done in the past.

"Umm... maybe in a little bit. I am going to go upstairs and freshen up." Tilly pulls out of my embrace, making her way up towards her bedroom.

"Dinner is ready whenever you are," I yell after her, in a lame attempt to entice her to come back downstairs again.

"Ok." Tilly grants me a weak smile. "I will be down in a few."

∞∞∞

Sitting at the dinner table the tension is so thick that it is almost suffocating. I want to do something to relieve this uneasy flutter I have in my chest, but I am not sure what to say. I know Tilly well enough, and I understand that she will only tell me what's wrong *if she wants to*. But at the same time (clearly) something is on her mind. She has barely touched her dinner, mostly using her fork to roll brussels sprouts around the ceramic dish.

"Do you not like it?" I attempt to make any level of small talk to break the ice. "I wasn't sure if you were over that whole *Ernest Scared Stupid* thing or not." I motion to the brussels sprouts on her plate.

"Huh...?" Tilly looks down and notices her practically full plate. "Oh, sorry. It is good. I guess I am just not very hungry."

Looking at Tilly, at first, I thought her behavior was as detached as it has been all week. But now as I pay closer attention, I see that she is nervously fidgeting. It is something Tilly has always done when she is embarrassed. Something happened today. I am not sure what, but I can see the gears turning in her head and trying to put all the pieces together.

"Is everything all right?" Tilly stops playing with her food and sets her fork down. Taking a deep breath and puffing out her chest, she looks up at me. Her amber eyes are ablaze. I am not sure what is fueling the flames exactly, but they are soaring.

Abruptly, Tilly stands from the table and commences to walk out of the room. There is no way I can let her walk away from me right now. That fire, it is something. It is the most emotion I have seen from her all week. I don't care if it is from anger or lust. While I hope it is the latter, I just want to feel something from her again.

My chair screeches as I slide it from the table. Almost instantaneously, I am behind Tilly, grabbing her arm and turning her back to me. "Tilly, wait—" The words are stolen from my mouth as Tilly pulls it down to meet hers.

"I'm sorry," she moans repeatedly in between strangled breaths.

My hands travel down her back, grabbing onto her ass and encouraging her legs to wrap around me. I contemplate carrying her upstairs, but the urgency in her kisses tells me we won't make it that far. If Jake comes home, he will get one hell of a show—but neither of us seem to care too much about that right now. I rush over to the couch in the living room, kicking my shoes off along the way. A primal urge takes over. Without thinking, I break our kiss to rip open her blouse. Buttons fly everywhere. When Tilly gasps, I worry for a split second that I have crossed the line; but when I see the flicker of hunger in her eyes, I know this is exactly what she needs.

Not wanting to waste another second overthinking what this might mean, I quickly strip Tilly and myself of our offensive apparel. Glancing down at Tilly's flushed body, I watch her breasts erratically falling and rising as she pants. Just the sight of her, like this, spirals me off the deep end. Burying my face in her neck, I begin kissing her firmly while giving her little love bites.

"Jax," she moans, "that feels so good." Her hands roam my back, as her nails trace roughly across my skin. This slight tinge of pain only encourages me to be rougher.

Kissing my way down to her rock-hard nipples, I take one fully in my mouth, sucking as hard as I can. I am instantly rewarded with Tilly running her fingers through my hair and pulling it so tightly that my scalp burns. "Fuck... I need more," she begs, practically ripping my hair from the root.

Before she has a moment to register what is happening, I pick her up and toss her down on her belly. Tilly raises her ass in the air, giving me a taunting little shake. Bending over, I punish her cheek with a light nibble. Tilly groans with encouragement. Tracing my finger down to her center, I slip it between her lips to check if she is wet and ready for me—which she is. Typically I would enjoy a bit more foreplay, but Tilly's body is begging me to fuck her good and proper right now.

Leaning forward, I grab a handful of Tilly's hair, tugging her head back slightly so that I can whisper in her ear. "Do you want me to fuck you?"

Tilly, as best she can, nods in approval. "Yes, please," she practically begs. It is all I wanted to hear before proceeding.

Without warning, I line up with her center and thrust deeply, sheathing myself fully inside of her. "Oh. God." Tilly cries in a mixture of pain and bliss. I give her a moment to adjust to the intrusion, before I begin pulling back and slamming forward again. My speed and tempo picking up with each thrust, it isn't long until I notice Tilly's desire boiling up. When I feel as though she is about to burst, I pull almost all the way out of her and hold myself in place. Tilly whines in frustration, begging me to continue, but I decide to let her suffer for a moment. I am not sure why. This isn't typically my style. But for some reason, in a way, I want her to feel a fraction of the agony I have felt for her this whole week.

Taking mercy on her, I resume my torturous thrusting. Tilly moans in appreciation and begins tensing up again. As I feel her on the verge of having a powerful orgasm, I pull back out. "God dammit. Jax—" Tilly starts to complain, but the protest is cutoff as I flip her onto her back.

"I'm sorry, Tilly. I can't do it..." A flash of concern on Tilly's face makes me realize that what I said came out wrong. Leaning down, I kiss her deeply... passionately. "I need to see your beautiful face as you fall apart around me."

Tilly's fear is immediately replaced with the intensity of her lust. Reaching lower, I hoist her hips up as I begin thrusting again, deep and steady strokes—savoring each moment I spend buried inside her wet heat. Tilly is practically vibrating in anticipation from the two orgasms I had previously denied her. "Please, don't stop," Tilly pleads.

I cover my mouth with hers as I continue pumping in and out, my tempo picking up slightly as I begin to lose control. Against my feral growls, Tilly whispers, "I love you." It sends me over the edge and into a monstrous spasm. Tilly tenses around me like a vice grip. I almost pass out from the sensation. It is seriously the most intense orgasm I have ever had.

Lying together, our limbs tangled up, I turn to nuzzle Tilly's face. "I love you too," I whisper softly in her ear.

Turning to look at me, Tilly searches my face. I can see that hint of nervousness again, so I lean closer and lightly kiss her nose—in exchange, she rewards me with a smile.

"I'm ready," Tilly says so softly, I almost don't hear her. I sit and think for a moment. She can't mean for sex again, can she? Because I am not sure if I can… to be honest. As if sensing my lack of understanding, she clarifies, "I am ready to give us a chance."

"Really?" I can't help but be a little cautious. I taper back my excitement, in fear that this is all a sex-induced dream.

"Yes…" Tilly hesitates for a moment. "I won't lie, Jax. I'm scared." Tilly's breath hitches at the admission. "Please, just don't hurt me?"

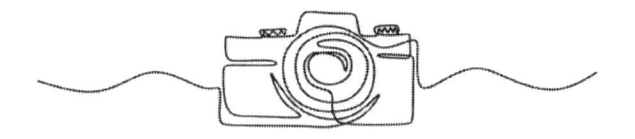

Chapter 16

Jackson

It has only been a few days since Tilly and I agreed to give this thing between us a real shot. That evening, she explained to me her fears and some of the guilt she has been carrying over the accident. It broke my heart to hear that Tilly has been blaming herself for the loss of her parents. It seems that whatever conversation she had with Robbie has helped her move past this giant burden she has been wielding. I won't lie. I was a little disappointed she didn't confide in me, but then again, I am grateful that she was able to talk to someone.

So far, things have been great. Fuck, I'd almost say perfect. We have basically had the house to ourselves. Jake is rarely ever around. When we are home, we binge *Buffy the Vampire Slayer*. Apparently, a ton happened after she graduated high school. I have decided that Spike is the biggest badass on the show, which has led to a few heated conversations over who is better—Angel or Spike? Then, we have some of the most amazing and crazy makeup sex afterwards.

When we are not at home, I go into the shop with Tilly and Scott. I have continued to help her, especially with social media and any heavy lifting. As she likes to put it, I am her "sexy muscle". In my downtime, I have even read through a few cookbooks and bookmarked some new recipes to try for us later.

It has been awesome spending so much time with Tilly; however—and though I hate to admit it—I still need more. Tilly is phenomenal and perfect, even better than what I could imagine. We just click. If that makes sense? But the shop is her thing, and while the social media is fun, it isn't enough to sustain me. I tried my hand in the café—and well, let's just say that those fancy coffees that Scott makes truly are works of art. It is amazing (with how big he is) that he can be so gentle and delicate with his creations. I felt like a giant with two left thumbs, fumbling those tiny espresso cups.

I need to find my place here in Tral Lake, something for me when I am not with Tilly. I know we are loving all this time together right now, but I also know that is just the honeymoon phase and we need to have our own things.

"Jackson Harris, is that you?" A warm voice says from behind me, while I am dusting some books. I turn around and see Patty Fitzgerald. She runs the local sweet shop here in town. It is one of those awesome places where all the candy is made in-house. The years have been good to her. She is probably in her late fifties now, but all that candy making has kept her in shape. Not to mention, she has this marvelous cotton candy pink pixie cut.

"Hi, Mrs. Fitzgerald." I put my duster down and give her a hug.

"Wow, you have grown so big, tall, and handsome." She winks at me. "I'm sorry for your loss." She frowns. "I know how close you are with the Moores. I wanted to say something at the service, but it didn't seem like the best time to catch up. I will admit I'm surprised that you are still here. I figured you would be off gallivanting and taking pictures around the world. How are you doing? Are you holding up okay?"

"I've been good. I know we are all still grieving. But I think each day it is getting a little easier. How are things going over at

Patty Cakes?" Yea, people in this town are pretty good at working their names into their shops. I still think Robbie's is the best though—*Moore Body and Lube.* Robbie hates it—but that is what he gets for betting against Jake. However, that's a story for another day.

"Oh, you know how it is—we have our ups and downs." She waves her hand, dismissing my inquiry. "How long are you in town for?"

"I am not sure exactly. I took some time off. And I'm... re-evaluating some things... I'm here at least for another week and a half." I look around and notice Tilly talking with customers. So I inch closer and whisper, "I am hoping to stick around permanently, but I'm still looking for work."

Patty glances over at Tilly; she knows exactly what I am trying to say. She leans in and whispers back, "Well, I know it isn't much. But maybe you could help me with something?"

"Sure thing, anything for you. What do you need help with?"

"Well, my sister who runs a candy shop over in Duluth has been hounding me about my social media. She is always telling me how much it has increased her business. But taking pictures and that posting nonsense, it isn't really my thing. I made an account, but it is so confusing. I saw some of the work you have been doing for the bookstore, and I was hoping maybe you could stop by, take some pictures and help me figure this stuff out?"

"Absolutely, does tomorrow work?" I offer gleefully.

"Oh, Jackson, you are a total lifesaver. Would you mind coming around 6am? That way you can get some pictures early in the day, when I do a lot of my cooking. I will even put together a special box of treats for Tilly," she adds with a knowing wink. That summer Tilly and I were together, I was in the shop almost daily buying her a treat. I know Tilly has never been the biggest fan of sweets, but she has a weak spot for dark chocolate.

"Sounds great. I will see you tomorrow morning, Mrs. Fitzgerald."

"*Patty*—please. Mrs. Fitzgerald makes me sound old, and I am not ready to be old yet. I will see you in the morning." She gives me a big smile before bringing her books up to the counter. I overhear her and Tilly chatting and shortly after, she offers her condolences.

I resume my dusting. Then a few minutes later, Tilly comes up behind me, wrapping her arms around my waist. "What was that all about?"

I turn around, pulling Tilly into my arms. "Oh, nothing really. Patty was just surprised to see me in town still. She asked if I could help her with a project."

Tilly smiles at me. I definitely want to see that smile every day. "Oh, yea? What kind of project? Are you going to learn how to make candy with her?"

I cannot help but laugh. "I do not think I am ready for that yet. No, she asked if I could come and take some pictures for her and help her learn social media. She mentioned her sister, and how much it has helped her business."

"Wow, Jax, that is amazing. It is absolutely perfect for you." A giant smile grows on Tilly's face.

"It is nothing much, just taking a few pictures." I shrug. "It will be fun, but it isn't exactly a career though."

"Yea, maybe not. Honestly, your help around here has been phenomenal. I am awful at taking pictures and doing posts. Scott is a bit better, but he doesn't have the time. Since you have been helping, we are getting so much engagement online—not to mention, an increase in orders." Tilly starts jumping up and down excitedly all of a sudden. "You know I am a member on our tourism board. Well, we could really use someone to help manage our town's social media, try to boost our tourism. You would be absolutely perfect for that. Would you come to our next meeting—it is Friday? I would love to pitch the idea to them."

Tilly might be onto something. It won't be as exciting as Greece or Hawaii. But at the same time, it is something I could do. If I could work with the town and help with the advertising, that would be right up my alley. Besides, it might be the best opportunity for me to stay here with Tilly and do something within my skill set at the same time. Which, in addition to getting to spend every day with her, is worth more than any exotic location I could imagine.

"Absolutely. I would love to go to your meeting."

Tilly leans up and gives me a big kiss. As if by their own accord, my hands travel down to her butt and respond with a small squeeze. Coughing off in the distance causes us to separate.

"Sorry to interrupt. I was just going to go pick up some lunch. I was curious if you wanted to go with me?" Scott asks in my direction.

"Yea, sure. Want the usual, babe?" I inquire with Tilly.

"Umm, actually, can you just get me some chicken soup and biscuits. I haven't been feeling so hot this morning," Tilly replies, a little hesitant to admit that she isn't feeling good.

"Sure thing, are you sure you don't need to go home and lie down?" I did notice she looked a little pale this morning. But we were up kind of late last night. I should start making sure she gets a good night's sleep. Instead of staying up too late watching *Buffy*, and then having amazingly awesome sex. I don't want her getting sick from exhaustion.

She waves her hand, dismissing my concern. "Oh, I'm fine. I am sure Sue's famous chicken soup will cure me." She offers me a small smile and returns to the counter.

I give her a brief kiss before leaving with Scott. As we make our way down to the diner, I notice we haven't really talked much since the fight. He has shown me some coffee stuff, but that is about it. While we have been pleasant with each other, it still feels as though this dark cloud hangs over our friendship.

"How is it going?" he inquires.

"So far, good. I am enjoying spending time with Tilly," I answer honestly.

"Hmm..." he ponders.

"Come on, Scott, subtlety has never been your strength. What is up?"

"Well, I was just curious if you have made any decisions yet. I know last week was a little tough with Tilly icing you out. But now that it seems you guys have gotten past whatever that issue was... well, you both seem really happy. I was kind of hoping to hear you have a plan for sticking around."

"Honestly, no, I don't have a plan yet. I want to stay. Being with Tilly has been incredible. I'm the happiest I have been in what seems like forever. But I haven't quite found my place yet, you know, my own thing? Outside of Tilly and me."

"Huh?" We both continue walking in silence for a moment. "I'm sorry about last week. You know, first, for giving you a hard time about staying. Then, about you almost giving up when Tilly put up her roadblock. Along with, well, you know..." Scott shrugs, not really sure how to bring up the fight. "You know I am just looking out for my little sister, right?"

"Yea, I know. As much as hearing what you said and getting punched in the face fucking sucked, I needed it. I needed my best friend to whip my ass into gear." I give him a teasing grin. I needed Scott's tough love.

"You are my best friend too, and it would really be awesome if you could stick around. If you need help with anything, let me know," Scott offers. I feel that metaphorical dark cloud start to move past us.

We both stop on the sidewalk and give each other a big hug. "Thanks, man. I will let you know if I need anything."

"Actually, I'm going over to Patty's tomorrow to do some photos for her and help with her social media. Tilly is really excited. She asked if I could come to her next tourism board meeting. Something about managing the town's social media? It isn't much right now, but it could be something." I shrug. I am hopeful, but I will not get excited yet.

"That is pretty awesome. I am sure a lot of people in this town would love the help of not only a professional photographer, but a professional travel photographer. Tilly is right. It is an untapped market around here." Scott pauses and thinks for a moment. "Hey, do you remember the Rigifords?"

"Hmm... yea, don't they have that farm on the edge of town?

Isn't that where we had the majority of our keggers?" I try to recall.

"Yea, that's the place. Well, his son Eli... I am not sure if you remember him—he was a couple years older than us. Anyway, he took over the orchard a few years ago after his dad retired. He has been wanting to get into some advertising and convert his old barn into an event area. You know how people go to vineyards and get married? He was thinking his orchard would be a nice spot as well."

"Oh, yea? That would be pretty cool. I always loved apple picking when we were young. I could sit out there and smell the orchard for hours." The Moores constantly took us to U-Pick Farms growing up. I loved going. The scenery was always beautiful and Mrs. Moore would reward us by cooking us a special treat with the produce we picked.

"Ha, that is exactly what he said. Yea, he actually got the permits to build a small chateau to rent out there, and is remodeling the big red barn. I know he could use some help with images and marketing."

"I will talk to him. Thanks, man." For the first time, I am starting to feel like maybe things are going to work out. "Hey, Saturday night, do you want to get together? Maybe we can all go out like we used to?"

Scott slaps me on the back. "Abso-fuckin-lutely, sir. Are you sure Tilly will let you come out and play?" he asks with his mischievous grin.

"Ha, I am sure I can convince her," I say, waggling my eyebrows. Scott elbows me in the gut. And it is nice. It feels like for the first time since I have been home, Scott and I are back to our old selves.

Chapter 17

Matilda

Watching Jax take pictures is one of the sexiest things I have ever seen. When photographing, he is totally in his element. Yesterday, he took pictures at Patty's. The images were absolutely amazing. I couldn't believe how well he captured her shop. Also (bonus) Jax brought me home a box of the most delectable dark fudge from Patty's. It has been forever since I had any fudge from her shop. It was always kind of Jax's and my thing, and well, it didn't feel right without him.

Today, Letty graciously agreed to help cover the shop. Granted, she doesn't take much convincing when extra money is involved. She has been saving up to buy Harper's. With Ted Harper not too far from retirement, she wants to be ready to invest. I'm excited. I have seen her plans for the bar and it will be amazing when she takes over.

Jax and I decide to get out of town, drive to the bluffs, and make a day of it. With the leaves changing and the clear blue sky, everything is stunning right now. Today has been absolutely perfect, getting to spend time with Jax away from the house and away from the shop. Not to mention, he has taken some exceptional photos. I cannot wait to get a few printed and hung up in the shop and at home.

Now, we are sitting on a log bench at a park, sipping some hot apple cider. We look like the classic Minnesota couple. I am wearing my light blue skinny jeans, a black t-shirt, a red and black plaid flannel, and tall tan hiking boots. Jax is wearing his grey dickies, a button-down black fleece shirt, his beanie, and boots. I've made sure to get a few pictures of us together, whereas Jax has made sure to get several of *me*. Some he asked me to pose for, but most he took on his own.

It is just like when we were younger. He was always taking my picture. At the time, it made me feel so beautiful, the way he was able to depict me. In each and every picture, I somehow looked pure. It was like he captured me, just how he saw me. After he was gone, I hated having my photo taken. I never looked the same again.

"I've been thinking," he states, breaking our comfortable silence.

"Uh oh, that can't be good." I smirk at him.

He chuckles and pushes my shoulder lightly with his own. "Well, I have a ton of vouchers to use at the resorts I photographed. And of course, a ridiculous amount of flyer miles. I was wondering if maybe you would want to go somewhere with me? Anywhere really?"

"Like a real vacation? Just you and I?" Besides camping up north or in Canada, I have never really been on a vacation before. Not to some exotic place, at least.

"Yea, just you and I. We can go wherever you like. I have vouchers for Hawaii, Greece, Spain, Ireland, Jamaica, Brazil, Japan, and more. Or if none of those resorts interest you, we can go wherever you want." He looks down at his hands before looking back up at me. "I just really would love to go somewhere with you."

"I would love that, Jax. I would need to work out the help to cover the shop. But I know it is doable. When were you thinking?" My mind is racing a million miles per minute. Does this mean he is sticking around? He only has about one week left of vacation here. The trips mean the future, some sort of future.

"Well, maybe we could go after the holidays? I understand this time of the year is still a little busy with fall tourism and then holiday shopping. I would say we could go away for Christmas, but I know how much you love celebrating the holidays with your family. I imagine this year will be difficult, and it will be important for all of you to be together."

I didn't think I could love him anymore than I already do, but then he says all this. He is right. I do love the holidays. They have always been a big deal in our home. Mom has totes full of decorations for the house and the shop to cover each holiday and then general seasonal decorations. She even has throw blankets and pillows to rotate through the year. I will admit I have been dreading the upcoming season a little, without mom and dad here. But I know it would honor them to continue with the traditions.

"That sounds wonderful Jax, thank you." I know this might kill the mood, but I need to ask. "Hey, Jax, what does this mean? Are you staying?"

Jax sits and ponders for a moment before sighing. "I am not sure yet."

"Oh." I know I shouldn't be surprised. But I was really hoping this was his creative way of telling me he wasn't going back.

Jax lifts my chin to look at him. "Hey, sweetheart, I am not saying I am leaving. Just that things are still a little uncertain right now. I have talked to folks around town about doing photographs and social media work for them. Patty has referred me to basically every shop on Main Street. I have also talked with Eli about his plans for the orchard. Then, we have the meeting tomorrow with the tourism board. But I still do not know what that all means yet. I am not sure how sustainable the work is."

I sniffle. "I know that makes sense. I am sorry I brought it up. I just—" He leans down and gives me a quick kiss.

"I get it. I am making plans for our future. You wanted to know what that meant. It does mean something, Tilly."

"But what *does* it mean?" A tear rolls down my cheek, and he wipes it away.

"Well, I have been contemplating a couple of things. If I don't find work in Tral Lake, it doesn't mean I need to leave town exactly. I know it would not be ideal, but I was thinking of getting rid of my apartment in New York. The lease is due for renewal anyway, and it is expensive real estate that I almost never visit. I was thinking maybe I should move back here. So, when I am not working, I can come home to you."

"How does that work exactly? You just said you are never at your apartment anyway?" I don't mean to downplay his idea. But while I enjoy seeing Jax, having him roll into town once every few months for a weekend is worse than him just being gone.

"That is by choice, Tilly. There was nothing to go home to. I would always show up to shoots early and stay longer, rarely ever going home. I was thinking I could balance my work and home life a little more. Sandra, one of the other travel photographers who works for the magazine... she works two weeks on and one week off. Then, she actually takes her vacation time and holidays off to spend with her family. She has three kids at home and a husband. I know it wouldn't be easy, and that the weeks apart would be tough—"

"But it would be something, right?" I try not to sound too disappointed. I know it isn't ideal, but this is better than what the military spouses go through. They manage to have happy healthy relationships, when their partner is gone six months to a year at a time.

Jax smiles at me. "I understand this isn't optimal, or likely what you wanted, but it could be workable if you are interested. We could video chat while I am gone, call or text each other daily, have amazing phone sex." He gives me his signature big smile. "Then, when I am home, I get to spend my time with you and help take pictures around the town. My ultimate goal would still be to find stable enough work locally. But at least this way, we could be together. I know I haven't figured everything out yet, Tilly. But spending this time home, the one thing I know for certain is that I am not ready to let you go. I might never be ready for that."

It would be difficult, but it is not impossible if we are both willing to put in the work. If Jax is willing to give up some of his traveling to be home more with me, I feel like I can compromise with him on wanting him here all of the time. But for how long? I know some can do it, but I've never thought of myself as a long-distance relationship kind of girl. Not to mention, I am getting older. I want to get married and have children. While Jax has always had the starring role in those fantasies, in those same dreams, he was also here. I am not sure I could handle a part-time spouse and father.

I set my cider down on the bench, and turn back to Jax. Straddling his lap and taking his face in the palm of my hands, I whisper, "Jax, I love you." I lean down and give him a deep passionate kiss. His mouth immediately opens for mine, allowing my tongue entry... allowing our entangled mouths to communicate how much we love each other, in a way words never could compare.

When our kiss breaks, we are both left breathless and panting. I rest my forehead on his as he confesses, "I love you, Matilda. I promise we will make this work."

I know Jax means well, but the only way this can work is if he is here all the time. I would never force him to stay or give him an ultimatum. But I am not sure if long-distance could ever work for me. I guess... we'll just have to cross that bridge when we get to it. I promised I would give this a shot, knowing the risks associated with it. I just hope in the end the gamble with my heart is worth it.

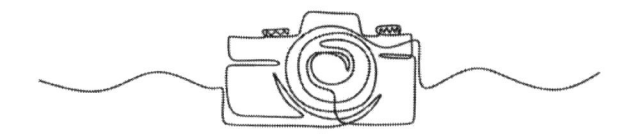

Chapter 18

Jackson

I'm not sure why, but I am really nervous for the tourism board meeting. I know I shouldn't be. Tilly seems on board with the idea that I still work for the magazine but make time to come home to her. It is not ideal. Honestly, the thought of not going to bed with her at night or waking up with her in my arms is like hell. Also, long-distance can be tough. And I worry that eventually, we won't be able to handle it anymore, especially Tilly. I just need to remember it will be temporary, until I find something local.

The meeting is taking place at the town hall. It is nothing large or fancy. I think it used to be a chapel back in the day. The board consists of ten members, most of whom own shops on Main Street. Then, there's the woman who runs the bed and breakfast; though, I haven't officially met her yet. I think she moved to town a few years ago. Tilly said her name is Scarlett and she is from California. How she ended up here, I have no idea.

"Matilda, you mentioned you have a proposition for the board?" Keith McCalester asks. Of course, fucking McCalester has to be on the damn board. And apparently, not just on the board, but the president of it. While I am pissed Tilly didn't warn me about this dipshit being here, I understand why she didn't. I probably would have never agreed to go to the meeting. The McCalesters are the richest family in town, and one of the founding families—along with the Moores and the Fitzgeralds. It doesn't mean much these days, but I remember granddad telling me all about it.

"Yes, Keith. We have been discussing how in order to increase our tourism, we needed a social media and marketing manager for the town. Jackson here, is a professional travel photographer. He has already been working with some of the shop owners in town, taking photos and assisting with social media. I propose hiring Jackson to fill the role as the town's social media and marketing manager."

"I love that idea. Jackson took pictures of my shop a few days ago and helped me do a couple of posts. I have already had ten new out-of-town orders. I usually only get ten of those a month," Patty adds.

"He is also helping me with a marketing plan for the orchard," Eli comments as well.

Keith sits there, rubbing his pointy chin. With his slicked-back black hair, he looks like a villain plotting to destroy the world. Don't get me wrong, I know by the usual standards he is "handsome" but that is only on the outside. On the inside, he is nothing but a weasel—the kind of man who hides behind both his last name and his daddy, who just so happens to be our town mayor.

Back in the day, I know he had an almost obsessive crush on Tilly. With the way he is looking at her, I am guessing that hasn't changed. Jake, Scott, and I made it our personal mission to keep him as far away as possible from Tilly. Not that she can't handle herself, but there is just something about that sleaze that has never sat well with us.

∞∞∞

Ten Years Ago

Tilly descends the stairs in a sparkling golden gown. Her hair is down in luscious waves, and her face is glowing with minimal makeup; all that I really notice is her plush ruby-red lips that I can't wait to kiss later tonight. She looks like a fucking goddess, and I am glad that I decided to finally take a chance on us. Scott was right, Tilly and I are meant to be. I have no doubt about that.

"Oh my, Tilly, you look beautiful," Mrs. Moore says, rushing into the room with her camera in hand. I can see the tears in her eyes… her children are now all grown up.

"She looks okay, but we both know that I am the better looking one though," Jake adds; he looks like Bond in his tuxedo, with his blonde hair slicked back and to the side. While they are twins, Tilly is definitely the more attractive sibling, at least to me.

"Whatever, Jake." Tilly rolls her eyes. "You are just jealous that I have a date to prom and you don't."

"Ha! Nope. Going stag is perfect. We all know I might be going there alone, but I will not be leaving that way," Jake replies, nudging my shoulder.

"Children, come on, now. I want to get some pictures before Letty shows up and rushes everyone out of here," Mrs. Moore says, ushering all of us to the living room.

"You look absolutely stunning, Tilly," I say, leaning down and whispering in her ear so only she could hear me. Tilly's pale complexion starts to flush, making her look even more beautiful.

Mrs. Moore takes what feels like a gazillion photos of us, before Letty finally shows up. Letty comes storming into the house, in her normal fashion. While Tilly chose a classic look, Letty went with a far more vibrant hot pink dress that leaves little to the imagination. Her dark hair is piled on her head in some curly mess. She also has the whole dark smokey eye thing going on with bright pink lipstick. While she is beautiful, I prefer Tilly's more natural and classic beauty.

"*Sorry I'm late. The limo got held up in some traffic,*" *Letty says, coming in and giving air kisses to Tilly on the cheek. "Wow, you look amazing, Tilly. I love the dress."*

"*Thanks,*" *Tilly replies, then looks confused. "Wait, limo? I thought we were just going to take Jake's van? Also, how the hell did you afford a limo?"*

"*One—there is no way we are showing up, as hot as we are, to our senior prom in Jake's Shaggin' Wagon." Letty gives Jake a look of disgust. "Two—I didn't have to afford anything. My date got the limo."*

"*Who was desperate enough to take you to prom, Letty?" Jake snarls at her.*

As if on cue, Keith walks through the doorway, wearing a classic tux with his ink hair slicked back. Upon entering, his eyes immediately lock onto Tilly like a predator. While his arm is around his date, he is shamelessly eye-fucking mine in front of everyone. Letty doesn't seem to realize, or care. But Jake and I take notice right away. Jake looks at him and then over to me, as if telepathically saying, "Is this guy fucking serious?" I wordlessly reply back, "We need to keep an eye on this scumbag tonight." Jake nods outwardly in agreement.

Mrs. Moore snaps a few more pictures of the whole group. Afterwards, Mr. Moore takes us boys to the side to give us his brief speech on respecting our dates; then he reminds us that he owns a shotgun and a shovel, in case any of us forgets. Though, the majority of that part of the conversation is directed to Keith.

The limo ride to prom is tense. Tilly keeps shifting uncomfortably next to me. I notice Keith has yet to take his eyes off of her. Letty doesn't appear to notice however. She has been too busy giving Jake the stink-eye, while he watches Keith as well. It seems he is just as uncomfortable as Tilly.

After finally getting to prom, we quickly find a table before making the rounds. As soon as I get Tilly onto the dance floor, she looks more relaxed.

"*Hey, is everything okay?" I ask Tilly. I know the issue is Keith. But she seems especially tense about it this time.*

Tilly looks up at me in a daze, almost as if my question didn't register with her. "Oh, yea, everything is really nice."

"No, Tilly, is everything okay with you? Ever since we left, you have seemed a little reserved."

Tilly looks around and sees Letty and Keith dancing on the other side of the room. She shakes her head and looks back at me before smiling. "No, sorry everything is fine. I think it just must be the whole senior prom, high school ending, nostalgia thing."

I know she is lying, but I drop it for now. Whatever was bothering her appears to have passed. For a while, Tilly and I dance and laugh, enjoying the night. Jake disappears, likely looking for his lonely girl who needs some cheering up. In between songs, we meet back up with Letty and Keith at the table.

"Hey, Tilly, let's go to the bathroom and freshen up after all that dancing?" *Letty asks, giving a come-hither look to Keith.*

When they walk off, it is just Keith and me sitting at the table. This is extremely awkward. I consider getting up and waiting by the restrooms, but eventually Keith speaks up. "It was sure nice of you willing to be Matilda's charity date this evening."

"Excuse me?" *Why the hell would Tilly ever need a charity date? If anything, I am grateful she wanted me to go with her.*

"Yea, I was worried tonight would be a little awkward. I had to turn down poor Matilda when she asked... well, practically begged me to go to the prom with her. She is a sweet girl and all, but Letitia is all woman," *he says, looking smug and drinking his punch.*

I sit there, clenching and unclenching my fist. I am pretty certain that Tilly would never have asked this sleazeball to the prom, but she has been acting a little weird about Keith tonight. I had thought that maybe she didn't like how he was staring at her. But maybe I am reading this all wrong? Maybe she is jealous of Letty? No, there is no way Tilly would ever give this douche the time of day. I cool my emotions before replying with a shit-eating grin, "Well, your loss is my gain I guess."

Keith laughs, a hollow soulless laugh. "Believe me, I am experiencing no loss this evening. As soon as Leticia gets back from freshening up, we are out of here. I got us a suite in the Twin Cities tonight, and well, let's just say neither one of us will be left unsatis-

fied tonight."

This guy is a complete pig, the exact stereotype of what no guy should ever be. I excuse myself before finding Tilly. Something isn't sitting right and I need to talk to her. I intercept as they exit the bathroom. "Hey, Tilly, can we talk for a second?" I ask, grabbing her elbow and leading her down the hall.

"I will meet you back at the table," Tilly says to Letty before walking with me. "Is something wrong?"

"Look, I don't know how to ask you this, but did you ask Keith to take you to the prom?" I can see the panic in her eyes. "It is okay if you did. He just mentioned something at the table, and well, you have seemed off since he showed up tonight. I was wondering if you were maybe jealous of Letty or something?"

Tilly has the look of complete disgust on her face. "I am not sure what the hell Keith said, but I can tell you I absolutely did not ask that jackass to the prom."

I let out a breath I didn't even realize I was holding. "Okay. Then, why have you been weird all night?"

She drops her shoulders, looking defeated. "This has to stay between us, okay? You can't tell my brothers. Promise?"

This can't be good, but I have no choice. "Okay, sure."

"Keith asked me to go to prom, and I turned him down," she says, looking towards her feet. "He didn't take it very well. At first, he played it off as no big deal. But then, he started showing up everywhere—at my locker, after my classes, and then eventually the shop. It was creepy. He kept asking me, telling me how great our night would be together and how we were perfect for each other. I don't know... a whole bunch of weird shit."

I knew the guy was a creeper... I just didn't realize how bad he really is.

"But that is not all. A couple of weeks ago, he asked me again. This time, he cornered me outside of the locker room. I told him no, again, that I already had a date. He flipped, started cursing, and even punched the wall next to my head. He scared the shit out of me. I know he has had a crush on me or whatever for a while, but I never realized just how psychotic he was." She takes a deep breath, shaking *the memory off.* "As far as tonight, I am absolutely not jealous. I am worried about Letty. I know for whatever reason she likes him, just like every other girl in the school who thinks he is mister prince charming. But I know he only asked her to try and get back at me. I am worried he is going to hurt Letty because I turned him down."

Tilly is practically shaking. Thinking back to what Keith said earlier, I am worried as well. I quickly let Tilly know what Keith told me. Before I finish, Tilly storms off and pulls Letty to the side. I am not sure what she says to her, but Letty returns to the table with a vengeance and Tilly on her heels.

"Hey, babe, ready to get out of here?" Keith asks Letty, giving her his deceptive smile.

Letty smiles right back, with venom practically dripping from her lips. She leans in to Keith, whispering something in his ear. Whatever she says, his mood changes dramatically. Before he even has a chance to react, she knees him in the balls. The squeal he makes as he collapses to the floor gets everyone's attention.

"You are a sick fuck, Keith. I hope I broke your needle dick, and maybe did the ladies in this town a favor." Letty then turns to the table, grabbing a couple cups of punch before dumping them on him.

As Jake approaches, he looks at the scene in front of him. "What the fuck just happened?"

I shake my head. It is best not to talk about it right now. Not to mention, I promised Tilly I wouldn't tell her brothers. He looks over at Letty, who is still fuming. I feel bad for her. If she does actually like the guy, it must suck to find out what he did to her best friend. And then, to discover that the only reason he was asking her out in the first place was in a failed attempt to make another girl jealous. It is fucking pathetic.

"Are you guys ready to go?" Letty asks, reaching for her purse.

We all grab our stuff and head towards the exit, leaving Keith on the floor embarrassed and in pain. The entire class is still standing around gossiping and laughing about the incident.

As a final fuck you to Keith, we take the limo to the Twin Cities. I buy us all some champagne and we continue partying. The rest of the night is amazing, even Letty and Jake seem to be getting along for a *change.*

∞∞∞

Present

"Hmm, it is not the worst idea I have ever heard," Keith replies, narrowing his eyes at me before smiling back at Tilly. "If you have a moment after the meeting, Matilda, maybe we can further discuss the position and what we would need to do to make it possible?"

Tilly tenses next to me. I am guessing the last thing she wants to do is be alone with Keith. I am about to say something, but Tilly places her hand on my arm and looks at me—pleading with her eyes—before turning back to Keith and giving him a shallow smile.

"Sure, we can talk after the meeting," Tilly replies meekly.

"Great." Keith smirks as though he just won some sort of victory. "Next order of business..."

Once the meeting is over, I walk with Tilly to the door. "Are you sure you don't want me to stay?"

"No, it's fine. Why don't you head over to Harper's and I will meet you there in a minute? I'll be all right." Tilly leans up and gives me a quick kiss on the cheek.

I don't like the idea of leaving her alone, but I don't want to cause a scene either. I mean, that shit happened over ten years ago. We are all adults now, and have moved on. Or, at least, I hope?

Chapter 19

Matilda

After Jax leaves, I take a deep calming breath. I am not sure why I am nervous about talking with Keith. We have both been on this board together for the past three years and have had no issues. Neither one of us has said much to the other, just shared casual pleasantries.

I walk back to the meeting area. Keith is sitting there on his phone. He holds his hand up to me, ordering me to pause—like whatever the hell he is doing is too damn important and I am beneath him. I know he is the Assistant City Manager and oversees many departments, but I can think of nothing that would be so important on a Friday evening.

After a moment, he looks up at me offering what (I can only assume) he thinks is his most charming smile. It likely melts the panties off most of the girls around here—well, those who don't know him, or those who don't care that he is a scumbag, and who just want to marry into his family money. Honestly, his last name is the only reason people kiss his ass.

"Oh, Matilda, thank you for waiting. Sorry, I had a last-minute city emergency. Please, sit." He gestures to the chair next to him. I reluctantly take a seat, angling my body in the opposite direction. "So, tell me, how are you holding up? I haven't spoken to you since the funeral."

"Okay, I guess. You know, each day gets a little better." I know it seems like he is just being nice, but I have a hard time trusting anything when it comes to him. This is exactly how things started when he asked me to prom. He was all nice and charming. But then, the second he didn't get his way, he snapped. "About the posi—"

He cuts me off. "Yes. Look, Matilda. I do agree we could use assistance when it comes to our town's social media and marketing. But I am just not sure Jackson Harris is... Well, I am just not sure he is what we are looking for."

"I don't understand. He has spent the last ten years working for a prestigious travel magazine. I know it isn't exactly marketing, but it is what he went to school for. Also, the few individuals he has helped around town, including myself, can speak for his skill set."

"Look, Matilda, can I be honest with you?" He tries to appear as though he is sympathetic, while he places a hand on my shoulder. "I am sure he takes good pictures and all, and maybe has helped people so far. But we really need someone with solid experience. Also, I think it would be beneficial to offer the position to someone local, who knows the area and is able to communicate the right message."

I shrug off his hand. "Jax is local and knows the area and, not to mention, most of the business owners. Also, experience is not everything. He has a true gift; he can capture the beauty of the most mundane things."

He sighs and shakes his head. "I understand he is a talented photographer. No one is denying that. But he is not qualified. I worry that your judgement is biased, given your *personal* relationship with Jackson. Offering the position to an unqualified individual—well, some might think you abused your role in this committee, just to help your friend get a job."

I abruptly stand up. "You have to be shitting me, Keith? At least two other board members both agree he would be ideal for the job, based on their own personal experiences. Then, of course, there's a number of other shops that are already interested in his assistance. It sounds like the only person who is passing judgement based on a *personal* relationship is you."

He scoffs and waves off my implication. "I'm not sure what you are talking about. Jackson and I have no personal history. I barely know him. I am only concerned about offering the position to an individual who has been absent from this town for a decade, and whose career involves a large amount of travel. You can't really think this job would keep him entertained enough to stick around, can you?"

"Whatever, Keith. Clearly, you are not interested in offering the position to Jackson." I get up to leave.

"Wait, Matilda." Keith stands a little too close to me. "I will admit I have some reservations about offering the position to Jackson, but I am not completely against it. How about this? Why don't we meet tomorrow night, and discuss it more over dinner?"

"I'm not sure, Keith. Why can't we just discuss it now?" I cross my arms. I really have a bad feeling about this.

"Look, I need some time to think about it. I will take tonight, and look at some of the work he has done. Then tomorrow, we can meet and talk about it more." Without giving me a chance to speak up, he quickly adds, "Look at the time. I need to get going. I will pick you up tomorrow at seven."

"Fine, but tomorrow I am working at the shop. I can meet you there instead," I agree. If having to suffer through dinner with Keith for one night can get Jax the job he needs to stay here with me, well then, it is worth it.

"Wonderful, it's a date," Keith says. He winks at me and immediately walks out the door, not even giving me a chance to reply.

Fuck! Hopefully, he doesn't actually think this is a real date?

It is just a dinner to discuss a business agreement. I quickly grab my purse to run after him. I need to clarify this fact. But when I get outside, he is already gone—the slimy little weasel.

∞∞∞

I see Jax, leaning on the bar and chatting with Letty. He looks so handsome—sitting there in his black pants, grey long-sleeve shirt, and his worn-out black and white chucks. Letty notices me enter the double doors and waves me over. Jax turns around, shooting me his giant megawatt smile.

"Hey, babe, how did it go?" He stands giving me a quick kiss. "I was about ready to run over there and rescue you."

I shrug and take the seat next to him. Jax plops back down on his own stool, before draping his arm over my shoulders. "That bad, huh?"

"I know what you need—a good dose of tequila will cheer you right up." Letty laughs, going for the bottle of Patrón.

"No, it isn't that bad. Can I actually just get a Sprite and maybe some chicken tenders?" I ask, while getting suspicious glances from both Letty and Jax.

"Are you sure? I figured you might want some sort of alcohol to sanitize yourself after interacting with that sleazeball." Letty crosses her arms, trying to read my mind.

"I agree, a hot shower does sound like heaven right now. But no tequila. My stomach still feels off and I just want something mellow."

Jax rubs my back. "You are still feeling sick? Why don't we go home and I can make some soup while you relax in the bath?"

He is so sweet. "Aw, thank you. But chicken tenders sound good. They are my comfort food and Harper's has the best ones in town."

"Okay, it's just that you haven't been feeling well all week. Maybe we should go and see the doctor?"

"That's okay. I am not sick. My stomach has just been a little queasy and I have been exhausted. I know it is just the stress getting to me. Don't worry. If I still feel sick next week, I have my checkup for my arm. I will mention it then."

Jax crosses his arms over his chest, analyzing me—almost as if he has x-ray vision and can see what is ailing me. "Fine. But if it gets worse, we are going in right away, okay?"

"Yes, I promise." I lean in and give him a kiss, which allows him to relax.

"So, what did douchenozzel have to say?" Letty inquires, as she gets my Sprite and Jax another beer.

"Umm, no decision was made yet." I better just tell Jax and get this over with. Maybe if I act nonchalant, he won't freak out. While I take a sip of my soda, I casually mention, "We are having dinner tomorrow night to discuss it more."

"Excuse me?" Jax whispers harshly, while Letty gives me a "what the hell did you just agree too" kind of stare.

"It is no big deal, Jax. He just wants time to look at your work and think about it. Then, we will meet tomorrow night for dinner to discuss it," I say, shrugging my shoulders and trying to downplay how really uncomfortable it all makes me. But if it will help Jax stay here, one night of hell is worth it.

"No, nuh-uh. You are not going on a date with him to get me a job," he says with complete finality. "I am not pimping out my girlfriend for work. We will find something else."

I laugh at his ridiculousness. "First, it is not a date. Second, you are not *pimping* me out. It is a casual business dinner. He had some concerns about offering you the position and I asked him to reconsider."

"Does he know it is not a date?" Letty adds to the conversation, still giving me the glare.

"Yea, what she said," Jax agrees. "This is Keith, the guy who harassed you for months to try and get you to go to prom with him. Then, when you denied him, he tried to manipulate you by taking Letty instead. And finally, he was made a fool in front of the whole class."

"I know what happened, Jax. But that was over a decade ago.

We have been on the council together for the past three years. Not once has that incident ever been brought up, or has he acted anything but professional with me." I understand his concern, but we have all grown up.

"I don't like this," Jax states as Letty echoes her agreement.

"Look, all that shit happened when we were stupid teenagers. He has not given me any reason to think he has any sort of ulterior motive. While I don't like what he said, he had valid business concerns. If going to dinner and discussing them with him is what I need to do, then I will." I give both of them the look that says, "I'm a big girl and I can make my own decisions."

"Fine, but let me go on record as saying, *I don't like this*. I have a bad feeling, Tilly." I know Jax is worried. But it is dinner, nothing bad is going to happen. Worst-case scenario, he doesn't give the job to Jax and we are back to the drawing board.

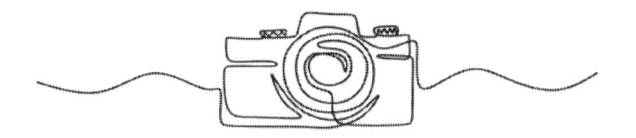

Chapter 20

Jackson

"Are you ready to go?" Scott asks from the archway that connects the shop to the cafe.

"Yea, just give me a minute." He nods and heads outside to wait for me. I quickly wrap up organizing the shelf I am working on before I leave. The next installment of some big paranormal romance was released today, and Tilly wanted to set up a display for the new book and the earlier installments. I quickly snap a few photos on my phone to post to the shop's Facebook.

I find Tilly in the back office working on the books. She looks like a sexy librarian right now. Her hair is up in a messy bun. She has on a simple cream button-up blouse, nothing too revealing. But all day, I've been imagining undoing each one of those buttons with my teeth. Then, to top it off, she is wearing these black slacks that hug her ass perfectly. I know it is not a particularly provocative outfit and that she was trying to make sure she looked "all business", but she could be wearing a burlap sack and she would still look sexy.

"Are you sure you don't want me to come with you? I can help convince Keith why I am good for the position," I offer for the hundredth time today. I really don't want her to go out to dinner with him. Even though she says he has been nothing but professional with her, I still get this weird vibe from him.

She sighs and closes the register. "I promise, I will be fine. Go have fun with Scott tonight. I don't think you guys have had any sort of boys' night out since you have been back." Coming around the desk, she gives me a quick kiss. "Have fun, and I will see you later tonight."

"Fine, but if anything feels off... If he makes you feel uncomfortable once, call me immediately," I sternly demand. I know Tilly is a grown woman and can take care of herself. I have absolutely no reason to be jealous. I honestly am worried the sleaze is going to try and pull something on her.

"Yes, I promise. Now go. I am sure Scott is getting impatient waiting for you." I give her one last good kiss before going outside and meeting Scott.

"Alright, man, what are we up to tonight?" I ask, slapping Scott on the back.

"I'm glad you asked. We have some business to settle," he says with a shit-eating grin.

"Business, huh? What business is this?" I play along with his banter.

"Well, Robbie and Jake seem to think that they are the reigning bowling champs. But as I recall, last time they lost... *quite embarrassingly*. So, we are going to meet them at Tral Lanes and remind them how inferior they are to us in the art of bowling."

I can't help but laugh. Those boys are horribly competitive. I don't think there was anything we ever did growing up that wasn't a competition. Even chores and yardwork ended in some sort of rivalry. I recall there was one summer when Mr. Moore was looking to build a new retaining wall. He had pallets of stone delivered that needed to be moved from the front to the back of the house. We decided to make it a race to see who could move the most stones the fastest. Scott ended up winning that one, and made sure to remind us for the next several weeks—frequently referring to himself as the "stone master".

"Let's go show them what real bowling is." I chuckle as we make our way to the bowling alley.

∞∞∞

Robbie and Jake are already at the bowling alley. I notice they snagged us our usual lane towards the back wall. Our table already has a couple pitchers of beer with accompanying glasses, a tray stacked with shots (of what I am assuming is tequila based on the salt and limes), baskets of wings, and mozzarella sticks—definitely the meal of champions.

"Alright, ladies, same rules apply," Jake announces acting official. "If you strike, you take a shot. Pick a spare, you take a drink. If your ass gets caught in the gutter, you take a double-shot. Finally, any genius who can pick up a 7-10 gets to decide who takes a shot and of what."

"You realize it is crazy to have rules that penalize you for playing well, right? Why should I have to take a shot because I bowl better than you?" Yea, as we got older our challenges turned into drinking games. While it is stupid, it did make things funnier.

"Are you worried, Jackie-boy? Not able to handle your balls properly after a couple of drinks?" Jake taunts.

"Your sister is well aware of how well I can handle my balls after a few drinks." Jake and I both burst out laughing, while Scott and Robbie pretend to vomit.

"New rule: Every time lover boy over here, mentions our sister, he has to take a shot," Robbie announces.

"Fine. But if we are altering the rules, then I want to add: if you cause a 7-10 split and can't pick it up, then your team needs to do a blizzard." It is a shot that can take down the best of us. It is made with Wild Turkey and Rumple Minze. That, mixed with the beer and tequila, and you are likely going to blackout. Luckily for me, Robbie is the biggest culprit for getting a 7-10 and, well, Jake isn't that good at holding his hard liquor. I'm guessing it is why he set up the rules the way he did. He rarely gets a strike, and usually ends up getting a ton of spares.

"Whatever. Let's play," Jake concedes.

Six frames into the first game and we each have finished a couple beers. Robbie has had to take two shots; Scott and I each have had three. Scott and I are leading... *as usual.* I am at one hundred and Scott is at ninety-seven. Jake's and Robbie's scores are both in the mid-seventies.

Jake is up to bowl and unfortunately, he has found himself stuck with a 7-10 split. If he picks it up, Scott or I will end up likely needing to take a blizzard shot. Because, of course, he would never pick anything easy. If he misses, then he and Robbie will end up taking one instead.

As Jake stands at the lane lining up his shot, Scott is being a jackass and hissing commentary into his beer. "'*He's got one foot in the frying pan and one in the pressure cooker. Believe me, as a bowler, I know that right about now, your bladder feels like an overstuffed vacuum cleaner bag and your butt is kinda like an about-to-explode bratwurst.*'" [1] We all chuckle (well, all except Jake) at Scott quoting *Kingpin* in his best Billy Murray impersonation; it's always been one of his favorite movies.

Jake looks back at Scott. "Shut up, man. I need to focus." He then goes back to lining up his shot.

Jake leans down to kiss his ball for luck. "Make sure all the holes get proper tongue there, Jakey-poo."

Without turning to look at us, Jake calls back, "Oh, believe me, my tongue is a pro when it comes to *all* three holes." We can't help but burst out laughing.

Jake starts as if he is going to throw the ball. "And there he goes. Oh, no, never mind," Scott says as Jake pulls the ball back, then realizes he is only doing practice throws. "Ah, now, here he... nope, sorry false alarm again. Come on, dude, throw the damn ball already."

Jake tosses the ball down the lane. It curves to the right going for the 7-pin. The ball slams into the pin with a mighty force. We all watch and, as if in slow motion, the 7-pin flies to the left and knocks down the 10-pin. We sit there, slack-jawed in disbelief, as Jake jumps up and down—celebrating and pumping his fists in the air. "Take that, bitches!"

"He cheated. I don't know how he did it, but he cheated," Scott mumbles under his breath. In all the games we ever played growing up, no one has ever picked up a 7-10 split.

Jake returns a moment later with a shot in his hand. Scott is the unfortunate soul who is required to take down the first blizzard for the night. This is how the game usually evens out. They suck and get us so wasted we can barely see straight. It gives them a chance to catch up.

Robbie is up to bowl next. I take the opportunity to check my phone for the hundredth time tonight. I know Tilly is out with Keith right now, and I am just waiting for her to call or text, telling me she is home and is okay. I seriously hope that asshat doesn't try to pull a fast one on Tilly. I will fucking beat his ass if he does.

"Whatcha doing?" Jake inquires.

"Checking to see if Tilly messaged," I reply, then immediately curse at myself as the guys point at me in unison, ordering me to take a shot. "Fuckers." I knock one back like a good sport, but Scott seems to notice me still scowling at my phone.

"What's going on?" he asks, taking a swig of his beer. "I swear, every minute you are checking your phone."

"Ha, nice try. I am not falling for that one again." I don't want to get too wasted... in case Tilly needs me.

Robbie is done with his frame and comes back to all of us. "Okay, timeout. Seriously, is something up? Every time you look at your phone, you get this weird somber expression on your face. Are you and Tilly fighting already?"

"What? No. We are fine. It's just..." Damn, I know the second I mention his name, they are going to flip. They don't know the whole prom story—well, unless Tilly eventually told them, which I doubt. But her brothers never liked Keith, and they sure won't like the fact that he is having dinner with her. They will probably kick my ass for letting her go with him, and then go kick his ass for forcing her in the first place. "Alright, so you know how Tilly wanted to talk to the tourism board about getting me some sort of official town marketing position?"

Scott nods. "Yea, wasn't that meeting yesterday? Did you not get the position?"

"Yea. No. Well, kind of. It is all fucked up." Sighing, I drop my face into the palms of my hands, rubbing my temples.

"I don't understand. Did you get the job or not?" Robbie asks.

"Tilly brought up the position during the meeting. And *Keith*, who is apparently the head of the committee, asked to talk to Tilly afterwards."

"I forgot fucknuts was on that damn committee," Robbie growls.

"Yea, well, Tilly said he wasn't super keen on me taking the position. I didn't have adequate experience or some shit."

"That is fucking BS. You have a bachelor's in marketing and have spent the past decade traveling the world for a prestigious travel magazine. They should be fucking licking your balls, begging you to take the job," Scott says, pacing back and forth. He understands how much this job would mean to Tilly and me.

"So, yea. Apparently, he needed the night to think it over and wanted to discuss things during dinner tonight with Tilly. I have been waiting to get some sort of text, telling me she is home or she needs backup."

"Hold up!" Jake hollers. "You allowed Tilly to go on a date with this douchecanoe? Are you a fucking idiot?"

"First off, this is not a date—it is a business dinner." It sounds even lamer than when Tilly said it. "Second, I didn't allow Tilly to do anything. She put her foot down and said she was going to go to this dinner. I tried to talk her out of it, but she wouldn't have it."

"Where are they?" Robbie inquires as he starts to put his

boots back on. I look up and notice Jake and Scott are doing the same thing.

"The steakhouse on Elm." When she texted me that, I shook my head laughing. Of course, he took her to the fanciest, most expensive restaurant in town.

"Alright, I ordered an Uber. They will be here in five minutes. Scott, you go closeout the tab and let's go pay fucknuts a visit," Robbie orders as he gets up to leave a tip at the table.

"Not that I am against rescuing Tilly from the assclown, but what is the plan? Show up there and beat his ass?" I stand, crossing my arms and scolding them like children. "If we show up there and start a fight, Tilly will get pissed—especially, if our actions prevent me from getting the job."

"Fine, good point. We will show up and get a table and eat dinner, like the civilized gentlemen we are. If we notice any shenanigans, then we drag his dumbass into the back alley and beat the living shit out of him," Robbie counters.

∞∞∞

Twenty minutes later we arrive at the steakhouse. Glancing around, I do not see Tilly anywhere. Maybe she is already home? I look at my text messages and still nothing. I try calling her and after a few rings, it goes to voicemail. I shake my head at the guys, letting them know I haven't heard from her still.

Jake approaches the hostess giving his award-winning, panty-melting smile. "Hi..." He looks down at her name tag. "Bethany, such a lovely name. Would you mind if I called you Beth?"

"All my friends call me Beth," she flirts back. God, she is young. I wouldn't be surprised if she was still in high school. But whatever, we need information and Jake is a professional flirt.

"Well, Beth, since we are *friends*. I was hoping you might be able to help me with a small problem?"

"Oh, sure. Anything," she replies, twirling her long auburn hair in her fingers.

"You see, my sister, Tilly Moore, was supposed to be here this evening with Keith McCalester, and we came here to join them but notice they are gone. Do you happen to know when they left?"

She looks down at her seating registrar, tapping her pen on the hostess stand. "Hmm... Oh yea, I remember them, such an adorable couple. Your sister sure got herself a true gentleman. But I'm sorry, they left here almost an hour ago. But I do have a table open, if you four are still interested in dinner?"

Couple? Gentleman? They left an hour ago? This makes no fucking sense. Scott puts his hand on my shoulder, telling me to calm down.

"Sorry, darling. We would love to stay for dinner, but we need to meet up with my sister and her boyfriend." Jake winks at me... just to piss me off.

"Oh, okay. Well, here." She slips him a piece of paper, presumably with her phone number on it. "Call me, if you feel *hungry*. I can always squeeze you in."

Jake pockets the number and smiles back at her. "Thank you, darling. I might take you up on that. I frequently find myself *famished*."

Robbie already has an Uber on the way to pick us up. At this point, all we can do is go home and hope Tilly is there. If she is not, we will have to find wherever her and fucknuts went.

Chapter 21

Matilda

This whole night has been nothing but a disaster. Keith took me to the priciest restaurant in town and reserved us the back, quiet, closed-off table. While one would think that the privacy is good for a business meeting, everyone knows it is essentially a lovers' nook. This way, you and your date can make-out discreetly in the dark, without disturbing the other guests. It was also one of those round booth-type tables, the kind that had Keith and I sitting practically next to each other. I tried to sit as far away from him as possible, but he took any opportunity he could to scoot closer.

During dinner, he practically refused to discuss the job. He constantly interrupted me to comment on the decor, or tell me how delicious the food was and then offer me a bite of his steak. To any casual observer, it appeared as though we were a couple on a special romantic date. It made me feel sick to my stomach. I could barely eat the chicken and wild rice soup I ordered. He tried to force me to order something bigger, more extravagant.

"Money is no object," he had said. While I would have loved to order the most expensive thing on the menu so I could fuck with him, I honestly couldn't stomach a big dinner.

He said we could discuss the job over dessert and ordered us a couple slices of their dark chocolate cake. I protested, letting him know I was full but he insisted that "business was best discussed over dessert". I finally gave up the battle, but I did not understand why we were taking the dessert to go. When I inquired about this, he just chuckled and told me "to be patient".

So now, here we are, parked on top of the hill that overlooks the town below. Basically, this is the town's "lovers' lane". I feel like such an idiot. I figured we were all adults now. High school was left back in high school. But here we are, Keith basically bullying me into a date. I've tried to text Jax to tell him where I am, but of course, there is no fucking signal up here.

"What are we doing here, Keith?" I am not even trying to hide the annoyance in my voice anymore.

"Come on, Matilda. Let's go enjoy our dessert," he says, grabbing the cake and a blanket from the back seat. I reluctantly follow him to where he lays down the blanket and pats for me to sit beside him. But I continue standing. I am done with his games. "You can stand if you want, but I imagine trying to hold your cake and eat it with that cast is going to be challenging."

I plop to the ground and grab the piece of cake. "So, about the position—"

"Isn't it beautiful out here?" he interrupts.

"Yes, now, about Jackson have you—"

"Wow, the skies are so clear tonight. Being up here, at this angle, you can see so many stars," he interrupts again. "I remembered how much you loved stargazing. I was thinking with the sky being so clear tonight, you might enjoy the view."

I am sure some woman out there might find this whole situation romantic—the local rich handsome bachelor takes her out for a fancy dinner and then stargazing while eating dessert. But this is not a date. This was a business meeting. Keith ignoring that, makes him an asshole and this whole situation, an abuse of power.

"Yes, the view is nice. But, Keith, I am here to talk about the job position for Jackson. I am not here to stargaze." I might sound like a bitch, but I don't care anymore. I just want to go home and back to Jax. "If you are not intending to discuss the job position, then I would kindly ask that you take me home now."

He sighs. "I brought you here because I was thinking this could potentially be a great marketing photo spot for the town. You know, a *'come stargaze here and enjoy our local culture'* type thing."

Great, now I feel like an ass. "So, does this mean Jackson has the job?" I ask, hoping this night wasn't a total waste.

"I haven't quite made up my mind on that yet," he provides.

"Okay, well, tell me what your concern is about hiring Jackson and let's see if we can figure something out." This is what I am here to do—get Jax this damn job so he can stay in town with me and still do something he loves.

"Hmm…" he ponders. "Why are you so adamant on Jackson having the position? I won't deny his photography skills. But we are not interested in hiring a photographer. We are interested in hiring a social media and marketing director."

"First of all, while Jackson's focus has been photography, in college he majored in marketing. Secondly, the type of photography he has been doing is to market for tourism. He knows what that market is looking for. And finally, Jackson grew up here. He knows the town and the people. Who better to represent and showcase us, than one of our own?" I'm out of breath by the time I finish listing all of the reasons Jax is perfect for this job. Keith would be an idiot to deny him the position.

"I can see you are very passionate about this… about the town," he says, with his voice getting low. Before I can understand what is happening, Keith leans over. Capturing my jaw, he turns my head towards him and puts his mouth to mine.

I work to push him away but his other hand goes behind my head, holding me close. His mouth opens and his tongue licks my lips, seeking further access. I try to turn my head to the side, but the bruising grip he has on my jaw is locking me in place. I want to tell him to get the fuck off of me, but I don't want to risk opening my mouth and allowing him entry.

I reach my hands between us and lay them on his chest—*an almost loving action.* But I only do it to feel around for his pecs. Finding what I am looking for, and with all my strength, I dig my nails through his shirt and into his flesh. I twist his nipples as hard as I possibly can. As I was hoping, he removes his mouth from mine to scream; and his hands leave my head and face to protect himself. I use the opportunity to quickly standup and get away.

"What the fuck is your problem, Matilda?" I can see the irritation and fury radiating off of him as he stands. Looking at his chest, I notice a few droplets of blood from where I dug my claws into him.

"No, Keith, what the fuck is your problem? What made you think that you had any right to kiss me?" I say, crossing my arms over my chest while trying to close myself off from him and keep my distance.

"Well, you've been giving me 'fuck-me' signals all night," he says, taking a step closer to me. I take a step back. "Besides, I was thinking you could use your *passion* to help me understand how Jackson is the best candidate for the job."

"Stay the hell away from me." I put my hand up and take another step back. There's no way I am letting him get close enough to touch me again.

"Oh, stop being dramatic, Matilda. It was just a little kiss," he says nonchalantly, and as though he didn't just hold my face still, while he assaulted me with his mouth.

"Did you not notice me trying to pull away from you? The last thing I would ever want is for you to kiss me, Keith. You fucking disgust me." I spit on the ground at his feet.

Keith's eyes go dark and his face contorts in rage, as he charges at me again. I try to back away but I end up being trapped between him and the car. Even though he is not exactly as tall as my brothers or Jax, he is still significantly taller than me.

"Look, Matilda, we both want something. You want your little boyfriend to get a job. And, well, I just want a taste of you." Keith raises one of his hands to gently caress my cheek. "Don't make such a big deal about it, Matilda. It is a mutually beneficial arrangement. If anything, you are getting the better end of the deal. I can promise you that when I am done with you, you will be so satisfied that you'll be begging me for more."

"I am not interested, Keith. There is nothing in this world that could compel me to ever allow you to touch me," I say, trying to escape the confinement he has me in. In response, he only steps closer, pressing his hard length into my stomach.

I am not sure if it is the situation, the stress, or what. But all of a sudden, a wave of nausea comes over me. I try to hold it in but I can't. One moment he is leaning in to kiss me again. And the next, I am projectile vomiting towards his face. Although it was not planned, it had the desired effect. Keith immediately steps away from me, completely repulsed by the situation.

"What. The. Fuck. Matilda?" he hollers, spitting vomit from his lips and trying to wipe his forehead.

Under normal circumstances, I would apologize or even feel embarrassed, but the scumbag deserves what happened to him. Instead, I wipe my mouth and regain my composure. I am actually feeling way better after expelling the dinner from my system. I quickly go, grab my purse, and check my phone. Still no signal, but that's fine. I will start walking home and as soon as I do get service, I will call for a ride. There's no way in hell I am getting in a confined space with him again.

"Matilda!" Keith yells. "If you walk away from me, the deal is off the table and I promise I will make you regret it. Jackson will never have a place in this town."

I stop and consider his words. No way would Jax want this job... if he knew what price it would come at. I quickly turn back to face him. "I am not afraid of you, Keith. We don't need your fucking job." Then I turn and walk away. I can hear him yell more in the distance but I ignore it, because I don't fucking care.

About a half mile away, I finally get a signal and call Letty.

While I know I should call Jax, I just need a moment to process whatever the hell just happened and to think of how to explain this to him. I know he is going to be furious and likely want to murder Keith. But I can't allow him to get thrown in prison over that scumbag.

As we drive home, Letty has a million questions and I notice a dozen missed calls and texts from Jax and my brothers. I am assuming that now, they are all panicking and wondering where I am. I will have to deal with that when I get home. I know Letty wants answers but I really just don't want to talk about it yet. I am still in shock Keith had the nerve to proposition me; but even more so, I am shaken he thought he had the right to lay his lips on me.

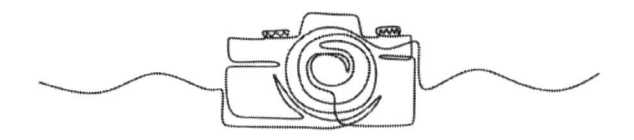

Chapter 22

Jackson

The morning sun is shining through the curtains, waking me up. I look down and notice Tilly resting her head on my chest with her casted-arm draped over me. While I feel like my bladder might explode, I can't bear the idea of moving. Instead, I lie here lightly caressing her back up and down, as she continues to sleep.

Last night, she came storming in the house and rushed to her room, avoiding all of us and the inquisition her brothers had planned. I will admit I want answers on what the hell happened last night. But when I entered her room, I was transported back to that first night I came home. Tilly was curled up on her bed... *crying*. All the questions I had, quickly seemed unimportant. I crawled in bed behind her and pulled her into my chest. Her hair and body were damp from taking a shower. The scent of her mango shampoo was intoxicating. As I held her, I could feel the tension leave her body. The sobbing subsided and she was finally able to sleep.

"Good morning," she whispers sleepily, nuzzling deeper into my chest.

"Morning," I reply, kissing the top of her head and giving her a light squeeze.

"How was your night with the boys?" she asks, obviously avoiding the elephant in the room.

"It was fine, but honestly, I am more interested in hearing about your evening?" As much as I want to give her time to tell me on her own, I need to know what happened last night. Based on how she stiffens, I am guessing it didn't go very well.

"Ugh, I don't really feel like talking about it right now. Can we talk about it later? Maybe after some coffee and breakfast?" she pleads.

"I'm sorry, babe, but I need you to talk to me. What happened last night?" Besides, I know her brothers did not go home and are all likely sitting downstairs, waiting for answers.

"Fine, but it stays between us?" Sitting up, she stares me down, letting me know this is non-negotiable. I nod in agreement. While I know we will need to tell her brothers something, more than that, I need her to tell me what happened. Before beginning, Tilly lets out a big sigh, her shoulders slumping in defeat. "You were right… Keith manipulated me. He had no intention of giving you that job." She then breaks down and starts sobbing into her hands.

I jump up, immediately on red alert, and pull her into my arms. I try to calm her down by brushing her hair back. "Shh… it's okay. What happened? What did he do?"

"I feel like such an idiot. I should have known the minute we got to the restaurant that something was off." As she continues to shake in my arms, my brain plays scenes of the worst things I can imagine.

"Tilly, you are anything but an idiot. But I need you to tell me the whole story. What happened last night?" I keep my voice calm and collected, even though inside I am screaming and practically pulling my hair out.

"Well, you know we went to that steakhouse, the fancy one. He reserved us that booth in the back of the restaurant. You know, the romantic one? All dark and secluded in the corner?" I nod in agreement, while biting the side of my cheek. "Well, at dinner he refused to talk about the job. He kept changing the subject whenever I brought it up. Then he mentioned something about 'business best being discussed over dessert', but he ordered the dessert to go."

We both take a moment as I process her story. The table location explains why the hostess thought they were a couple. But I have a feeling that isn't the worst part of the story. "Okay, what happened after you left the restaurant?"

"He drove us out to the overlook," she whispers, staring down in shame.

"He drove you out to lovers' lane?" I try to rein in my anger but it is starting to become difficult. I had no doubt he was going to try and make the meeting a date. But I never expected this level of manipulation. If I had any inkling that he might have brought her somewhere private like that, I would have never let her go with him.

"Yea, at first he was mostly talking about the view. How it would be a good place to capture images of the town for marketing. But then..." She takes a deep breath, trying to steady herself. "I don't know what happened, Jax. One minute, I was explaining to him why you are perfect for this job, and he was appreciating my passion on the subject. Then, before I knew what was happening, he was kissing me. He basically told me the only way you would get the job is if I would fuck him."

I am not sure when it happened. But the next thing I know, I am standing in Tilly's room with my fist red and bloody, and there's a new dent in her wall. Tilly is sitting in her bed, crying hysterically and telling me not to be mad at her. Fuck, I drop back down next to her, taking Tilly's hands in mine.

"Shh, babe. I'm sorry. I promise I am not mad at you. I am mad at that fucking psychopath. I am frustrated at myself for allowing you to go to that fucking dinner with him. I am pissed that

I was not there to protect you from him. Fuck, what happened? Did he...?" I suddenly realize I didn't hear anything about how she got out of there or how far he took it.

She chuckles, clearly amused by something. I can't imagine what though, given the fact that there is nothing funny about this situation. "Well, at first, to get him to stop kissing me—because he was holding my head in place—I used all my strength to give him the fucking goriest purple-nurple." Involuntarily I chuckle as well, imagining Tilly getting him good. That used to be her number one move in the many wrestling matches her and Jake got into as children. "After that, he cornered me again, trying to convince me to accept his proposal. As he leaned down to kiss me again, I am not exactly sure why it happened, but I got super nauseous and Linda Blair-ed him. I mean, *badly*. it was all over his face and in his mouth. It was fucking disgusting and hilarious, all at the same time." We both cringe at the imagery she describes. Granted, I would have loved to have seen it though.

"Why didn't you call me?" Although I am relieved that she got out of that situation, I can't help but be hurt that she was in trouble and didn't even bother to call me.

She looks down sheepishly picking fake lint off the blanket. "I'm sorry, Jax. It was nothing personal. I just needed time to process everything. I know if I would have called you and you would have seen the situation... Well, you would have ended up beating his ass and getting yourself thrown in prison."

"I'm not some sort of neanderthal, Tilly."

"You literally just punched my wall, Jackson, from only hearing my story. Imagine how you would have reacted... picking me up on the side of the road, crying and with vomit all over me? You would have hunted him down and made sure he paid for what he did."

Fuck, I hate when she is right. But still, I would like to think that when there is a problem, I would be the first person she would contact.

"Please understand, Jax. I didn't call any of my brothers either. I called Letty because I needed someone with a level head, who could get me home. Also, let's not forget, I know you guys were out bowling and drinking last night. I doubt that any of you would have been in any position to drive."

I huff. While she is completely right, it still sucks. I should have never allowed her to go out in the first place. "Okay, so, what now? We need to report this."

"Absolutely not! It will only cause more problems for us."

"Tilly," I say sternly, "he needs to be reported. What he is doing is illegal. You can't just let him get away with it. This isn't like high school. We can't just ignore it and pretend it never happened."

"It will just be a he-said-she-said situation. In the end, nothing will happen except for having to relive one of the most embarrassing nights of my life over and over again. I will end up being the talk of the town. Because he is Keith McCalester, whose daddy is the mayor. It will all get swept under the rug. Fuck, they might even twist it that it was my fault. It just isn't worth it, Jax. Nothing happened. He made a douchey move and I handled it. The only thing that sucks is that now we are back to the drawing board on you getting a job."

"Fine then… what now?" I don't like her not reporting this. But then again and at the same time, I understand her concern. The McCalesters hold a lot of power in this town. Without concrete proof, her complaint would fall on deaf ears or be twisted to make her the aggressor in this situation.

"There isn't much of anything. Look, I'll handle my brothers and give them an abbreviated rundown of the events of last night. Then we will keep working on finding you a new job. I mean, if that is still what you want?"

"I don't care about the job…" Tilly tenses pulling away from me. I realize what I said and try to gather my thoughts. "Of course, that is what I want." She lets out a relieved breath. "I just don't like that he is getting away with this. But it is your choice, and I will respect it." I bend down and kiss the top of her head and gently pull her out of bed. "Come on, we better get downstairs and eat some breakfast.

"Okay," she says, leaning in and kissing me. "I will meet you downstairs. I am just going to freshen up real quick."

Chapter 23

Matilda

After breakfast this morning, I decided I needed to get out of the house. We gave my brothers the abbreviated version of the events that occurred last night. I know Jax isn't happy with me; but based on the rage they displayed from the story I did give them, I know it was the right choice to make. I hate that Jax is disappointed in my decision, but I know he will understand after he has had a chance to cool off.

Thankfully, it is Sunday. Letty and I both don't have to work today so we decided to take a trip to the Mall of America. I am hoping that getting away for the afternoon will help clear my head a little. That, and I really need this opportunity to talk with Letty about what happened. I tell Letty everything, down to every last embarrassing detail.

"I cannot believe that needle-dick," Letty curses. She hasn't been able to stop since I told her. "Jax is right. You need to report this."

I shake my head. "Come on, we both know nothing will come of it, besides town gossip. I have no proof of anything." I would love nothing more than to report the asshole; but without proof, no one in this town would do anything about my allegation. They would start some awful gossip that ended with me being the villain in the story.

"We can't let this go, Tilly. He is clearly still obsessed with you, and now has crossed the line. What if he tries to corner you again, or worse?" She removes her right hand from the steering wheel to hold my left hand. "I know you just want to forget about it and move on, just like you did in high school. But you can't this time. The boundaries he has crossed are unforgivable."

"Letty, I understand what you are saying. And if I had anything more than my word, I would be down at the station right now. But let's face the facts… Keith is the wealthy, loved bachelor in this town. The majority of the women would think I am just lying to get a paycheck. Then Derek, his best friend, happens to be a lieutenant at the Sheriff's department and his daddy is the Sheriff. Oh yea, and I almost forgot, Keith's dad is the mayor." I list the reasons that this is a terrible idea, counting them off on my fingers. "I need to be smart about this. If I go in, guns blazing, with nothing other than my word, I would lose more than just this job for Jax."

"I agree. You need to be smart about this. However, I still think reporting it is the right thing to do." She puts up her hand defensively. "But I understand your concern. I won't force you to do anything you don't want to do. I will support you no matter what. Just promise me, you will truly think about reporting it?"

"I promise. I just need to think this through a little more." Fortunately, she drops the topic after that. The rest of the ride to the mall we sing along to our road trip playlist. Neither one of us can sing well, but it is a blast singing along to the classics.

At the mall, we walk around and mostly window shop. Of course, Letty ends up buying six bottles of her body spray, since there was a buy-three-get-three deal going on. Honestly, I am amazed she didn't buy twelve. I decided to buy myself a new cute bra and pantie set to surprise Jax with—nothing too sexy, because that has never been my thing.

After we are done shopping, we decide to stop at one of the food courts to grab something to eat. It is crazy. This mall is so big. It not only has several large chain-restaurants, it also has two food courts. We decided to stop at the burger and shake place that has an awesome 50's theme with little jukeboxes at the table, where we can select a song for a quarter.

Letty catches me up on what's going on with the bar. It sounds like Ted will be retiring any minute now. He has already started negotiating with her about the purchase of Harper's.

"I don't have quite enough saved up yet, and I don't think I will have enough by the time he retires. But we have already discussed having me make a down payment and taking over daily operations... and having him just be a figurehead. Then, I'll cover the mortgage until it is paid off—which is better than me having to go and try to get a mortgage on my own. While we were looking at the numbers, I think it will take me maybe five years to pay it off. Four, if I am lucky."

"That is awesome, but how are you going to be able to afford this all? Rent for the apartment, plus covering the mortgage? When you take over, you won't get a regular paycheck anymore."

"We already figured that out. Since the bar is unofficially mine, Ted showed me a space upstairs—which is a large lofty studio apartment that I am going to clean up and renovate. I will move in there and my rent will technically be covered by the mortgage, since it is my building anyway." Letty is grinning from ear to ear. I am so excited to see her dreams finally coming true. "It is going to be awesome, Tilly. Ted will still be involved in the bar until I officially take ownership, but ultimately, he is stepping down. He said all decisions will go through me and he will only speak up if he thinks I am about to make a fatal error."

"Let me know if you need help with anything. I will do whatever I can."

∞∞∞

Back home, Letty drops me off. We have been gone all day. It is almost six at night. I am surprised to see all of my brothers are still here. I figured they would have gone home by now (well, except Jake). I look around at the kitchen counter and notice an assortment of toppings spread around, along with mini pizza crusts.

I set down my bags and stand in the archway. "Hey, what's going on in here?"

Jax looks up, giving me his panty-melting smile. "Hey, we didn't hear you come in. Hurry up and assemble your pizza."

"We couldn't decide on a pizza to order, so I whipped together some dough and figured we could do our own personal sized ones. That way, we can all get what we want," Scott says with a satisfied grin. Ordering out has always been a headache in the family. Mom and dad rarely did it—because instead of being able to order two large pizzas that we would all share, they would have to order seven small ones to ensure everyone got what they wanted. Sometimes, we could compromise and get five mediums. But that was rare.

"Huh, not that I am complaining, but what brought all this on?"

"We were talking about the old days, and how we used to do Friday night dinners until we basically all grew up. I was thinking that most of us don't work Sunday evenings and we should re-institute weekly dinners," Robbie says, while piling his crust with every meat option available.

I feel a tear roll down my face and I quickly wipe it away. "Mom and dad would love that."

"That's what we were thinking as well." Jake walks over to me and drapes his arm over my shoulder. "Now, come on, sis. Help me figure out what monstrosity of a pizza I will make this evening." This elicits a laugh from everyone. Jake will eat just about anything, and used to pick random toppings every time we ordered out.

It was fun creating our own variations. I am usually pretty boring with mine and stick to pepperoni and green olives. Robbie makes his meat-madness pizza. I don't think the term "too much meat" registers with him. Scott goes fancy gourmet with his. He uses a white sauce, spinach, chicken, bacon, and peppers. Jax surprises me. He ends up doing a fancier version as well; it has white sauce, balsamic, caramelized onions, prosciutto, and goat cheese. Then Jake was... well, *Jake*. He ended up topping his with grilled chicken, pineapple, jalapenos, and mushrooms, before drizzling it with buffalo sauce.

While Scott works on baking our creations, I take the opportunity to bring my bags upstairs. The last thing I need is to have the boys snooping around to see what I bought. I quickly change into my leggings and one of my big comfy sleep shirts. There is no need to be dressed up to sit and eat dinner with the guys.

Downstairs, Jake and Robbie are arguing over what to watch —*typical*. Robbie wants to play some mindless action flick, while Jake wants a horror movie. With Halloween around the corner, I agree with Jake. We should definitely choose something scary, but we are the only two who seem to enjoy the genre. Jax will tolerate the funnier ones with minimal gore. But Jake and I love the more gruesome titles with way too much fake blood and guts.

"Jax won bowling last night, so I say it is up to him," Scott adds to the argument. Jake and Robbie look downright terrified, and they have every reason to be. Scott and Jax have this ridiculous obsession with sappy chick-flicks. Some aren't too bad, but these guys can go pretty deep down the romance rabbit-hole. Like the only reason I have seen *The Notebook* as many times as I have is because Jax and Scott dragged me there almost every week (when it was still in theaters). Then, when they bought the DVD... Well, let's just say, we avoided movie night for a long while.

Jax gives a devilish grin, rubbing his chin as he contemplates what he will torture us with tonight. "Fine," Jake says, "but no fucking *Notebook*. I see that evil glint in your eyes and you are not making me watch that shit again."

Everyone bursts out laughing. "Oh, you know you love that shit, and use the fact you have seen it a hundred times to pick up chicks," Jax retorts. "But whatever. *Moulin Rouge*, it is." Jake and Robbie groan, while Scott and Jax give each other high-fives. Fortunately, I actually like this one. I do have a weakness for musicals and it used to be one of my favorites in junior high.

Once the pizzas are finished, we all settle in to watch the movie and eat. While the last twenty-four hours have been a nightmare, sitting here with my brothers and Jax—watching a movie and eating dinner like we used to—well, it is amazing. I really wish mom and dad were here to see it. But like Letty said, they are here in spirit.

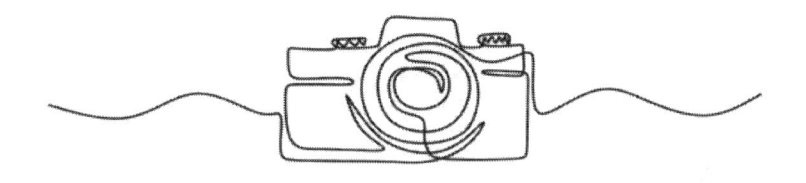

Chapter 24

Jackson

Once Moulin Rouge is over, Robbie and Scott go back to their respective homes. Jake, Tilly, and I stay up longer to watch another movie. They are able to convince me to watch Shaun of the Dead. Although I am not big into horror or anything, this one is too hilarious to skip. Half-way through, Jake passes out in the recliner, and Tilly is not far behind him. We end up snuggling onto the couch together and she is out like a light.

I carefully separate myself from Tilly and get off the couch. As quietly as possible, I work my way around the downstairs: straightening up, locking the door, and shutting off the lights. I will leave Jake in the recliner. He looks comfy, and well, he can get his own ass up to bed. Tilly on the other hand, I gently carry upstairs to her room. With the exception of cuddling into my chest, she barely stirs on the journey.

After laying her on the bed and tucking her in, I quickly change into some shorts and a t-shirt to sleep in. Crawling under the covers, I try not to disturb her and snuggle closer. I pull her into my chest and I can't help but lie there, watching her sleeping form like a total creeper. I am still upset that she will not report the incident, but I do understand her point. I just wish there was something I could do to help protect her. Because I do not doubt for a minute that captain-dipshit isn't going to try and pull some shit again.

The next morning Tilly and I wake to her alarm. She groans, reaching over to shut off the offending sound. I look down and notice that as she does, her shirt raises and reveals a sliver of her flat stomach. It takes all my willpower to not immediately mount her and take care of my morning erection. As Tilly rolls back over, she seems to notice my predicament and a sultry smile spreads across her face.

"Morning, handsome," she says, leaning over and kissing me. I feel her hand travel down my chest to my stomach, then to the waistband of my shorts. Unavoidably, I groan.

"You are playing with fire, babe." My warning seems to fall on deaf ears. That, or she doesn't care. The next thing I know, she is straddling me and grinding her hot center over my erection.

My hands slip under her leggings and panties to squeeze her delectable ass. She rewards me with a deep moan that almost sends me over the edge. Her hands go to the hem of my shirt and start pulling it up. "Off," she demands. We quickly separate to rid each other of our clothing.

Tilly resumes her vantage point on top of me. Reaching between us, she positions my erection to slide through her wet folds. As she grinds me, she uses my cock to rub against her clit. I can tell she is close, based on her increased breathing and speed. I put my hands on her waist to help keep her steady during her orgasm. I continue the motion she has started while she comes back down.

"Fuck," she whispers in my ear. "I need you inside me." Tilly sits up and perches her center over my erection, before impaling herself in one thrust. Being sheathed deep inside her is the best feeling on earth. I will never get over the sensation. After she adjusts to my intrusion, she begins rocking back and forth. Then, supporting her weight on the top of my thighs, she angles herself backwards.

The view from below is mind-blowing. Her ample breasts and perky pink nipples are on full display for me. Looking down, with her legs spread over me, I can clearly see her swollen clit and the joining of our bodies. The sight alone is enough to make me come, but I am not ready to end this quite yet. I steady one hand on her hip to help support her and maintain the tempo, while my other hand reaches between us to rub circles on her clit. Within seconds, she is moaning loudly. Her vagina strangles my cock as she comes. It takes all my willpower to keep fucking her through the orgasm.

Noticing she is becoming physically exhausted, but without separating our bodies, I flip us so that I am on top now. I quickly throw one of her legs over my shoulder and begin pounding into her. Tilly's hands reach up, her nails digging into the taut meat of my deltoid muscles. I am excited to wear the battle scars I have received today. After a few more thrusts, she lets out a silent scream as her body begins to spasm again. Her climax sets me off this time. My vision goes white and all I can see are fireworks exploding around us.

Lying in bed—sweaty, sticky, and with our limbs entangled—I wish we could lie here forever and never leave this bed. But as I glance at the clock, I know that is not possible. Tilly needs to get to the shop and open up soon. Giving her a quick kiss, I reluctantly disentangle myself from her and get up. "Come on, babe. We better get you into the shower and dressed for the day."

"Do we have to?" she asks with a seductive smile that almost makes me forget she needs to get to work.

"Unfortunately. But hey, at least there is a shipment of new books today. That is exciting, right?" I grab her hands to pull her up from the bed.

"Yea, usually. I just feel too exhausted to work today," she sighs. "I guess that is the downside to running the shop—sick days aren't really an option."

I kiss her forehead. "Yea, it sucks. But at least I will be there with you today. You can sit there and be lazy, ordering me around like your puppet."

"Hmm, that does sound nice, my sexy puppet." I chuckle and lightly slap her ass. "Hey!"

"Come on, we need to shower. As sexy as the 'just fucked' look is on you, it probably isn't the best look for work." Standing behind her with my hands on her hips, I lead her into the bathroom.

∞∞∞

Once we finally get to the shop, I head over to the cafe to get us some coffee and muffins. "Late night?" Scott inquires with a knowing look.

"Nah, those two passed out halfway through the movie. Tilly has been exhausted all week, though. I think it is all the stress getting to her. I really wish I could take her away for a bit. We talked about going somewhere after the holidays, but I don't think that will be soon enough."

Scott ponders this for a moment. "Well, I mean, you guys could maybe get away for a weekend? It might not be whatever exotic vacation you have planned. But I am sure she can manage a three or four-day weekend trip."

"That sounds like a good idea. Thanks, man." I immediately start thinking of all the places I could take Tilly for a quick getaway.

After I grab our drinks and muffins, I find Tilly in her office, resting her head on her desk. "Hey, babe. Are you feeling okay?"

"Huh, yea." She sits up, rubbing the sleep from her eyes. "Sorry, I am just feeling a little rundown this morning." She grabs her cup of coffee from me and takes a big whiff. "Hmm, nectar of the gods," she mumbles, before taking a gulp.

"I've been thinking. I know we talked about going on vacation after the holidays, but how would you feel about getting away for a long weekend? We could go to the Keys? Relax on the beach, while enjoying umbrella drinks and reading books?" I offer her.

"Oh, that does sound really nice. I have my appointment on Friday to have my arm looked at. Let's hear what the doctor says, then plan from there. I would love to go to the beach with you, but with this stupid cast..." She lifts her arm. "...I am not going to be able to enjoy much. Also, weird tan lines," she chuckles, shaking her head.

I lean down and give her a quick kiss. "Perfect. After your appointment Friday, I will start looking at flights and stuff." Tilly smiles up at me, before giving me a big yawn. "How about you relax back here and I will man the front of the store?"

"Thank you. Let me know if you have any issues, okay?"

"Sure thing, babe. Just get some rest." I take my coffee and muffin to the front of the shop and grab my laptop. Since the town social media and marketing position will not be working out, I need to start looking for something else. I am not going to let that jackass keep me from moving home full time. Fuck, at this point, I might see if Robbie needs a lube tech or something at the garage. I may not know as much about cars as he does, but I can at least change my oil and a tire.

Chapter 25

Matilda

After I relax in the back office for a bit, I decide to get up and move around. As much as I love Jax for helping to run the front of the shop today, there is still work I need to get done. Making my way to the counter, I see Jax on his laptop clicking away. He is so focused on what he is doing, I'm able to sneak up and wrap my arms around him from behind. "Hey, whatcha looking at?"

"Oh, not much. Just some possible marketing positions in the Twin Cities." He closes his laptop and looks back at me. "Are you feeling better?"

"Yea, thanks for letting me rest for a bit. I was thinking I better come out here and try and get some work done." I hate that he has to look for jobs in the Twin Cities. The commute would be brutal, especially during the winter months. I know it would be better than him having to travel, but it just doesn't feel right. His heart has always been in photography. I can't imagine him sitting behind a desk all day.

The bell rings as the shop door opens and Robbie walks in. "Hey, how's it going?"

"Good. What brings you in today?" It is rare that Robbie ever stops by the bookstore. He is usually so busy with his own shop that he doesn't have the time to spare.

"I got a call from the lawyer. They wanted to see if everyone could meet today and go over the will. I was hoping maybe we could all meet here, say around two?"

"Yea, sure. I'm amazed that they haven't asked for us to meet with them sooner."

Robbie looks sheepish as he rubs the back of his neck. "Yea, that is kind of my fault. The lawyer called me a couple of times to try and set up a meeting and I honestly just spaced it." Sounds like typical Robbie. He really needs more help at that shop. He is always so busy and barely has time for himself.

"How do you space something like that?" Jax chuckles, shaking his head.

"I don't know. I've been busy, I guess. Anyway, does two work for the both of you?" Robbie presses on.

"Yea, I have no plans today. I can help watch the shop while you guys meet," Jax mentions.

"Actually, no, you need to be present. You are in the will too, brother."

Jax seems taken aback by this. "Don't be so surprised. Mom and dad loved you as if you were their own," I say, giving his shoulder a reassuring squeeze.

Jax and I work around the shop, putting out the new releases and arranging a few new displays. After everything is all set up, he focuses on taking some pictures to post on the shop's social media. Pre-Jax, I had a Facebook account. Now, we have Facebook, Instagram, and Twitter. I had no idea there were so many platforms. It baffles me how he is able to manage all that. But whatever he is doing, it's working. My online orders have been at a steady increase.

Two o'clock approaches quickly. Jake and Robbie show up a

hair before the scheduled meeting time. After they arrive, Scott comes over from the café, leaving one of his baristas in charge. Letty is kind enough to stop in for a little bit (prior to her shift at the bar) to help cover the front of the shop. Fortunately, Mr. Reed (the lawyer) is on time. We decide to all meet in my back office for some additional privacy. It is a tight fit, but it will do.

"Thank you for taking the time to meet with me today. I understand you are all busy individuals," Mr. Reed starts off.

"Sorry for the delay, Mr. Reed. I'm glad we were able to all meet today," I reply, trying to smooth over Robbie's forgetfulness.

"Anyway, your parents had everything very well planned out in regards to their assets. If you are all ready, we can proceed with the reading of the will?"

We nod in unison. Jax holds my hand for support, which I greatly appreciate. Mr. Reed runs through a bunch of legal stuff but at the end of the day, Jake and I were left the house—which makes sense, since we both currently live there. We can choose to sell it if we want, but we are required to split any profits. Scott and I are both left Moore Books and Coffee with the same stipulation—if we want to sell, we can; but we need to share the proceeds. Robbie was left my dad's storage unit. It houses a few classic cars my dad inherited from his father and never really got around to working on. Jax was left with a private letter and some property that I am not familiar with, but it seems he is. Some other key items are divided out between us, but the real kicker is the money.

I knew mom and dad had life insurance and investments. I just never realized how much it would be. The total cash value is split between the five of us, leaving each of us roughly a hundred thousand. It isn't life changing money, but it is a lot. There is so much I can do to the shop with that sum. Even though, there was a comment added from my dad asking us not to spend all of our inheritance on our shops; instead, he suggested we try and do something fun and frivolous… something more personal and that we would actually enjoy.

After the reading, we have to sign some legal documents and then we are handed our respective checks. We thank Mr. Reed for agreeing to come down to the shop and apologize again for not meeting with him sooner. Letty rushes out quickly to get to the bar. Her shift starts in just a few minutes.

"What's with the property and letter, Jax?" Scott asks, not out of jealousy or anything but likely because of the same extreme curiosity we all have.

"I'm not sure. I'll read the letter and stuff later. Tilly, we better get back to work. There is still a lot we need to get done in the shop today. Plus, there are a bunch of orders we need to bring to the post office," Jax says, trying to avoid the subject of his inheritance.

My brothers seem to take the hint and drop it. As much as I want to know as well, I will give him some time to figure it all out.

"Well, shit. Anyone know what they plan to do with the money?" Jake asks, trying to break the tension. Robbie, Scott, and I are all about to answer when Jake interjects, "Plans that don't involve spending it at the shops?"

We all laugh, knowing our only plans have been on how to improve our businesses. But honestly, I am not sure what else to do. I already have a home and a car. School is paid for... Sure, I could use a little of the money on a vacation, but no way am I spending that much on a trip. Scott and I have both been eyeing up the shop behind ours; and if we could get our hands on it, we would own this whole corner of Main Street. We could expand, and Scott could take over the kitchen there. It seems like it would be the best use of our money, if that is what he wants to do as well.

"Ha, that is what I thought. I don't blame you guys, though. My only thoughts are investing or helping you expand the shop to add my video store," he chuckles, bringing up his rental store idea again.

"Yea, I was thinking of the place behind the shop," Scott says, having the same idea I do. "If all three of us went in on it together, we would only need maybe fifty thousand a piece. Then, we could use the rest for whatever."

"That sounds like an awesome plan. I'd be interested if Tilly is." Jake seems uncharacteristically enthusiastic about this video store concept.

"I like the idea. But before we do anything, let's check on things... look at the space. It has been abandoned for a while and we should make sure it is worth investing in. If the kitchen needs a complete overhaul or cannot easily be integrated into our space, I'm not sure if it is worth it or not." While I am excited over the prospect, I know we need to all slow down and think about it.

After my brothers take off, Jax and I are left in the shop. I want nothing more than to hound him about what my parents left him, but he seems a little closed off right now. I know that when I need space, he usually gives it to me and so, I need to do the same for him.

"Hey, would you mind if I head out? I've got some shit I need to take care of," Jax says suddenly.

"Umm, yea, sure. All the hard stuff is done for the day."

"Thanks, babe," he says, giving me a quick kiss on the cheek. "I will bring these orders to the post office for you."

"Thank you. I will see you tonight at home." He gives me a quick nod, before grabbing his stuff and the orders and heading out.

I hate that something is bothering him... and that I don't know what it is. Is it just grief? Is it guilt? Or is it something else altogether? I will give him some time to process everything. I just hope it isn't that much time.

I spend the rest of the afternoon working around the store. A few customers come in, and I get a few more online orders that I prep for tomorrow. Scott has already shut down the cafe for the day and gone home. Sometimes I envy the fact he finishes his day at five, but then I remember he starts at like four in the morning. So, yea, I will handle closing at seven since I get to sleep in and not show up until nine.

About half an hour before closing, the chime above the door rings and I see Keith. Immediately, all the blood drains from my face. What the hell is he doing here? What right does he have to come into my shop? I mean, I know it is a public establishment and all, but still he has no business being here.

"What do you want?" I skip all pleasantries and cross my arms over my chest. Thankfully, I have the counter separating us; so, if he tries anything, it will be easy to evade him this time.

Keith holds his hands up in surrender. "Hey, no reason to be so hostile. I just came by to deliver this notice." He slowly approaches the counter, as if he is approaching a wild animal, and lays a letter down in front of me.

"What is this?" I ask, refusing to even touch the white envelope; because frankly, I am not sure I want to touch anything that he has had in his possession. "It is not common for you to go around delivering notices."

"Martha was out sick today, and well, these are urgent. They contain time-sensitive information that I needed to get passed on to the shops."

I raise a curious eyebrow at him. "What is so important?"

"Well, you can read it yourself. It is right in front of you," he says, patronizing me like I wasn't already aware that was an option.

"Yea, but you are here. Might as well tell me. That way, if necessary, I can ensure you get my complaint."

He huffs and puts his hands in his pockets, before looking up at me with a shit-eating grin. "Fine, it is a cease and desist notice, along with a warning to any shops who are using Jackson Harris's service."

"What in the actual fuck, Keith? What bullshit is this?" It takes all of my willpower to not jump across the counter and punch him in his stupid smug face. "It isn't bad enough that you are refusing to employ Jax, now you are trying to eliminate his personal business on top of it?"

"Whoa, calm down, Matilda. This is nothing personal. As I have explained to you, he is not qualified for the position you have been trying to force me to—"

"Don't you dare talk about *force*, Keith. You fucking assaulted me with your mouth and told me that if I don't fuck you Jax couldn't have the job." I cannot believe this fucking asshole. What the hell is his fucking issue?

"No one *forced* anything. We went out and had a lovely evening. One minute, we are sitting there discussing Jackson's qualifications. And then, all of a sudden, you were throwing yourself at me. I am guessing you had a little too much to drink at dinner. Because you got so upset when I rejected you that you vomited. I wanted to make sure you were well… but by the time I looked up, you must have run off in embarrassment." Keith offers his retelling of the evening; and exactly as I had suspected, he would spin the story to make me seem like an incompetent fool. "I know you really wanted to get Jackson that job… But, Matilda, throwing yourself at someone—it is beneath you."

"You fucking lying—" Keith holds up his hands.

"Let's not play this game, Matilda. We both know you will lose. No one will believe anything you have to say. I promised that you would regret your decision. And, well, I am someone who always keeps his promises."

I want to protest, but it is a waste of oxygen. "You know that is not what happened, Keith. But whatever. Why can't Jax help the shops?" Clearly, he feels no remorse for his actions and has already concocted his story.

"Well, according to local ordinances all businesses must work with approved and authorized and licensed vendors. Jackson is not licensed for the services he is offering nor is he an approved vendor." Well, fuck me. Of course, he would go home and dig through the fucking ordinances to find anything to nitpick us about.

"Well, Jax is my employee. Therefore, taking and posting images on my social media is within the scope of his position." Ha! Take that, asshat! It doesn't cover Jax for the other shops but at least I can keep him here with me.

"He is an official employee? On payroll? Filled out the necessary documentation? I'd hate for you to get into legal trouble, for paying an undocumented employee cash under the table." He feigns concern for me and my business.

"It isn't necessary. He is a volunteer and is not being paid. But we have been discussing creating a permanent paid position for him and will ensure that it is legal, as we always do with any of my other staff."

He huffs. "Fine. But ensure he is working within the legal volunteer limits, which is no more than twenty hours per week. If I find he is working more frequently than that, then I will have no choice but to report you. This could cost you your business license, and I would hate to do that to such a keystone in our community."

"Sure. Anything else, Keith? I'm about to close up."

"That's all. Have a good evening." He turns and strolls out of the shop, whistling and clearly pleased with himself.

I take the notice and quickly shove it into my purse. I need to go home and talk with Jax. He needs to figure something out. We can't let Keith keep him from doing his freelance work. Granted, I am worried that even if we get him as a licensed business, Keith could still block him as a vendor.

Gathering my items, I rush to lock up and get home. However, once I do get there, I am surprised to find the house dark and empty. There is no delicious smelling dinner cooking. There is no Jax. There is nothing. I try to give him a call, but it just rings a few times and then goes to his voicemail. Where the hell is he? I'm about to text him when Letty calls.

I answer quickly. As much as I want to talk with her about this shit, I need to figure out where Jax is and discuss it with him first. "Hey, Letty, can I call you back? I need—"

She cuts me off. "Let me guess… you are looking for Jax?"

"Yea, do you know where he is?"

"Yup. He is sitting in the bar. Unfortunately, he is pretty wasted and I know he is in no condition to drive home. Why don't you come here and I will get some dinner for you guys? He needs something in his stomach to absorb the shit ton of alcohol he has been drinking."

Dammit, did he already hear about this shit with Keith? No, even if he did, this wouldn't cause him to drink heavily. It has to be something to do with the will reading today. That is the only thing that makes sense. Or maybe, work has called him and he needs to go back? Anyway, I don't have time to debate this. I just need to get to the bar and make sure that he is okay.

"Thanks, I'm on my way. Chicken tenders, please."

Letty laughs at me. "You are still on a chicken tenders kick? Sure thing, I will get them dropped in the fryer for you."

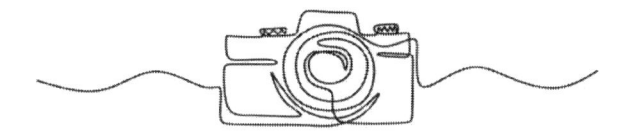

Chapter 26

Jackson

To say today hasn't exactly gone as planned is an understatement. When Robbie mentioned that I was included in the will, well, I couldn't believe it. Then, I figured it was going to be something small and sentimental. You know, like a t-shirt or a vinyl record? I was absolutely not prepared for what they left me. The second Mr. Reed said it, it was like everything else just faded into the background.

I feel bad for leaving Tilly alone at the shop, but I just had to get away for a moment and try to clear my head. Unfortunately, that journey led me to Harper's... and turning to the bottle to help me solve all my problems. I know that this is not the proper solution, but I just needed something to help me think straight. However, that one drink has almost turned into one too many.

As I sit here and swirl my glass of amber liquid, I cannot stop myself from thinking this whole month has been nothing but a whirlwind. First, the passing of Mr. and Mrs. Moore. Then, seeing

Tilly for the first time after so many years, falling in love with her all over again... (*and twice as hard*) and worrying I'm having a midlife crisis over my career and my desires. And, now, there's *this*. At this point, I am wondering what else the world might try to throw at me.

A light, delicate hand touches my shoulder. I don't need to turn around to know it is Tilly. I can smell her mango shampoo and body spray. She always smells like a tropical paradise. Fuck, I cannot wait to take her to an actual tropical paradise. "Hey, Jax," she whispers softly in my ear. Damn her... *Not really*... It's just that out of all the shit going on, she is the only thing I am certain about. I want Matilda Moore. I want her in every way possible.

I turn and try to give her my best smile. Though, I'm aware I am slightly too intoxicated, and looking just as much like a fool. But oh well, she has seen me hammered before—maybe not nearly as emotionally hammered, but hammered nonetheless. "Hey, babe," I hiccup.

"I was worried. When I got home, you were not there and you weren't answering your phone. Is everything okay?" She asks delicately. Damn, I am such an asshole. I told her I would meet her at home and like a dick, I came to the bar and started drinking instead. I'm guessing that Letty called her. And for that reason, I'm not sure if I like or hate her right now... Part of me says like, because Tilly always makes everything better. But the other part says hate, because I really don't want Tilly to see me this way.

"I'm sorry. I came here to unwind and lost track of time," I only slightly slur. While I am drunk, at least I am pretty good at holding my alcohol.

"What's going on? After the meeting today, you seemed pretty distraught and now, here you are... drinking at the bar. I'm worried, Jax. Please, let me in," Tilly begs, holding onto one of my hands. I really didn't mean to make her worry. I was just caught off-guard.

"Here ya go." Letty replaces my whiskey with a coffee and

brings me a giant burger, likely in an attempt to get me sober. I notice Tilly has a Sprite and chicken tenders again. Now I feel even more like an ass. She has been so sick from stress and instead of trying to make her life less stressful, I am making it worse by being a whiny bitch.

I grab her parents' letter out of my pocket and look down at it again. "You know that when my grandpa died, I was the only remaining family he had left, right?"

"Yea, that is why mom and dad insisted you come live with us. None of us wanted to see you end up in the system." That was the best and worst day of my life. I was so terrified I was going to be torn from everyone and everything I knew. But the Moores wouldn't let that happen, and they "adopted" me. They took me in, raised me as their own, and never treated me any differently.

"Well, when my grandpa died, all of his properties and possessions became mine. But I was too young to manage them. So as my legal guardians, your parents took control until my eighteenth birthday." Tilly sits there, listening to me intently; she hasn't even touched her food yet. "Well, when I turned eighteen, I asked for your parents' help to sell the house and liquidate any assets so I could use the money for college, travel, and whatever."

"Okay, I knew my parents gave you money for college, but I didn't realize it was really just your own money. But I am guessing that there is more to this story?" *Smart cookie.*

"Technically your parents did loan me money for college, but as soon as everything was liquidated, I paid them back." I felt so proud—eighteen, and I was able to pay the majority of my schooling out of pocket, and pick up the rest with my job. Most kids my age would have blown the money on stupid shit. "They lied to me, Tilly..."

"I don't understand, Jax. What did they lie to you about?" Tilly is immediately on red alert. Her parents were genuinely the nicest people in the world. To hear they lied about anything, to even think they would lie about anything, is like hearing a lie in of itself.

"That property they gave me... it was my grandpa's." Recognition shines across her face over what I am trying to say. "Your parents never sold or liquidated anything... Well, not *technically*. I mean, they did sell it. But not like I thought... They sold it to themselves. They fucking purchased all of it and kept it for me." Tears well up in my eyes. The fucking Moores... just when you think they can't do anything else to make you feel like the most important person in the damn world, they say "hold my beer" and prove you wrong.

"Oh, Jax..." She rubs my shoulder. "I'm sorry. I honestly don't know what to say."

I hand her the letter to read for herself. I am genuinely too emotional to convey it all to her right now. But I still think about their words:

Dear Jackson,

I hope this letter finds you well. I am aware that you may be reading this due to unfortunate circumstances. Though, I really hope you are reading it for a joyous one.

We still remember when you turned eighteen and were ready to go off to college. We wanted to help you just as much as we helped all of our other children. Because, while you may not have been related to us by blood, you were our child nonetheless. But much like your grandfather, you were too stubborn and too proud to accept our help.

When you begged us to help you liquidate everything, it broke our hearts. We knew how much your grandfather's home meant to you and your family, and well, we didn't have the heart to let you get rid of it. At least not at eighteen and when you were so desperate to make your own way. So, we decided to invest the money we wanted to give you for college, plus some other funds we had set aside, to purchase the home for you. That way, you still got the money you wanted, but the home could still be there when you were ready. Because one day, when you are older and ready to settle down and raise your own family, you will wish you had this home.

This home, as you are well aware, was built by your great-great grandfather. And from then on, it was continuously built upon by each son who inherited it thereafter. Knowing your grandfather, he would have wanted you to continue this tradition; and knowing you as we do, when you are ready, you too will want to do the same.

We apologize for deceiving you, but please do not worry about the personal money we invested. We know you would have never wanted to owe us anything. After we purchased the property, we decided to rent it out. This way, someone would live there to help keep everything up and running. Anyway, we used the initial rental income to pay back the money we invested. And then, the rest of the rental income has been deposited into a savings account for you. The details of the account are enclosed in this letter, along with the current lease.

Now that you are older and more mature, the decision is yours as to what you want to do with the home. You can continue to use it as a rental property and collect income. Or if you honestly do not think you will ever return to Tral Lake, then it is yours to sell. Or if you are ready to settle down (hopefully with Tilly, hint-hint) it is ready for you.

Just remember we love you, Jax, and we never thought of you as anything less than our own son. That being said, as our son, we will love and support whatever decision you make.

Love,

Mom and Dad

I look over to Tilly, who is sobbing as she is reading the letter. Although I am sure the contents have her tearing up, seeing the words of her parents may just as likely be the culprit. Unfortunately, none of the Moore siblings received any sort of letter. But given their parents were young and in good health, they probably didn't think they needed to write one. Looking at the date, it appears they wrote it a few months after I left for the travel magazine. And (I can only assume) it was after one of the many phone calls I had with them, crying about how much I missed home and loved Tilly. I wonder if they were just waiting for me to come home, before finally giving it to me? As if knowing that the moment that I did, I would never want to leave. Consequently, if that was their thought, they were correct. I already knew I wanted Tilly. But now, knowing that I have the option of marrying Tilly and raising our family in my family home, it just seems almost too perfect.

When I first came home, I drove out to my grandpa's place. There was no way I could not check in on it. I remember feeling sad seeing a family of five playing in the yard. The dad was pushing his son in the old tire swing mine had hung up for me. Looking at them, I almost felt as though I was transported back in time, and that man was my dad pushing me. While it made me sad to see a new family in our home, I was also happy to see it in good condition and filled with love.

In the lease, I notice that the Moores were gracious. Because my grandpa's house had long since been paid off (well, the land was paid off... the house itself was built by hand) there was no mortgage to cover, just property taxes and upkeep. The home is a large stone farmhouse with five bedrooms and three bathrooms, situated on five acres of land. There is a heated three-car garage (because this is Minnesota and winters get cold) and a giant pole barn. Not to mention, a pond is situated on the property as well, along with an established personal farm with produce and chickens. They could have charged, even in this small town, two grand a month. But no, not the Moores. They only asked for fifteen hundred a month, and that was with all utilities included. So, the profit that went into savings was not a lot. After a decade, there was only around a hundred thousand in the account.

"Wow," Tilly comments. I assume she has finished reading the letter. "This is crazy. I'm not sure what to say. Are you okay?"

"Yea, I couldn't believe it. I think I'm still in shock to be honest. When I first came here and saw a family living there, I was a little heartbroken and regretted my choice. But now, knowing your parents did this... Well, it is just so unbelievable."

"You are happy?" she asks cautiously.

"Yes and no. I am happy that something I thought I lost—because I was young and desperate—is not gone for good. Finding out I didn't truly lose it... it is nice. But now, I am not sure what I want to do with it. I read the current lease. It is up in six months, so I have four months to decide what to do. As much as I want to say I will come home and take over the house, seeing how happy that family is there... Well, I don't want to kick them out. Especially since it is such a big home. It is meant for a family. I would feel selfish living there by myself."

I look over. For a brief moment, I see a hurt expression on Tilly's face. "Shit. I'm sorry, Tilly. I didn't mean it like that. It's just it is a lot to think about, and I am still trying to find work here. I know right now money isn't that much of a concern. But it isn't like this is 'never have to work again' money. It can help me do a lot of things, but I will still need work." Dammit, she looks hurt. I am drunk and I am fucking this up—*I know it.* "Besides, let's say I find work and I stay. Would you really want to leave your family home to come live in mine? It is not fair for me to assume that of you."

"I guess you are right. It is a lot to think about. Because I am not sure what I would want either."

Chapter 27

Matilda

Last night was difficult. I felt heartbroken for Jax. There is so much on his plate right now, and all I can really do is be there to support him. I can't... No, I won't make his choices for him. I am not sure what that means for our relationship. But I do know that whatever becomes of us, it will be for the best. At first, when I read that letter and saw what my parents had hinted at (they were hoping he would raise his family there and ideally with me) I was so excited. I could already picture him and me in that big home, raising our family. I know when I settle down, I definitely want three (maybe four) children. Growing up in a big family with my siblings has been wonderful, especially now; having that bond is priceless.

But when it didn't even sound like he was considering us in that home... it hurt. At first, when he had asked me if I would be willing to leave my family home to live there, I was uncertain. Then, after thinking about it more last night, I realized that I would. I love my home. It has so many good memories. But then, sometimes those memories are a little overbearing. I look at the door to my parents' bedroom and think to myself—*would I ever live in that room?* What would I do with it? Maybe that is the same problem for Jax. Would moving there be like living with an overwhelming amount of good and bad memories?

Given the circumstances, I guess that house has a lot of tragic memories for him. For instance, I'm sure memories of watching his father die slowly and painfully from Lou Gehrig's disease still linger there. I was too young when that happened. I was only three, but Scott has told me about it. He said it was hard being there with Jax, who was watching his father wither away to nothing. Then, to be twelve and go to wake your grandpa one morning, only to find a cold lifeless body... I guess I would never want to live there either.

I think momentarily, I was just being selfish and reading into things. In fact, the more I consider it, Jax living in that home or not has nothing to do with us. It really is his choice and (like my parents said) I will support him no matter what he decides.

I still need to talk to him about the notice Keith dropped off yesterday. But last night, I really didn't have the chance. Then this morning I came to the shop, allowing him to sleep in. Although he sobered up before we got home, my guess is that he is going to have one hell of a hangover when he wakes up. I made sure to leave him a note next to the coffee pot, letting him know where I was and that he didn't need to come in.

"Where's Jax?" Scott stands between the cafe and the shop.

"Oh, I let him sleep in. He had kind of a rough night last night."

"Is this about the will reading?" I can tell Scott is both concerned and curious.

"Yea, but it isn't my place to explain." While they are best friends and basically brothers, I don't feel comfortable telling his story. I have had Jax keep enough of my stories private, so it is the least I can do for him in return.

"Okay, sorry. I guess, I don't know..." Scott rubs a hand over his face. "I was thinking maybe you two were fighting or something. I know his vacation is almost over. And well, I just... you know?"

Yes, I know. I have been trying not to think about that. Obviously, the town marketing job is not happening. I have a feeling that Keith will block him on starting his own private business as best he can. So, the only thing he can really do is become employed with someone else. I would love it if he wanted to help run the shop with me, but I don't think that would ever be enough. I've noticed him working here, and he always seems bored.

"I understand. We haven't really talked about it," I tell him honestly. I am not going to panic over "what if's" and "maybe's" right now. Especially since Scott helped me so much the first time Jax left. I would hate to put him out like that again. Not that he wouldn't do it anyway. Hell, all my brothers would be there. But I am an adult now. I can't afford to breakdown over any guy, no matter how much I love him.

"Just let me know if you need anything, okay?" I nod in reply and he goes back into the cafe to resume working.

I try hard to focus on work today, and to think about all of the things I want to do with the bookstore, especially now that I have the extra money. We have talked about expanding the shop; but really, I don't need much space. A majority of it would be for storage, which I could do anywhere. I mostly just want to expand so that Scott can have his industrial kitchen and open a full-blown restaurant. It has been his dream for so long, and I would do anything to help him fulfill it.

As I glance around, I try to make note of where improvements could be made. I could invest money into making a better reading corner? Or a nice place for the children's story time? There is so much I can do... While in the back of the shop, I hear the ding above the door and rush to the front. When I get up there, I see a disheveled looking Jax.

"Hi, I didn't expect you to come in today." It all feels really strained between us right now. My mind is overanalyzing everything, coming up with each possible worst-case scenario. On top of that, I am terrified that he is pulling away from me.

I know it sounds silly... But except for the few times when I touched him last night to comfort him, he didn't touch me at all, even when we went to bed. Normally, he would snuggle against me. Last night he felt so far away. I keep trying to tell myself he was just overemotional and drunk, but another nagging part of me is saying it is more than that.

"Did you not want me to come in?" Clearly, he is having the same "off" feeling about us.

I drop my head and sigh. "No, it is not that, Jax. I just figured after last night... maybe coming into the shop is not what you wanted to do today. If you want to be here, I am happy to see you. But if you don't want to be here, you don't need to be." Fuck, even though I know we are talking about today, I also feel like I am talking about "us" in general.

"I'm sorry, Tilly. I didn't mean to be a dick. I guess you are right. I am still a little shell-shocked from yesterday and then the hangover isn't helping."

I walk up to him slowly, to place a quick kiss on his cheek. I hate this horribly awkward feeling. Normally we are in sync. But right now, I feel like we are two magnets pushing each other apart. "Then go home and rest. I can handle things here. I will see you later, okay?"

"Sure, okay. I will see you tonight." He turns and walks out of the shop. I can already feel my fragile heart start to crack. No kiss, no hug, no anything. He just feels like a robot. Although I want to believe there's just a lot weighing on his mind... there is that voice in my head, reminding me that this might be our end.

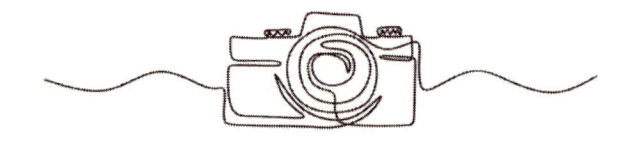

Chapter 28

Jackson

Shit, ever since that will reading, I feel like I am fucking everything up. My mind is so overloaded that I can't think straight. Do I quit my job and stay here? Or keep my job and move back? If I quit, what will I do? If I don't quit, could we survive the strain a long-distance relationship would put on us? I know other people in my line of work have families, but I am not sure if I could raise my own like that. I don't think Tilly would want to either. Then the next questions are: If I stay, Tilly and I together, would we live at her house? Or my grandpa's house? Or should we just buy a new one and be done with it?

There is just too much damn shit to consider. I know Tilly and I should talk more, but ever since last night when we were discussing my inheritance, she has felt distant. Maybe it is just me... But I feel like there's this invisible force field around her, and she is untouchable. The worst part is I think I put the fucking barrier there myself.

Come on, Jax, pull your shit together. My vacation is almost up.

While there are so many uncertainties right now, I know I want Tilly. So, I need to pull my head out of my ass, and fix this distance issue that I caused by being a drunk shit last night.

I take out my laptop and start looking at some dinner options to make for her. Flipping through, I notice there are a lot of great recipes. But with running to the store, I wouldn't have enough time to cook something up, so I bookmark them for later. Even though a nice steak and lobster dinner sounds good, Tilly really hasn't been eating anything too heavy. *Shit, I need to do something.* That's when I find it. It is simple but I can make it from scratch easily enough.

I found a recipe for creamy tomato soup. Although it may not be fancy, growing up with the Moores, I know for a fact that tomato soup is the automatic go-to whenever someone feels sick or down. *Actually...* I think for a moment, then go look in the pantry. I remembered seeing a recipe box in there the other day. *Bingo!* I find Mrs. Moore's recipe for tomato soup. This is perfect and I know Tilly will love it.

∞∞∞

Around seven thirty, Tilly comes home and puts her stuff up. I rush out to the living room to greet her and try to push through that invisible barrier I built. I stroll up to her and give her a kiss on the cheek. "Hi, babe. How was the shop today?"

Tilly still seems a little guarded, but she smiles at me. "It was good. What did you make? It smells great."

I smile back at her. "It's a surprise. I'll meet you in the dining room, okay?"

I head back to the kitchen. I stir and taste the soup—*it's perfect*. Quickly, I fry up a couple of grilled cheese sandwiches I had prepped. I didn't want to make them too early and chance them getting cold. Bringing the dishes into the dining room, I call out, "Close your eyes."

I hear her chuckle. "You are ridiculous. Okay, they are closed."

I stroll in, setting our bowls and sandwiches on the table. She sniffs the air and then smiles. "God, this smells so good. I can't quite figure it out, but it reminds me of mom." That makes me smile in turn. Even though she doesn't know what I made or how it tastes, the smell is at least right.

"Okay, open!" I say, taking a seat in my chair.

Tilly slowly opens her eyes. Looking down at the table, she grins, a single tear running down her face. "You made me tomato soup and grilled cheese?" I reach over and wipe her damp cheek. "It smells just like the soup she used to make us as kids."

"I actually used her recipe," I say. Another tear is shed. "I hope that was okay?" Damn, I didn't think about how this might upset her. Maybe it is making her sad thinking about them.

"It's perfect, Jax. Thank you, I really needed this today." She leans down and smells the soup before she takes a spoonful into her mouth. The moan she makes in approval sends signals down below. I shift slightly in my seat to try and relieve some of the pressure. "It is perfect, Jax."

"I'm glad you like it. I wanted to cook you a nice dinner. To make up for last night... and today. Then, I thought about how you haven't felt well and how your mom's tomato soup cures everything. So, I don't know... I thought maybe this would help make you feel better. But also, maybe it would cure whatever damage I caused as well."

"Jax, you didn't damage anything. It was a very emotional day for all of us. Regardless, though, I love the soup. It was exactly what I needed," Tilly praises, digging in.

"So, we are okay? I didn't fuck us up?" I feel like an insecure idiot right now. But I worry that hiding my fears and letting them simmer will only hurt us more. If Tilly and I end up doing this long-distance thing for a while, communication is key.

"No, you didn't fuck us up. I will admit I was scared. I felt like you were more distant since yesterday. But I realize we both had stuff to think about and work through."

We continue eating our dinner. Taking into account the little moans Tilly keeps torturing me with, she is enjoying the meal.

But something still feels off. Tilly still seems to have reservations. About what, I have no idea. "Is something else bothering you?"

"Huh?" She looks up at me confused for a moment.

"I'm just wondering what's on your mind? While I feel like we cleared the air about us, I am still sensing that something else is bothering you."

"Oh, yea. I guess there is." She starts playing with her soup, clearly stalling. "Keith stopped by the shop last night."

I drop my spoon, and try to rein in my anger. "Why didn't you tell me?" She gives me a pointed look that says—*do I really need to answer that?* "Sorry... are you okay? Did he try to pull anything?"

"I am fine. He did not touch me or attempt to. But he did deliver me and a bunch of shops... a notice."

"What was the notice?"

"Umm... well... you can read it. But it basically says shops can't use your services, because you are not licensed or an approved vendor. Anyone who does is at risk of losing their business license. I did justify that you are technically my employee —well, volunteer—and it is just a job responsibility. So, I am not in trouble as long as you don't work more than twenty hours, or until I officially hire you on. But that means the other shops can't contract you, unless they hire you as staff."

That fucking weasel. Of course, he would pull some stupid stunt like this. I am sure that even if I get licensed, he would make it hell to do so. Then, who knows if he would allow me to be a vendor... It seems pretty obvious that finding work around here won't be easy. Well, at least independently. I could get a job somewhere else. He really can't mess with that. It's just one more damn thing to deal with.

"I'm sorry, Jax. I know that puts a wrench in your plan. But we will figure something out, okay?"

I take her hand and smile. "It will be fine. I will find something. Honestly, I wasn't sure if that is what I wanted to do anyway. I have been thinking about doing general photography— you know, weddings and portraits? But maybe I'll do something else altogether."

"I know. I would ask if you wanted to join me at the shop. But that isn't what you want full time. I can tell you don't mind helping out, but it really isn't your thing," Tilly mentions. There is no resentment in her tone. She is only stating what she has observed—unfortunately, she is not wrong.

"It really isn't. I wish it was though. I enjoy being at the shop with you and spending time together. I also like helping with your social media. But, no, I don't feel like running a bookshop is what I want to do," I say in somber agreement.

"It's okay, Jax. I am not angry. It is slow and boring work. Even if you stop doing photography, you need something fast-paced and challenging. The bookshop isn't that. Also…" She sighs. "…please don't take this the wrong way, but I don't think one of those marketing jobs in the Twin Cities is the right thing for you either. Besides the horrendous commute, I think you would be miserable sitting behind a desk all day."

I let out this deep breath I didn't realize I was holding in. "Thank you." I take her hand into mine. "I was worried about the same thing, but honestly, I have just been desperately trying to figure out what to do."

"We will figure it out. I hate to bring this sensitive subject up again, but do you really need to work right now?" Tilly says softly, verbally walking on eggshells.

"I know I've got some money, but it isn't enough to not work."

"No, but with the house being rented you are generating income. If you did freelance photography work, that would be more income. I guess I am not sure about your finances, but living here with me, the expenses would be almost nothing."

I guess I never thought about that. I mean, except for the rent on my apartment, I don't have much in the way of expenses. I don't own a car, but would have enough money to buy one. I have one travel miles credit card that I don't really keep a balance on. I pay it off every statement. I have no student loans either. While maybe only making a thousand to fifteen hundred a month sounds like very little (especially since the rent of my apartment is eighteen hundred alone) if I stayed here, she is right. I wouldn't need much to live.

"Let me think about it, okay? I mean, it sounds like a good possibility. But there are some things I need to think about—like insurance and what the hell I would do with all my free time?" I try to make a joke to ease the tension.

"I understand." She looks a little sad. "If I didn't have the shop, I don't know what I would do."

"Can I ask you something, Tilly? And I need your honest answer..."

She gulps. "Okay?"

"Is the possibility of me working my current job, but coming home to you... is it not going to work for you?" I ask the question I have been dreading.

"I honestly don't know, Jax. I want it to work. But it scares me. I feel selfish because I know there are military spouses who have it a lot harder than what you are proposing. But when I think of a partner, well, I think of someone who is here." She shakes her head. "I want a family. And I have always imagined that family having a husband and a father, who would be here."

Fuck, I knew this long-distance thing was going to be a stretch. I am not even angry with her. Tilly wants what her mom and dad had. I've always known that. I think she could handle the separation temporarily. But long term, with marriage and children, she would never do that kind of arrangement. And neither would I. I couldn't imagine missing so much being gone.

I take her hand in mine and give it a quick kiss. "It's okay, babe. Nothing to be sorry about. We will figure everything out, okay?"

Chapter 29

Matilda

Wednesdays are one of my favorite days of the week. A couple years ago, I started a local reading group and we meet on Wednesday evenings. Scott usually heats up a carafe of coffee and puts out hot water with an assortment of tea options, along with a delectable spread of cookies and finger-sandwiches he makes.

Our group sure has grown over the last year. When it started, there were only three of us. Now, we officially have seven members. Our newest is Scarlett Valentine. She moved here a few months back and took over the bed and breakfast. It has been a blast to have her in the group. Let's just say, she has really expanded the book genres we read.

"Well..." Sally clears her throat. "...that book was interesting." This is the Minnesotan nice way to indicate that you do not like something, but don't want to be rude and flat out say it. Sally is one of our more conservative members, and I was concerned that the book Scarlett recommended last week wouldn't sit well with a few, her included.

"Interesting? Please..." Patty interjects, blowing air through her pursed lips. "It was brilliant." Patty (although she is almost sixty) is pretty hip with the times. I wasn't too worried about her.

"Patricia, seriously? Some of the scenes were anatomically impossible," Michelle, likely the most conservative member of our group, adds.

"Not really. I haven't personally tried many of the positions but I know friends who have," Scarlett intervenes. I can tell she is enjoying seeing some ruffled feathers.

"Don't be ridiculous, Scarlett. There is no way..." Michelle looks around to make sure no one is near, then whispers, "...she had two men enter her at once, in the same location." She shivers, recalling the scene.

Yea, I haven't known Scarlett for very long and we do not get to hang out much, each of us having busy work schedules and all. But we are becoming fast friends. That's right, last week she suggested a reverse harem to the group. I couldn't believe it! It wasn't the fact that she reads them, more so that she would suggest it for open discussion. Not only that, but the book itself was fairly erotic.

"It is a stretchable muscle that is designed to expand. Given that a woman can accommodate child birth, I am not sure this is much different?" Scarlett retorts. Yes, she is making some of the most conservative members in our community talk about a girl being double-stuffed by two guys—who, by the description, have "long cocks as thick as her wrist". I am a fairly petite woman and, well, that definitely sounds like an undertaking. *That's for sure.*

"That may be true, but childbirth is not an easy or enjoyable experience. Then, couple that with her giving fellatio to a third male..." Michelle arches her eyebrow. "I am sorry but only a professional sex-worker might be able to handle that. The woman claimed to have been a virgin and had never done a sexual act beyond kissing, before engaging in intercourse with these men. It was all highly improbable."

I try my hardest to suppress my laughter. Hearing Michelle, the Sunday school teacher, talk about the probability of a menage sexual position is almost too much.

"Though I find the intercourse impractical, I do understand the appeal of the polyamorous relationship." My jaw drops as Michelle tosses that bomb at the group. "The three men were all very similar but different. While I love my Hughie with all my heart and would never cheat on him, there are times where as a partner, I feel he is lacking. The other week I wanted to go try this new restaurant. It was some sort of Japanese fusion and he refused, complaining about how awful going out to eat is and how he would rather save the money and have me buy him a takeout burger. Then, he mentioned wanting to use the money saved to purchase more model plane kits. To be able to have my Hughie and then another man or two, who are able to satisfy my other needs, would be wonderful."

"Absolutely. All I want is for Steve to give me a back rub," Amanda joins in the conversation. "But it ends up being a half-assed one-handed massage that lasts five minutes, before his hand starts wandering to a different region. Then, he is too turned on to continue, so we need to take care of him. And of course, afterwards, he is too *exhausted* to resume the back rub."

We all laugh as the women in the group discuss the issues they have with their partners. I won't deny that I would find some aspects appealing. But I honestly can't imagine myself with anyone but Jax. It would maybe be cool if he had a best friend that we could be a throuple with. That way he could keep his career and I wouldn't be alone. But his best friend is my brother. And, well, I am not even going to travel down how very wrong that road is.

"So, what is our next read?" Sally inquires.

"Scarlett, I know it is technically my turn to pick. But your suggestion last week was so wonderful, I'd be happy to let you pick again this week," Michelle offers.

"Sure." Scarlett smiles. "Let me think about it for a minute."

We resumed the discussion on last week's book, talking about the advantages and disadvantages associated with a polyamorous relationship and the impracticalities of multi-person sex acts. I almost wish Jake was here tonight. I am sure he has some stories he could share about his experiences. Although I wish I didn't know, I am aware he has participated in a few menages. While Scarlett's book suggestion was a little unconventional for this group, it seemed to go over better than I had expected. I was honestly prepared for pitchforks and the flagrant cries for a book burning.

As we wrap up the evening, Scarlett suggests a less controversial enemy-to-lovers romantic comedy. I'm sure everyone expected her to choose another risqué book, but I don't doubt she will shock everyone later. Besides, we can't overload these ladies too much. "Hey, do you need any help picking up?" Scarlett asks me as I work on putting things away.

"Sure, would you mind stacking up the chairs?" I ask as I gather the leftover coffee and snacks. "How are you enjoying Tral Lake so far?"

"Oh, it is nice and quiet. Nothing like LA," Scarlett mentions absentmindedly.

"LA must be nice though?" I have never been but it looks so glamorous on the TV, with all the celebrities and the beaches.

"It isn't terrible, but I needed somewhere more mellow. Everything there is so fast-paced and busy. I was ready to slow down." I understand that. Although I have always lived in Tral Lake, whenever I go visit the Twin Cities, I feel like I need to decompress.

"How'd you end up at the bed and breakfast?" It isn't often that we get new people who move here, especially those who are not already local to the area.

"Oh, my grandfather left it to me," Scarlett replies quietly.

"I didn't know that Mr. Peterson had a granddaughter."

"Yea, he and my mom weren't very close. She left Tral Lake for LA before I was born." That explains why I never heard about her. Tral Lake is a fairly small town with a population of about five thousand. It is big enough to have a slight economy, but small enough that you tend to know the majority of people who live here... *especially when it comes to business owners.*

"Thank you for letting me join the reading group. I was worried about moving to a small town where I didn't know anyone."

"Absolutely. Fortunately, we aren't one of those weird towns where all outsiders are avoided like the plague." I give her a big smile. "If you are interested, Sunday Letty and I are going to get mani-pedis. Then, we usually grab a bite at the diner afterwards."

Scarlett looks down at her hands. "That sounds wonderful. Letty... she works at Harper's, right?"

"Yea, she is actually about to own it soon." I can't help but gloat about my bestie's dream coming true.

"Oh, wow. That is awesome. Good for her," Scarlett says with genuine excitement.

"She is really hyped. It has been a dream of hers ever since she started working there. I know she has a ton of plans for the place."

"Hey, babe. About finished?" Jax asks, strolling in. With the whole Keith situation, he isn't comfortable with the idea of me being alone anywhere, and insisted on meeting me at closing.

"Yes, just about. You remember Scarlett, right?" I motion to Scarlett, who just finished putting away the chairs.

"Yes, we met Friday at the meeting. How are you enjoying Tral Lake so far? Tilly mentioned you were fairly new to town," he asks, shaking her hand.

"It has been pleasant, a nice change of pace. I was actually hoping to talk to you. Would you possibly mind coming to take some photos of the Inn for me? The ones my grandfather has out there are really outdated, and I have made some improvements since taking over."

"Honestly, I would love to. But I was recently advised I am not an approved vendor and cannot take images for shops anymore, unless I am an official employee." Jax gives her a remorseful smile.

"Well, technically, I am licensed by the department of health—not local ordinances like other shops. So... that rule doesn't apply to me. I told Keith as much when he tried to serve me that ridiculous notice." Scarlett is clearly happy with herself. "I have actually seen some of your stuff in the past. The resort I worked at in LA was always messaging your magazine, hoping to get a feature. Unfortunately, they have yet to accept. But compared to other resorts in SoCal, ours was nothing special. I was really surprised to see you in such a small town and looking for work. No offense, but that Keith who runs the committee is an idiot. I couldn't believe that he didn't hire someone of your caliber on the spot."

Jax stands there, awkwardly rubbing the back of his neck. I shift uncomfortably at the topic of Keith and the job. "Yea, well, it is what it is. I am looking at some other options as well. But if it won't affect your license, I'd be happy to help."

"I would appreciate it. I was looking at some freelance photographers in the area. But their specialties are more weddings and portraits. I know I need someone with a real eye for architecture to help capture the historic beauty of the Inn."

Jax and Scarlett exchange contact information and will look to schedule a shoot soon. She still has some improvement projects to wrap up before he takes photos. Jax and I lock up and make our way home.

Once inside the house, I can smell the delicious aroma of whatever Jax decided to cook for dinner tonight. "That smells amazing. What did you make?"

"I made a chicken pot pie. Some southern lady on the cooking network was making one yesterday. I figured that while you were at your book group, I would try my hand at it." He pulls the pot pie out of the warmth of the oven. "I think it has had enough time to rest... if you are ready to eat?"

"Yes, I am." I stretch up on my tippytoes to give him a quick kiss. "I'm just gonna go upstairs and change and will be back down."

"Okay, I will get the table set."

Upstairs, I quickly change into my leggings and a light sweater. Then I throw my hair up into a messy bun. I try to freshen up a little bit before heading back down.

Downstairs, Jax has the table set again for our dinner. I swear since he has been home and taken up cooking, our dining room has gotten more use then it has in years. Usually, we would end up just sitting around the kitchen counter. But that was after Jax moved away. When he used to live here, we would always eat at the big table.

Jax dishes me a big serving of pot pie and then passes me a couple of dinner rolls, which (by the looks of them) he made from scratch. Then, grabbing my wine glass (though I am about to protest, letting him know water is fine) he goes to the kitchen and comes back a minute later. When he returns, my glass has clear bubbling liquid inside.

"I don't think champagne goes well with pot pie, Jax?" He just chuckles at me and sets the glass down.

"I did not serve you champagne. It's Sprite. I bought some for you today at the market. I figured it has been your drink of choice recently."

"Oh, thank you. How thoughtful."

Dinner is amazing. I swear, every dish he makes gets better. I won't lie... I could absolutely get used to these delicious home-cooked meals. I was worried that with mom gone, I would never have one again. After we are done eating, I help Jax clean up the kitchen before we settle down on the couch to continue watching *Buffy the Vampire Slayer*. I have to admit, re-watching this as an adult, Jax is right. I might be team Spike now. But because I enjoy our heated debates on the subject, I will never tell him that.

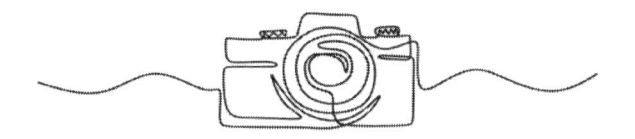

Chapter 30

Jackson

"How's it going?" Jake asks, flopping down on the couch.

"Eh..." I shrug in response.

I have been looking around for some possible work in town. So far, I haven't found much in my field. My small freelance operation idea is kind of dead in the water with Keith threatening the shops. Fortunately, I can help Scarlett and Tilly, but that isn't really a career. I put in my resume with a few marketing firms in the Twin Cities, but Tilly was right... The commute would be awful and not to mention, sitting at a desk all day would be absolute hell.

"I am sure there is something out there, maybe Robbie..." I cut off Jake shaking my head.

"I was already desperate enough to ask Robbie about a job. He laughed at me like I was insane." I tried to tell him I was serious, which just elicited more laughter. He told me that unless I can do books and manage a back office, there was nothing for me in his shop. We both very well know that I would be awful as an office manager.

"I am getting nervous," I admit. "I know any day now my boss is going to call me for an assignment. My three weeks is almost up. And unfortunately, I don't have a solid enough plan to justify leaving my career just yet." I know without a doubt I want to stay here with Tilly, but first I need to find something. I've got some money, but I feel like it would be wasted if I used it just to live off of. I'd rather use it to put into some sort of business, invest it for the future, or even take Tilly on an amazing trip. But to use it just to survive seems ridiculous.

"Don't worry, man. Tilly really doesn't need your money. You could live here, be her house-husband. Cooking and cleaning—*she would love it.*" Jake chuckles, "She can be your sugar momma."

I roll my eyes at Jake before shutting down my laptop. There is nothing more I can do right now. Looking at the clock, I notice it is almost six. I need to pick Tilly up from the shop. "Well, I better get going. I told Tilly I'd meet her at closing." I came home early today to prepare another dinner. This time, I went with roasted chicken and vegetables. The recipe looked really awesome. I did something called a brine. I basically soaked the chicken overnight in a pot with herbs, spices, and orange peels. It is supposed to make it super flavorful and moist. I heard it is common to do for turkey also. Maybe I can convince everyone to let me take over the turkey this year.

"Sure thing, just make sure you lock the door before getting freaky in the shop," Jake teases as I grab my coat and keys. I don't even bother dignifying his lame joke with a response and instead, I head out the door.

As I approach the storefront, I admire our handiwork. We have been so caught up in everything going on, we almost didn't realize that Halloween is this weekend. I helped Scott and Tilly hang up all the decor for the bookstore and the cafe. They have a pretty cool spooky-chic thing going on. Cobwebs are strung about, decorative pumpkins are placed around the shop, and Tilly set-up a display for some of the old worn books she keeps in the back. They kind of look like old spell books. In fact, I wouldn't be surprised if she had a couple of them thrown in there.

Entering the shop, I notice Tilly sitting at the counter with her head in her hands, looking down at some sort of paperwork. Whatever she is looking at has caused her to cry. Her eyes are still red and puffy. I sneak around the counter and place an arm over her shoulder. "Hey, babe, what's the matter?"

She looks up at me with tear-stained cheeks. "He can't do this," she murmurs.

"Who can't do what?" I ask, alarm bells sounding off inside my head.

"Keith," Tilly whispers.

"Was he here? Did he do something to you? I told you we needed to fucking report his ass. This shit is ridiculous." I am furious. I knew he wasn't done with Tilly. There is only one way to stop a guy like him (well, *two ways,* but still…). Sitting and doing nothing wasn't going to fix the issue.

"Yes, he was here. But he didn't do anything. Well, anything like what you are thinking." She sits up and hands me the piece of paper in her hand. I quickly read over the document. It is some formal notice, advising her that she is no longer welcome on the board of tourism due to misconduct.

"What the shit is this?" I can feel my blood boiling. How the fuck can he kick Tilly off the board for misconduct, when he was the one who attacked her?

"The letter claims that I abused my power on the board, basically trying to force the town to give a position to an unqualified candidate for my own personal gain." Tilly sits there, wiping tears from her face.

"Fuck, Tilly, I'm sorry. This is all of my fault." I pull her into a tight embrace, in an attempt to calm her down, as she shakes her head no. "Yes, it is. The only reason any of this is happening to you is because I came back to Tral Lake. Everything was better before I came here."

Tilly stiffens in my arms, before pulling away and looking up at me. "What are you trying to say, Jackson?"

"I don't know what I am trying to say." I rub my hand over my face. I don't want to go, but I also don't want to destroy Tilly's life by being here. Ever since I returned home and talked about staying, it has caused her nothing but issues. The more I think about it, leaving might be best. As much as I want Tilly, the only option seems to be long-distance, which she doesn't want. She loved me enough once to give me up, so I could pursue my own dreams. Maybe it is time I return the favor. This shop... this *town*... is her whole life. I can't take that away from her.

"You are leaving, aren't you?" Tilly looks me in the eyes, no longer crying. I can see she is furious with me. I stand there in silence. The last thing I want to do is leave, but I just don't know how I can stay.

"Tilly, please listen. I am not sure what I am trying to say. But it is one thing for him to keep me from working in this town. But now messing with you, what's next? I am terrified that I move here, and then the next thing we know, your shop is being torn apart by this asshole." I try to reason with Tilly.

"So that's it, you give up? He wins? Keith McCalester doesn't want you in this town, so you might as well obey?" Tilly taunts me.

"Don't be ridiculous, Tilly. That isn't what I am saying. But this town, your shop, it is your life. I can't be what takes that away from you." I grab her shoulders and try to have her look me in the eyes. "I love you, Tilly. I want nothing more than to be with you. But at what cost?"

"So, what? I'm just not worth it? We are not worth it?" Tilly pushes away from me. I can see that wall going back up. The same one I put there the other night and tore back down. Clearly, I am fucking this all up again.

"That is not at all what I am saying—" I attempt to rectify this disastrous conversation with Tilly, but it is no use.

"Stop." She cuts me off. "Listen to yourself, Jax. You are okay with letting us go, because of Keith."

"I'm not sure how this is any different than when you pushed me out the door... to take the job with the magazine. Because you couldn't ask me to give that up. If I don't go, what if he takes all your dreams away."

"This is not the same, Jackson," Tilly cries. "I wasn't *pushing* you out the door to punish you. We were young, I wanted to ensure you took advantage of an amazing opportunity. I didn't want you resenting me for making you give that up." Tilly struggles to maintain her composure and not scream at me in frustration. Taking a deep breath, Tilly continues. "Don't you get it, Jax. If you leave, it's *you* who is taking my dreams away," she whispers, turning before walking off.

I quickly rush over and wrap my arms around her. "I'm so sorry, Tilly. I love you." Fuck, I don't know why I would even imply that it would be better for me to leave. I am just not sure how to have Tilly, and not ruin her life at the same time. I will figure it out and fix this. I don't care what I have to do.

She shrugs out of my embrace and looks over her shoulder at me. "Jax, you know I would give you my whole world... if only you would take it." Then she walks away from me towards the back office. Before I can say anything or try to apologize, she is gone.

I'm about to follow her, when I feel my phone vibrate in my pocket. I glance down and look at the screen. It is my boss calling. Dread washes over me. I feel like everything is about to fall apart. Hopefully, I am not too late to fix the damage and doubt that I just caused between Tilly and me.

Chapter 31

Matilda

Slamming the door to my office, I try to cool off before going back out to Jax. The last thing I want to do is say something I might regret. Or even worse, have him say something he might regret... and will never be able to take back. I know this isn't all Jax's fault, and that he is concerned about me and my shop. Although I love the bookstore, it isn't everything.

Until Jax, I hadn't realized how much was missing from my life. I was very much "all work, no play" Tilly. With the exception of Letty and my family, I really didn't have much going on in the form of social interactions. I'd go to work, go home, think of work, then repeat. My dad had been pushing me to expand my personal life. In fact, his influence was what encouraged me to start my weekly reader group. But that can't be it? Can it?

Come on, Tilly, pull up your big girl panties and get back out there, I tell myself. I quickly grab my stuff and walk back out front. I slow down as I hear Jax on the phone. I don't mean to eavesdrop but I do.

"What's the assignment?... How long?... Hmm, okay. I will be honest I was hoping to slow down on my workload... Yea, I understand. When do I have to go?... Sure, just send me the details." Jax hangs up the phone then whispers, "*Fuck.*"

"Hi," I say meekly, pretending I didn't just listen in on his call. "Who was that?"

"My boss," he says grimly.

"Oh." I know this is hard for him, but honestly, he was just talking about leaving anyway. Maybe this is a sign and just like ten years ago, it is up to me to be the strong one again. As much as I want forever with Jax, I guess it just isn't in the cards we were dealt. "When do you have to leave?"

"Officially, I have to be on site Monday. But I need to go home and get some stuff together. So, I'll have to fly out Saturday," Jax mentions cautiously.

There it is—*home.* And *home* is not here. For Jax, it is out there, far away from this town... and from me. Keeping Jax in Tral Lake is like poaching a wild animal and locking it in a zoo. No matter how much I love him, he isn't mine to keep... and never will be. I was stupid to ever think this would work. But that is what love does to you, it makes you stupid.

"Well, we should get back to my house. I am sure you need to get things together." I pull my purse strap up and head to the door to lead him out. Jax grabs my arm as I walk past, forcing me to turn and look at him.

"This isn't the end, Tilly, but I think this came at a good time. With Keith breathing down your neck, not finding work, my grandpa's place, your parents—a lot is going on right now. Maybe taking a breather will help put things into perspective?" Jax attempts to reassure me.

"I get it," I say, shrugging out of his embrace. "It's been a long day. I'm exhausted."

"Yea, let's get you home," Jax agrees solemnly.

For the rest of the evening, the distance between us is evident. I know I am not the only one hurting. Part of me also knows that Jax is likely waiting and hoping I will break down and beg him to stay. Honestly, I might have… But after he was already questioning if this relationship was a good idea because of Keith, I'm not sure I should really be the one begging. I told him I would give him my whole world if he would take it—*and I meant it*. But I am not sure he is strong enough to reach out and grab hold.

We could try this long-distance thing, and enjoy the time he is home. But we both know that is not sustainable. Then there's his concern about Keith… Well, Keith is an ass and will always be one. But Jax was already taking a step back because of him. If we are going to do this, especially with the long distance, we both need to be all in. And after earlier, I am not convinced that Jax is anymore.

I'm terrified that if Keith pulls one more stunt, or there is one more speed bump, Jax will bolt. Unfortunately, in the real world there are always going to be things that go wrong. It is just life. But what matters is how we handle the things that go wrong… *as a couple.* It is crucial to face those issues together. While the timing with his boss is super inconvenient and we knew it was coming soon, I can't help but feel like he is using this opportunity to escape his problems. Jax has spent the last decade living one long vacation—no strings, no real responsibilities, no one to care for, no one to care for him. He has been free. I doubt he knows how to be tied down, or even how to handle day-to-day conflicts.

∞∞∞

"Are you sure I can't take you to the doctor's?" Jax asks me over breakfast. I know he wants to go with me, and part of me wants him to come with. But after yesterday, I feel like I should start to let go. Every minute that I hold on, feels like it will make the pain that is about to come, cut that much more deeply.

"My appointment is all the way in the Cities. With you needing to pack and get ready for your flight tomorrow morning, it just seems like a bad idea." I dismiss his request to attend again.

"Tilly, it isn't like I have a ton to pack. I really only need my gear. Most of my clothes I will just leave here. It will honestly take me a half an hour, if that." Jax thinks for a moment. "Hey, why don't I go pack my stuff quickly, and then you can get an overnight bag together? We can just both stay the night in the Cities. Then you can bring me to the airport in the morning. This way we can spend as much time as possible together?" Jax offers with a slight lift in his spirits.

This is so hard. A part of me wants to spend one more great night with him, especially since last night we barely spoke to each other. The other part reminds me that the longer I hold onto him, the more it will hurt when this is over. Despite his mini freak-out yesterday over Keith, it sounds like he still wants to go through with this long-distance plan. *Fuck!* Is love always this difficult? But then again, don't they say the hardest things end up being the best things?

Fuck it. "That would be nice. Jake was going to cover the shop today for me anyway, since I didn't know how long the appointment would be."

"See? Perfect!" he says, getting up and putting his plate in the sink. "I will go get my stuff together real quick, and then book us a hotel room and look for a nice restaurant to go to. We will make tonight as special as possible, even better than prom night," he says, wiggling his eyebrows at me. *Prom night was pretty epic...* I blush at the memory.

∞∞∞

"How have you been feeling, Ms. Moore? Any major pain or discomfort?" Doctor Holt asks as he is checking the movement of my arm. I wince as he raises it higher.

"Yea. I mean, it's not as bad as after the accident. But I struggle to lift my arm up. And after a day of working, it continues to throb throughout the night," I admit hesitantly. Fingers crossed, I am healing okay and can finally take this cast off.

"I see. It's likely all just your body adjusting during the normal recovery process, but I'd still like to take some imaging and see how things have progressed. Before we do that, we will need to remove your current cast. Hopefully, if everything looks good, we can have you fit for a brace. This will allow you to take it on and off for brief periods of time as needed."

"That would be wonderful. I absolutely hate this thing. It has made showering so awkward." I chuckle with a self-deprecating laugh.

"Besides the arm, is everything else feeling well? How are you doing?" the doctor asks, plugging notes into the computer.

"Umm, fine. I mean, as well as expected." I fidget. I have never been a big fan of doctors. They always freak me out. It's not that they are bad... It's just so hard to determine what to share with them, verses what is just normal and doesn't need to be mentioned. I never want to be that patient that complains about every ailment and has to be subjected to a million tests.

"Tilly, what about feeling sick?" Jax interjects. I knew I should have had him stay in the waiting room. But I caved, knowing the support would be nice. Being back in this hospital is hard enough, I really didn't want to face the doctor alone.

"Sick, tell me about this? What kind of symptoms?" The doctor is giving me his whole focus now.

"It is nothing serious. I have mostly just been a little tired and my appetite has been funny. With all the stress of my parents, work, and healing... I'm sure it is no big deal." I try to dismiss this whole thing. I know Jax has wanted me to get checked out. But there is nothing this doctor can do for my stress level.

"Hmm, it could be stress but you did have internal damage as well. I think, to be safe, I'd like to take some bloodwork and do a body scan. Even if there hasn't been pain, it doesn't mean that something else can't be going on in there. I'd rather be safe and not overlook anything."

A short while later, the nurse comes back for a blood draw and removes my cast. God, having fresh air on my arm feels so amazing. This is also the first time I've been able to see my incision from the accident, or at least the first time that I can really remember. I have this giant (maybe six-inch) scar down my right forearm. It is still red and healing. I'm sure it will fade over time, but it will be a constant reminder of the worst day of my life.

While we wait, Jax is a good sport. He tries to keep me entertained by showing me information about the Keys and the resorts he has been to in Hawaii. He is still planning our mini weekend getaway. We cannot exactly commit to anything yet but it is fun to plan. Although I am reserved over how everything will work when he is gone, it is encouraging to see him trying.

"Ms. Moore, sorry about the wait. There were some delays at the lab," the doctor says apologetically, re-entering the room and taking a seat.

"No worries. I expected to possibly be here all day," I say with a smile, letting him know I am not one of those patients who expects to be in and out in ten minutes. Especially since this isn't a normal doctor's office. It is a hospital, and I am sure emergency cases take precedent. "Everything look good? Do we still need to do the body scan?" It would be nice to not have to deal with that bill as well. I know the lawyer said not to pay anything and that we will submit it all in the lawsuit. But still, I know those things can get expensive.

"Ms. Moore, before we discuss any of your test results, I need to ask... Are you comfortable having your boyfriend, I presume, present?" The doctor gives me a curious look.

"Yea, it is fine. Is there something wrong?" I question, starting to panic. Jax takes my hand in his, passing his strength and support to me.

"Very well. Do you happen to recall when your last menstrual cycle started?" the doctor inquires awkwardly.

I blush. Maybe I should have had Jax step out... I didn't think we were going to talk about menses. "Umm, I guess I really don't know. I don't exactly pay attention." I stop and think about it for a moment. My cycles aren't consistent. And well, with my IUD I really don't keep track, since I don't have to worry about pills or anything. "I'm sorry I have an IUD and don't mark down the dates. I don't remember anything recently. I'd guess maybe six or seven weeks ago? But I'm never regular," I say shyly in front of Jax. Based on his stiff posture, I can tell he is uncomfortable with this conversation. This is the last thing any guy wants to think about.

"Hmm. Well, looking at your bloodwork, we cannot perform a full-body scan at this time. We will still be able to x-ray your arm. We have safety measures we can take. Your test results indicate you are about..." He pauses to double-check his clipboard. "I'd estimate you are about six or seven weeks pregnant, depending on when your last menstrual cycle started."

"Six or seven weeks pregnant?" I whisper, looking down at my flat stomach.

"Usually, we base the fetal age off of the date of your last menstrual cycle. However, we will do an ultrasound and get a better idea. We will also look for your IUD. It is possible it fell out and you might not have noticed, or it might have gotten dislodged. Regardless, we need to remove it if it is still intact."

I look over to Jax who is still holding my hand. I cannot read his expression right now. I can't tell if he is panicking, or if he is excited, or just in shock. I am not even sure how I feel right now. A baby? A little bit of me and Jax rolled into one. I've always wanted to start a family. I want a big family, like what I had growing up. I just assumed I would be married first. Granted, the dad is who I hoped it would be, but not like this...

"I have some literature for you. You can read about your options. It is still early enough if you—"

"I'm keeping the baby!" I yell, cutting the doctor off. I don't even want to hear what he was going to suggest.

"Okay, well then, review this literature and I'd suggest speaking with your OBGYN for any prenatal care. We will make sure everything is safe for the baby today. But assuming that nothing is wrong... I would recommend that you start a prenatal vitamin, avoid alcohol, maintain a healthy diet, and continue to get plenty of rest and fluids. The pregnancy is the most likely culprit for your exhaustion and food aversions." The doctor glances between us, both still slightly in a state of shock. "We will get you in for your ultrasound. Then after we verify everything is okay with the baby, we will move onto the x-ray. In the meantime, congratulations."

After the doctor leaves, Jax and I continue to sit in silence. He is still holding my hand and I am honestly still in shock over the whole ordeal. I guess it's more like a mixture of shock, fear, excitement... just everything. I really wish he would say something, anything.

"A baby..." he whispers.

"Yea, a baby," I verify.

"A baby..." he repeats.

"I'm sorry." I am not sure what he is thinking. I can only assume he is mostly still in shock. But my doubt is creeping in again... Maybe this isn't what he wanted?

"What... sorry?" He shakes his head as if he is trying to knock some sense back into it. "Shit... Tilly, no, *I'm* sorry. You have nothing to apologize for. I guess I am just a little stunned. Not in a bad way! It's just that this is not what I was expecting today."

"Yea, I can agree with you on that..."

A knock at the door interrupts Jax from what he was about to say. "Ms. Moore, we are ready to take you for the ultrasound. Will your boyfriend be coming with you?"

Jax shakes his head again, finally coming back to reality. He immediately stands, pulling me up with him. He smiles back at me. "Yes, I would love to. If that is alright with you, of course?"

"Yes, please," I beg, squeezing his hand tighter.

Okay, so early pregnancy ultrasounds are nothing like in the movies. When she asks me to disrobe from the waist down, I am shocked. Then when I am instructed to lie on the table, and see a long probe lubed-up and ready to be shoved inside me... (well, *uncomfortable* doesn't even begin to describe how I feel). I'm both glad and mortified that Jax is here to witness this. Looking up at him, I can tell he is suppressing his laughter over whatever sick and twisted joke he has running through his head right now.

As this probe is inserted into me, the tech keeps apologizing for "any discomfort"—which there absolutely is plenty of. Besides the pressure it is putting on my insides (and not in the sexy way) the ridge on the plastic covering scratches a little. As she moves the device around, she explains which organs we are looking at, before confirming that they indeed look healthy. Finally, she gets to the uterus and I can see tiny flickers.

Ah, there we go." She makes some marks on the screen to indicate a baby is there. "The flicker you see is the heartbeat. Oh wait... Well, look at that... Hello, there!"

"What?" *What is happening?* "Did you find the IUD?"

"Nope, I haven't seen that yet. I will do another look around, but I assume it fell out. If you had a heavy cycle with lots of cramping, you might not have even noticed. It was likely the reason why. Nope, what I am seeing here... are twins."

I sit up straight as I can. "TWINS!?"

"Yea, do twins run in your family?" The nurse inquires while making a few more notes on the images.

"I'm a twin actually," I say quietly, afraid to even look at Jax now. We were just in shock over the idea of one baby, but now *two...*

"That makes sense then. Twins are usually hereditary through the mother. You have greater odds for twins, given that you are one. Well, double congratulations. Would you like to hear their heartbeats?"

"Yes," Jax proclaims, before I even have the opportunity to respond.

The technician turns on the sound, and you know that scene in the *Grinch* when his heart expands and starts beating? That is exactly how I feel as soon as the sound, of what seemed like a stampede of horses, started running through the room. Immediately, my heart doubled—no, tripled—in size for these two little surprise babies.

"The doctor will review the images, but I didn't see anything alarming. The heart rates are strong for both babies. Based off of their size, I'd agree with the estimate that they are about six to seven weeks old. Which would put your due date at the end of June. Here, let me print off some images for you. Afterwards, I'll have you get cleaned up and take you to x-ray. Your boyfriend can head back to the exam room."

I quickly put myself back together when she leaves, and stare down at the babies in the pictures that she has just handed me. I can't believe it. I'm not sure how to process this or what this means for Jax and me. But ultimately, I am excited and happy. Because even though I only learned about them an hour ago, I am absolutely in love with them both.

Chapter 32

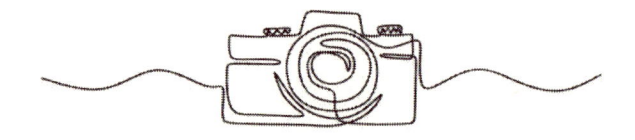

Jackson

Wow, just wow. That is the only thought that runs through my mind the rest of the time at the appointment. I cannot seem to find the words to describe what I am feeling. We are going to have a baby. No, correction—we are going to have babies. I have thought about having babies with Tilly so many times over the years, but I always assumed we would be married. I guess that is life. It never goes the way you plan it to.

We have barely spoken since the doctor's office. I am sure she is in just as much shock as I am. Thankfully, she doesn't need another cast. She just needs to wear a brace at all times, except when showering or taking a bath. I know she was excited to be free of the monstrous thing. We got out of there pretty late, and ended up leaving the office and heading right over to our dinner reservations. Here we are, sitting in a romantic little restaurant and not able to say a word to each other. I know she is happy about the babies. I knew that fact the moment she yelled that she wanted to keep them. Then, as we were hearing their heartbeats, I saw the look of love and adoration in her eyes. I'm sure if she would have looked at me, she would have seen the very same reflected back at her.

"Tilly." She turns her gaze to me. "Please, tell me what you are thinking."

"That is difficult. I am thinking so many things right now. I am still in shock, but I know I am happy. It is just a lot to process and a lot to think about. What about you? How do you feel about this?"

"To be honest… while I am shocked, I am also excited. The second I heard their hearts beating, I was blown away. I couldn't believe it."

"Yea. That was incredible, wasn't it?" She smiles at me.

I smile back at her. "I don't even have words to describe how amazing it was."

She continues smiling at me. Then a flicker of sadness passes over her eyes, before she frowns and looks away. "Tilly, talk to me. What's going through that brain of yours?"

"It's just… you are leaving tomorrow. We find out we are having babies, barely have anytime to process it, and you have to leave. I know you didn't plan it this way, but still… I am sad to think about how much you are going to miss. I am also scared of doing this alone. One baby is a lot of work, but two newborns at the same time…" She severs her own words and shakes her head.

Fuck, I literally forgot about the fact I need to fly out tomorrow. My boss assures me the assignment should only be three weeks and that I should be home for Thanksgiving. But then, I might be out again until Christmas. Apparently, another photographer left while I was on leave, so the workload has really piled up.

I reach across the table and take Tilly's hand in mine—noticing that, unintentionally, I had grabbed her left hand. I start to rub circles over her ring finger, knowing that soon I will put one there. I knew she was my forever, but with the babies there is no doubt in my mind. We are meant to be. It's as if fate intervened before I had to leave, telling me that no matter what I need to come home to Tilly and come home to her fast.

"I know this is hard, Tilly. I want nothing more than to call my boss and tell him to shove the assignment up his ass. But I cannot do that. Apparently while I was gone, we lost a photographer, so the work is extremely backlogged. I can't just up and leave them right now, as much as I would love to. They have been nothing but good to me over the years and I don't want to leave like that."

She squeezes my hand and smiles at me. "I understand. It sucks, but I get it. How long will you be gone?"

"Well, this first assignment will be roughly three weeks. I will be doing a circuit of hotels and resorts in Asia. But I will be home for Thanksgiving... for at least the week. Then, I need to go back out again for another few weeks and do a circuit in South America, but I will be back for Christmas."

"That is such a long time." I notice a tear rolling down her cheek and I quickly wipe it away.

"I know, babe. But I promise tomorrow I will message my boss and turn in my notice. I will help out on these assignments, and hopefully they should have a replacement figured out by the time the second one is done. I might have to do one more assignment to help train, but I will only do it if absolutely necessary. I will make sure he knows I am done. I promise, Tilly, you will not go through this pregnancy by yourself. I will not leave you to raise these babies alone. I will be there every step of the way."

"I don't know. This is a lot, Jax. Yesterday, you were talking about it maybe being best if you left. Now today, you are willing to throw everything to the wind. What will you do about work? Keith—"

"I don't care about Keith. He can have his fucking social media and marketing job that he covets so much. I still might do some freelance, but honestly, I don't care. I will work as a barista with Scott... work at the bookshop with you... Fuck, I'll stay home cooking, cleaning, caring for the kids..." I plead with Tilly.

"I want you, Jax. I never want to keep you from your babies. But I don't want you to stick around out of obligation. I would hate it if you ended up resenting me or the babies one day, because we forced you to stay when you didn't want to." I can see in Tilly's face she is still doubting my intentions.

"Please, Tilly, can we forget about yesterday? I was upset and confused over the whole Keith thing and not finding work. I didn't mean to take it out on you or to imply that we are not worth it. We are absolutely worth it, and I wanted to be with you even before the babies. This isn't a whim or obligation. It is what I want. As long as I am with you and our babies, nothing else matters. You understand that? You are—and these babies are—it for me. I love you, Tilly, and we will be a family." I pour everything I have into those words, hoping Tilly can finally see I am all in.

"Oh my god, Jax. I love you too. I am so sorry about the fight yesterday. I am sorry for being distant. It's just... I love you and I want this—*I want you.* I can't bear the thought of doing this without you." At Tilly's words, I can feel the barrier that has always kept us separated finally crumble.

I stand, walk around the table and drop to one knee, looking up at her while still holding onto her hand. "You will never be without me, you understand? I am not going anywhere. Well, not anywhere permanently. I will finish my obligations with work and then I will come home to you. I know we have a lot to figure out. But none of that matters right now. Just know that I intend to come home and marry the fuck out of you and raise our children."

"A-are you proposing?" The blush on her face makes me want to.

"No, this is more of an IOU..." I smirk at her. "But I will. And when I do, it will take your breath away." I want to make sure I have an actual ring to slip on her finger and that we are somewhere romantic. I don't want to do some sort of spontaneous thing. Not that she likely cares. Tilly isn't that kind of girl. But it is what she deserves. She doesn't deserve a proposal in the heat of the moment, in the middle of a restaurant and on a pretty crazy day at that.

We spend the rest of the dinner just casually talking. I think that in order to give our brains a break, we avoid the big topics. But it doesn't feel like we are avoiding anything in particular. Instead, it feels like we are trying to have a nice evening, just the two of us. Like it or not, tomorrow I will be out of the country and I will not be able to see her for a while. I don't want to spend our last night together discussing things we can't control or change.

After dinner, I take us over to the hotel, and Tilly's eyes immediately light up in recognition. Although they have made some updates since we were here last, it is still unmistakable. After checking in and getting our room keys, we take the elevator upstairs. Tilly is practically vibrating with excitement. Once in the room, Tilly gasps looking around the suite.

"Seriously, Jax. It isn't only the same hotel but the same room?" I was lucky the room number was available. When I saw that it hadn't been booked, there was no way I could pass up the opportunity to step back in time. "This is amazing. It is almost better than I remember."

Tilly walks around, taking in the king-size bed with white linens. I paid extra to have rose petals sprinkled on it. The "romance" package also included some champagne, chocolate-covered strawberries, and bath oils. When Tilly was in the bathroom at the restaurant, I was able to call and they kindly replaced the champagne with sparkling cider.

"Oh my god, I still have dreams about this bathroom," Tilly yells from the adjoining en suite. I go and follow her inside. *It is pretty impressive*, I think to myself, eyeing up the giant jacuzzi tub. "This is incredible, Jax. Thank you." She presses down on her tippytoes to give me a kiss.

The last time we were in this room, it was the night of prom. Tilly and I had already been dating for a couple of months. She had mentioned to me that she was ready to lose her virginity, and I wanted to make sure it was as spectacular as possible. I looked for the nicest hotel I could find in the Cities that also had some sort of in-room jacuzzi or hot tub. Just like this time, I purchased what they called a "romance" package as well. While I barely had the money for it, especially with needing to rent a tux, it was worth every penny to see the look on her face. We spent the entire weekend of prom here, basically naked and living off of room service. We had originally intended to go around the city, but as soon as we had sex once, it was like we couldn't stop.

I reach around Tilly, pulling her back to my chest before resting my hands on her still flat stomach. Leaning down, I whisper in her ear, "I love you, Matilda Moore." She sinks into me and clasps her hands over mine.

"I love you, Jackson Harris." Turning in my embrace, she places my palms on her ass. I give it a gentle squeeze as she wraps her arms around my neck. Granting me a quick and soft kiss, she pulls back and looks at me. "I want to cash in my IOU. I know you want to plan some extravagant proposal and probably want to have a ring first. But honestly, Jax, I cannot think of anything more special than this. This room was where I realized I loved you more than I would ever love anyone else. It was a major milestone in our relationship. I think it is only perfect that it is the benchmark for the next phase of our life. I don't care about you showing off with some big fancy ring or shooting fireworks in the sky. While those things are nice, all I want is you—*is us.*" She pulls her arm down and places a hand on her stomach. "All that matters is that we are forever."

God, she is the most perfect woman in the world. Besides, she is right. This is the perfect place to propose and all I had wanted to do was make sure that the moment was special. Honestly, now that she mentions it, I cannot imagine any moment more special than this one.

I bring my hands back around, taking hers in mine before dropping to one knee. "Matilda Rose Moore, I have loved you all of my life, even before I understood what love was. You are so kind and loving that it radiates from you, giving off an ethereal look. I remember the first time I took a picture of you and my breath was taken away. I thought I had captured the image of an angel. You once said your world was mine... if only I would take it. If that offer is still on the table, I would love nothing more than to take your world into my own. In return, I would give you my everything. I can't promise it will always be easy, but I will promise you my forever. Will you marry me?"

Tilly is looking down at me, tears pouring from her eyes. "Yes. Absolutely, yes." I quickly stand to kiss her, tugging her closer to me. "You are my forever," she whispers between breaths.

Chapter 33

Matilda

I can't believe it. Jackson Harris proposed to me, in the same hotel he took me to on one of the most magical nights... no, one of the most magical weekends of my life. I never thought any other moment would be able to top it. But of course, he somehow does. He clearly didn't need to prepare any proposal; he seemed to have that completely figured out. It was perfect and I honestly don't care about a ring. We could get one from a gumball machine for what it's worth. This... us... is all I want.

Kissing me, Jax reaches down to pull me up. I instinctively wrap my legs around him as he walks us back to the bed, laying me down gently. His mouth consumes mine. We have had some amazing kisses, but I think this is by far my favorite. His hand reaches to the hem of my shirt. He breaks contact for a second to pull the fabric barrier off me. I barely have a moment to capture my breath before he returns his lips to mine.

He kisses a trail down from my mouth, to my neck, then to

my collarbone as he seeks to unclasp the front of my bra. Taking one of my pert nipples into his mouth, he slides his hand over and begins to lightly squeeze and massage the other one. Alternating between kissing and lightly nibbling my nipple, the stimulation sends sparks down to my core, which is begging for relief. Sensing my desire, he reaches between us and slips his hand below my waistband and into my panties.

His fingertips lightly caress my sensitive clit before he sinks two of his large digits inside of me, while using the palm of his hand to rub against my clit. With the mix of sensations going on, I climax hard and almost immediately, clenching around his fingers. As I come down from my orgasm, I whisper, "Please, Jax. I need you inside of me now."

In a flurry, he somehow manages to remove my pants and underwear while undressing himself. Almost instantaneously, he is back on top of me, devouring my mouth as his firm erection teases my entrance. He enters me in one slow motion, allowing me to feel my muscles expand around his throbbing cock. While hard and fast is fun, this just feels otherworldly. Once fully sheathed inside of me, he whispers in between kisses, "I love you."

As Jax slowly pulls almost all the way out, I long for the sensation of him so full inside me. But before I have a chance to miss him too much, he thrusts forward again. Jax continues the painfully slow and delectable sensation of almost pulling out and slamming in. A dozen or so repetitions later, we are both panting and close to climax. My hands claw into his back and my legs wrap around his waist, while my heels dig into his ass. I pull him into me, and we both come at the same time in a spectacular glory. It feels like hours before I finally stop vibrating from the intense orgasm.

∞∞∞

We reluctantly wake up early in the morning. I wish we could ignore the alarm but that would make Jax late for his flight. After turning off the intrusive beeping, I look at him still with sleep in his eyes and disheveled sex hair. While we barely slept last night, due to the multiple sessions of love-making, I don't regret it one bit. I will have plenty of time to sleep at home. I try to mentally engrave this image into my mind to remember when he is gone. Though I know it will only be temporary…

"Good morning, beautiful." He gives me the sexy lazy smile I have come to love each morning. I am going to miss him when he is gone.

"Good morning, sexy." I give him a playful wink, before leaning down and giving him a quick kiss. "While I never want to leave this bed, we need to get moving."

He stretches and groans. The sheet slips down, giving me a glimpse of his morning erection. I glance over at the clock and try to calculate if we have time for a quickie and breakfast. *Nope, unfortunately we don't.* Based on the grumbling of our stomachs, we both need to eat and recover from last night. I lightly pat him on the chest as I get up. "Come on, big guy. Let's get a move on." He chuckles, getting out of bed and slipping his briefs back on. I make sure to take a quick glimpse of his ass, and add the image to the mental scrapbook I am making.

We rush to get dressed and check out of the room, before making our way to the little restaurant inside the lobby. We are able to order and enjoy our quick breakfast before it gets too crowded.

"So, what do we tell your brothers? I mean, do we wait?" Jax inquires, taking a bite of his toast.

I contemplate this while taking a bite of my oatmeal. I want to relay the news immediately, but I think it should really be more of a joint effort. "I'm excited to tell everyone and I don't want to keep it a secret for long. But I think we should be together when we do tell. So, how about when you are home for Thanksgiving?"

"That sounds good. I was dreading the idea of you telling all of this to your brothers alone. I really wanted to be there."

We finish up our breakfast and make our way to the airport. I'm grateful that it is still early enough in the morning that there is no line at the drop-off, and I am easily able to find a place to stop and put on my hazards. Standing on the sidewalk, I give him one last big hug and kiss.

"I promise we will talk every day, okay? I should be twelve hours ahead of you, so I will plan on contacting you around 8 pm?"

"Okay." I try to hold back my tears. I am going to miss him so much when he is gone.

"Good, I will be in New York tonight and tomorrow. I will let you know when I land, and then I will call you tonight." He leans down giving me one more deep kiss.

A cough distracts us both and we look at a security guard observing us from the corner, who will likely yell at us at any moment to get moving. "I better go," Jax says reluctantly.

"I will miss you," I say, giving him one more kiss. "I love you, Jax."

"I love you, Tilly."

We avoid the word "goodbye", because it would make it sound as though he is not coming back. And we both know, without a doubt, he will be home soon.

Chapter 34

Matilda

Fortunately, Jake is not on call at the firehouse this weekend. He took some time off, not only to help at the shop while I was gone, but also to ensure that I am not alone. Sunday, all of my brothers were home and Letty came over. We spent the whole day together, which was nice. I only wish they would stop treating me as though Jax and I broke up.

Yes, I have been a little sad due to a mixture of hormones and missing Jax. But I haven't been breaking down and crying or anything. For some reason though, they still all treat me like I am fragile glass and about to break. Jake insists on helping me at the shop during the day this week, since he is on call at night. Then Scott was adamant that he would bunk here the nights that Jake was on call. While it is a little annoying, I do appreciate the fact they love me so much.

It has been tough, but Jax has kept to his word. We either call or video chat every evening, then send texts throughout the day. He has been sending me the most beautiful images of Vietnam. He is in Nha Trang currently shooting for a resort that has recently undergone major updates. The photos are absolutely breathtaking—crisp blue water, white sand beaches, and palm trees. Then the pictures of the local cuisine are mouthwatering. He says this location is definitely on his list of places to take me. He has also been rubbing in his eighty-two-degree weather; the highs here have been in the mid-forties. But honestly, I don't care. I have always loved the cooler weather. I have lived with it all my life.

It's Thursday and I am at the shop working on a quick display for a photo to add to our social media. Jax started this throwback Thursday thing, where we feature classic must-reads on the page. While it is a lot of work to maintain, I cannot deny that Jax's social media strategy has been very successful for us. It isn't even officially the holidays yet and we are already in the black. With the volume of online orders that I am getting, I need to set up some sort of mail pickup arrangement with the post office.

Hearing a ding above the door, I quickly make my way to the front of the shop. Jake is out grabbing us some lunch from the diner. I stop dead in my tracks when I notice Keith inside, holding a letter. "Good evening, Matilda. How are you today?"

"Fine, how can I help you?" I just want him to say whatever he has to say and get the hell out of my store.

"I haven't noticed Jackson around recently. He already wander off to bigger and better things?"

The nerve of this asshole. "What do you want, Keith? I have a business to run."

"Sorry, didn't mean to strike up a nerve. I know breakups can be hard." While we are very much not broken up, I do not feel any need to dignify his curiosity with an answer. "Anyway, I came by to deliver you this notice." He holds up the letter in his hand.

"What is it this time?" I ask, keeping my arms crossed and not even attempting to take the envelope from him. I don't want to be within touching distance of that man.

He motions to the letter. "Well, if you read it, you would know."

I cautiously inch forward to take it from him, ensuring I only get close enough to grab it from his outstretched arm. As I get within reach, he pulls the letter back. "You know, Matilda, all this could be avoided."

I cross my arms again over my chest, cock my hip and begin tapping my foot. "Give me the fucking notice or get the hell out, Keith."

"The hostility is completely uncalled for, Matilda. I would like to think our local shop owners were more hospitable in their establishments." He extends the letter to me. I quickly snatch it from him, then take a few steps back. "Have a good night, Matilda. I'm sure I will be seeing you soon." Keith goes to exit, bumping into Jake on his way out. "Jacob," he says, jutting his chin in acknowledgement before finally leaving.

After Keith is gone, Jake asks, "What the fuck did that twat want?"

I wave the notice in front of him, before tearing open the envelope and reading it. "That fucking asshole!"

Jake grabs the notice from me and reads it over. "What the hell is this?" The letter contains a list of violations my shop has that need to be corrected within thirty days. Failure to do so would result in the suspension of my business license. If it is suspended, I would have to go through an appeal's process to get it reinstated. Not to mention, I'd be forced to pay a hefty fine, and I'll give you one guess who would review my appeal. All the violations are absolutely ridiculous. Some are miniscule—like a fine for still having Halloween decor up, even though Halloween was over three days ago. But looking down Main Street, my storefront is only one of many to meet that criteria. Another violation is that the layout of my store is considered a fire hazard, due to my bookshelves. The notice states that they "block and/or prohibit access to the emergency exits". However, that one is easy to resolve because I know we are within regulations, given that my brother is a fireman and would be the first to tell me if something was wrong. Even so, this will make me go through the hassle of getting a sign-off from the inspector. Some others are bigger, such as my awning is too faded and needs to be replaced, and my door needs to be repainted. The citations go on and on.

I sit down, put my hands in my face, and begin to cry. That asshole, even with thinking Jax is gone, is still trying to manipulate me. "Tilly, this notice is bullshit. What aren't you telling me? I know something is going on with you and Keith. I know there is more to that bullshit story than what you told us."

Shit, I don't want to lie to Jake. Honestly, it is almost impossible. Even if I want to lie to him, with our twin-link, he would know right away. "Fine, but you have to keep it a secret."

"I don't like keeping things from Scott and Robbie, Tilly, and you shouldn't either." He crosses his arms over his chest, looking down at me.

"Please, Jake. This has to be a super special twin secret. You can't tell Robbie or Scott," I plead with him.

"Fine, I promise. Now tell me what's going on. Don't skimp on the details. If I get any inkling you are holding back, I am telling Scott and Robbie."

I agree and proceed to tell him everything about Keith. How he insinuated that in order to get Jax the job, I would need to sleep with him. How he has essentially banned Jax from helping shops around town. How he kicked me off the board of tourism. Then today, how he implied this notice could be forgotten, if I would just give into him. I even went back to high school and explained what happened that night of prom.

As I told Jake the story of all the assholery that is Keith, he was furious. He paced back and forth for a half an hour before talking. "Why did you keep this from me?" I can see the hurt in his eyes. "I always thought that out of all of us, we were the closest? I thought that no matter what, you would always confide in me. We used to tell each other everything. I would have never kept something like this from you."

Fuck, now I feel guilty. I didn't want to hurt anyone. I just didn't want my brothers getting all riled up and causing problems. "I'm sorry, Jake," I say quickly, hugging him. I immediately feel better when he wraps his arms around me. "I wasn't doing it to hurt you. It's just… I was embarrassed and then I didn't want you guys going to prison after you killed him."

He chuckles. "Tilly… if we killed him, I promise that between the three of us, we would cover our tracks and no body would ever be found." I can't help but chuckle as well. "We need to do something about this. He is trying to destroy your business over not getting some. Besides being a next level douche, what he is doing is also illegal."

"I know. Jax and Letty both wanted me to report him. But it would just be a battle of he-said-she-said, and I would end up being the guilty party when it was all over."

Jake steps away from me. "You fucking told Letty and not me?"

"Seriously? Get over it, Jake. She is my best friend and was there the night it happened. If it makes you feel any better, she doesn't know about him kicking me off the board."

"It only makes me feel *a little bit* better. But seriously, moving forward, you tell me anything and everything before you tell Letty. I don't care what it is. Jax only gets a pass because he is your boyfriend."

I roll my eyes at him. "Sure, Jake, whatever. Well, I better get working on this list. Do you think you can help me get the chief to come here and sign off on fire safety?"

"Seriously, Tilly, are you just going to roll over for him like a good puppy?"

"Well, I am not going to let him shut down my business."

He shakes his head at me. "Tilly, Tilly, Tilly… you see, you should have come to me first. Of course, Jax and Letty were no help. You are right—reporting dickwad with nothing more than your story wasn't going to go anywhere. But if you would have come to me, I could have helped you resolve this, and we could have prevented him from scaring Jax off."

"Seriously, Jax is not scared off. He is going to be gone for a bit, but it is just temporary. Hopefully after these couple assignments, he will be done."

"Are you sure?"

"Without a doubt, Jax is going to come home and he will come home for good. I know it." I don't tell Jake about the pregnancy or the proposal, but I know there is no way Jax would break his promise to me.

"Alright then, are you ready to fix this shit and get back at the fucker?" Jake asks with the grin of an evil mastermind about ready to conquer the world.

Chapter 35

Matilda

"How is Akihabara?" I ask, looking into Jax's cerulean eyes on the video chat. I wonder if our babies will end up with my amber or Jax's bright blue eyes?

"It is good. This hotel is amazing. I really want to bring you here. I think you would love the city. It's crazy with all the technology and manga. I went to a maid cafe yesterday. It was great. I will send you pictures when we are done." I smile at him. So far in the past two weeks that he has been gone, every place he has stayed at he also wants to bring me to.

"You are such a dork. With the list of places that you want us to travel to, I'm not sure when we will have the time to work... *or raise our children.*" Internally, I worry. While traveling, he has been so happy. I wonder if he could truly be satisfied here with me and the babies full time... Guilt has me feeling bad for wanting him home all the time. I know he would never ask me to give up the bookshop, so it seems unfair for me to ask him to give up traveling.

"Hey, what's that look?" Damn, he reads me too well.

I try to wave him off. "Nothing. Everything is fine."

"No, Tilly. Something is bothering you. I need you to talk to me... Tell me what you are thinking," he pleads with his bright blue puppy-dog eyes (which are still trying to shed sleep). God, he looks so sexy when he wakes up. Damn, these hormones. I am horny all the damn time. I read it is normal and I think (because of the twins) it is even worse—because well, double the dosage.

"It is nothing, really. It is just my stupid hormones. I am just feeling guilty for expecting you to give up your career to be here with us all of the time. Since you've been traveling, you have seemed so happy."

"That's because I am."

"Oh." I try not to let the disappointment show on my face.

"I'm happy because the love of my life is pregnant with my twins. I'm happy because I am going to marry the girl I have loved as long as I can remember. I'm happy because in a week I will be back home in time to go with my beautiful pregnant fiancée to her first official doctor's appointment and see our beautiful babies. The only thing that is getting me through being away from you right now... is trying to imagine how much you and I might enjoy one of these places together, *as a family*."

I can feel the tears running down my cheeks. "Ugh, I hate these stupid side effects. I never used to cry."

"Ah, it's okay, babe. I still think you are the most beautiful and radiant woman ever." I snort—*yes, very attractive*. "Don't worry. Tomorrow, I leave Japan and I am heading to the Maldives. After that, I will be coming home. I verified I have a whole week home with you before I have to take off again. It sounds like Greg has a couple photographers lined up, who should be replacing me and the other guy. I promise, this distance... it is almost over."

We chat a little more about Akihabara and the crazy tech culture there. Today, he is actually going to some sort of anime convention; and he is completely geeking-out about it. I haven't told him about Keith's most recent visit. I really don't want to worry him. Not to mention, Jake and I have a plan to handle it. Once everything is settled and Keith is no longer an issue, I will fill him in.

∞∞∞

Tonight is the night. Jake and I have everything set. While my stomach has nothing more than the smallest baby bump, pregnancy has already made my breasts fuller. Which makes showing off my cleavage in this button-down shirt much easier. Jake thought it would be good to dress sexy, but not too sexy. If I went overboard, Keith might get suspicious. I went for a sexy librarian look: an almost sheer button-down blouse with too many top buttons open and my black lace bra peeking through, a tight black pencil skirt with a slit up my thigh, and tall stilettos that I had to borrow from Letty. I have my hair lazily piled on top of my head and held up there by a pen. I kept my makeup to a minimum, since I never wear it. But I did put on bright red lipstick.

"Okay, you remember what to do right?" Jake asks for the millionth time.

"Yes, I remember. Now go in the back. He will be here any minute." Jake scurries off to the back office to monitor the exchange.

A few moments later, the bell over the door rings as Keith enters the shop. I look him over and it is a shame… He could be an attractive man, if his soul was not so black on the inside. He comes in, wearing pressed black slacks and a grey cashmere sweater. His dark hair is pushed back. He is definitely trying to dress up for this interaction.

"Matilda," he says in greeting, as he is looking me up and down and practically eye-fucking me. It makes me sick to my stomach, but I need to hold it in. "I was surprised you called and wanted to see me. How may I be of service to you this evening?" I don't miss his innuendo.

"Well, Keith I wanted to discuss this list of violations with you." I try to say calmly. If I get hostile, he will bolt.

"Let me see." He walks over, grabbing the list I hold in my hands; his fingers purposefully caress my wrist. "It is a lot of work, Tilly. You only have a few more weeks to get everything wrapped up. I would hate to have to suspend the license of one of our primary businesses."

"Keith." I try to give him my best puppy-dog eyes. "This list is ridiculous. My shop has been running the same way it always has for the past almost thirty-five years now. With the exception of my tardy removal of Halloween decor, all of this seems to be coming out of the blue. Then, with you removing me from the board of tourism… because I suggested Jax as a possible candidate for a position… Well, I am just curious as to what you are hoping to get out of all of this?"

"Matilda, I think you know very well what I am hoping to get out of this?" Keith says, stepping into my space and lightly caressing my cheek.

"And what is that, exactly?" I ask, pretending to be coy.

"I just want you. I've always wanted you. I've watched you since we were small children. You are kind, loving, compassionate—exactly the type of woman a McCalester should have by his side. I have tried to be nice about this over the years. Be friendly. Be professional. Hoped that you would get over this silly little crush on Jackson and come to your senses. I apologize. But when I saw how the grief over losing your parents was messing with your judgement and that he was taking advantage of you, I needed to intervene. You are too special to waste your life with someone like him."

God, he is a complete psychopath. "What are you proposing?"

"It's simple. You are mine, completely. We will get married. You will become a McCalester and produce me a worthy heir. Together, we will rule this town. If you agree to this, you will be put back on the board. All these silly little violations will disappear, and that property next door that you and your brother have been looking at is yours. My family maintains the holdings, so you can consider it an engagement gift."

"Let me get this straight... I marry you, and all of the issues with my store are gone? My life goes back to normal?"

"Well, I mean mostly normal. Obviously, there will be some changes. But yes, as far as your role on the board and your shop, everything will be forgotten."

"Perfect," I say, giving him my most evil smile. "Did you get all that?" I yell back to Jake.

Jake strolls out from the office (very casually) with his hands in his pockets. "Sure did." He smiles at Keith, who looks as pale as a ghost.

"What did you do?" Keith asks, panicked.

"I did nothing." I continue to smile at him. "You, on the other hand, did everything. You tried to convince me to sleep with you to give Jax a job. Then, you removed me from the board for refusing. Finally, you give me this bullshit to-do list in hopes that I what? Marry you?"

"No one will ever believe you. All you have is your brother as a witness."

"And me." Derek Lafferty, a lieutenant with our Sheriff's department, walks out. "I heard everything Keith. I can't fucking believe it. To think when Tilly and Jake came to me with this story, I thought it was a prank or something. But to hear it from your own mouth... I feel sick calling you a friend for all of these years."

"Derek, it isn't what you think. She baited me to say it all wrong, to make me sound guilty."

"No, she didn't. Everything came directly from the ass's mouth." Derek looks over to me. "You have the tapes as well, right?"

I look at Keith, who is about to have a heart attack. "Yes, I do. From tonight and the night he came to my shop to give me his to-do list, and mentioned again, about how I could make it all go away."

"Perfect, get me copies." Derek walks up to Keith, grabbing his arm. "In the meantime, you are coming with me..." Derek reads him his Miranda rights as he is taken away.

Jake rushes over and embraces me, picking me up and twirling me in the air. "I told you we could take care of that fucker. By tomorrow, his name will be all over the news. I am sure he won't get the sexual assault charges he deserves. But blackmail and abuse of power—well, he is for sure going to get into a load of trouble for those."

"I can't thank you enough, Jake."

"No need to thank me. Just remember that out of the three of us, I am going to be the best uncle ever. I maybe even deserve the role of godfather. Or if it is a boy, he should be named after me. I mean any or all of those things would be acceptable." I look at him stunned. How did he know? "Come on, Tilly. Twins, remember? I've suspected it for weeks. You were giving off this vibe. Not to mention, how sick you've been. Then after your doctor's visit a couple of weeks ago, you are eating crazy healthy and taking vitamins, and you touch your stomach every two seconds. It wasn't difficult to figure out. But once again, you are keeping things from me, Tilly, and I don't like it."

I give him a big hug. "I'm sorry, Jake. I promise you, this time I was only keeping it a secret because Jax and I found out right before he was leaving. We wanted to tell everyone together. I promise, with the exception of Jax who only found out because he was there... Granted, I would have told him anyway... But as I was saying, I haven't told anyone else. Not even Letty."

Jake gives me a giant smile, relishing in his victory over Letty. Those two... you'd think this childhood rivalry for my attention would be done by now. "Well, as long as Letty doesn't know. Is there more? Any more secrets you are keeping from me, Tilly?"

"Yes, but don't get angry. Like I said, there is stuff Jax and I want to share with everyone at Thanksgiving. Please, don't say anything to Scott or Robbie. I don't want Jax to feel left out of the announcements."

"Hmm..." Jake rubs his chin, considering my request. "Fine, you can keep your secrets until Thanksgiving, and I won't mention anything to Scott or Robbie. I can't promise I won't rub it into Letty's face after the reveal though. Also, I want godfather rights."

"I will try. We both know that Jax is going to want Scott as the godfather, but I promise you I will try."

"Well, if you would like, I can give you a few pointers on how to be more persuasive," he says, wiggling his eyebrows at me.

I push him away. "Eww, no. I do not want any sex advice from my brother."

"Come on, Tilly. I promise you will blow his mind."

"Ugh, fine. But please, don't be a creep about it."

Jake breaks out into a sinister smile before giving me his "tips". While my brother talks with me about sex (a conversation I hoped to never have with my brother) I cannot help but think, given his experience and expertise, he should really write a manual or something about it.

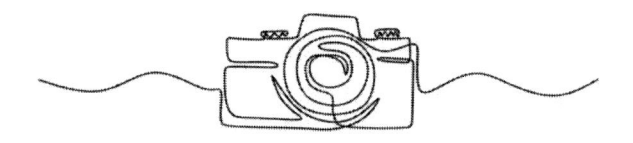

Chapter 36

Jackson

Walking up to the two-story farmhouse, I take everything in. Coming home feels different somehow. Last time, I rushed back here because of a tragic accident. Because I didn't have a choice. It was what was needed of me. This time, I am excited to see my fiancée and spend time with my family. I am here because I want to be and it has nothing to do with obligation.

Tilly has all of the fall decorations out on display. It is cute with hay bales, scarecrows, and this awesome door wreath—offering varied shades of red and orange. I've only been gone a few weeks, but everything looks different. The ground is brown and muddy, and the leaves are pretty much gone from the trees. Minnesota is (unfortunately) one of those states that has an ugly time twice per year. A time when everything is dead and brown. But then, you get the most spectacular sights the rest of the year. Like those postcard winters with white blankets of snow (which most people can only dream about). It looks like a winter wonderland. Or when everything is in full bloom and you are given all those lush greens. Then finally, the beginning of fall when the colors change (but before everything dies). It is utterly breathtaking.

I'm home a day early to surprise Tilly. I was able to wrap up the Maldives ahead of schedule and couldn't wait to get back. I rush up the steps and ring the doorbell. Tilly answers. Her hair's a mess on top of her head, she is wearing grey jogging pants with a black t-shirt, and tied around her waist is a bright teal apron with this whimsical cupcake pattern on it. Her makeupless face has flour smeared everywhere. The brace is still on her arm, but she is hoping she won't need to wear it at all in a couple more weeks. Needless to say, she is absolutely gorgeous. Especially when she smiles realizing that I'm home.

"Oh my god, you are home!" she yells, jumping up and wrapping her arms and legs around me. Before I can say anything, she is devouring my mouth. Fuck, I missed her. While I enjoyed my travels in Asia, I knew that those days were behind me. They do not give me the same sense of fulfillment anymore. Everywhere I visited, I couldn't help thinking how much better it would be with Tilly and our babies. "I missed you so much," she manages to get out, still kissing me.

I hear a male cough in the background, making his presence known. We break our mouths apart. I peer around Tilly's head to see Scott standing there, looking much like Tilly in grey sweatpants and a black t-shirt. I can barely contain my laughter when I notice he and Tilly are wearing matching aprons.

Tilly separates from me. I miss her warmth already. But I know I will get to fully embrace her before the evening is over. I look between her and Scott, trying not to laugh. Directing my question to Scott, I offer, "Do I need to ask?" He shakes his head, indicating he doesn't want to talk about it.

Tilly pulls me into the house. She is all-smiles, leading me by the hand into the kitchen. "Scott is teaching me to make pies."

"Trying to at least," Scott says under his breath. I love Tilly, but cooking has never been her skill. But I guess it was never mine either, until I started to learn.

"Hey, I am not that bad," Tilly defends herself.

Scott laughs at her. He gets back to the counter to roll out dough. "She has destroyed four pies," he says, shaking his head in disappointment.

Well, pie crust is tricky, but I am really good at adding filling," Tilly announces proudly.

"Yea, you at least got that part right. Look, I'll finish up here. Why don't you go upstairs and get Jax settled?"

"You don't need to tell me twice. Come on, Jax, I got something to show you anyway." As Tilly tugs me out of the kitchen, I glance back at Scott and mouth "thank you" to him. As cute as she is with flour on her face, I was looking forward to getting some alone time with her. Tomorrow will be hectic with her checkup and everyone prepping for the holiday dinner. And of course, the following day is Thanksgiving. Then on Friday, I'm sure her and Letty will want to go shopping. That means it could be three or four days before we get any alone time again.

In the room, Tilly motions for me to sit on the bed next to her. "Come here. I have something to show you." *Nice, right to business.* I can't wait. I sit down next to her, kissing her neck. "Not that, silly." She leans down and grabs a newspaper, handing it to me. "Here, read this."

I skim over the headline "Scandal in Tral Lake". I don't read too in depth. But from a brief glance, I can see that last week Keith McCalester was arrested for attempted blackmail and abuse of power in his role as Assistant City Manager. At this time, he is suspended from his position within the town and they are launching a full investigation. There is mention of a nameless shop owner who came forward, after he leveraged sexual favors in order to save her business. While they didn't say her name, I know it is Tilly. "What is this? What happened?"

Tilly goes on to explain how Jake was there when Keith dropped by a couple of weeks ago with a laundry list of bogus violations. How he had insisted by sleeping with him, they could all go away. How she had to fill in Jake on everything that was going on with Keith. And how (besides being furious for her not telling him sooner) he came up with a plan to expose the asshole. I guess over the years, Jake and Derek have become friends and so, he and Tilly explained everything to the lieutenant. They had Derek hide in the shop while they got Keith to confess everything in front of the officer; and for good measure, they made sure to catch it all on the shop surveillance.

"Wow, I don't know what to say. I mean, part of me is angry you didn't tell me he was harassing you again. But the other part of me is proud that you and Jake stuck it to the asshole."

"I know. I'm sorry." She leans in and kisses me. "I just didn't want you to stress while you were away working and couldn't do anything. But Jake was here and was able to back me up. I am honestly not sure what will happen legally, but I know for certain he will never return to any city-held position. I wouldn't doubt that his dad will ship him out of town and try and sweep this embarrassment under the rug."

"Well, I guess, since you gave me a surprise tonight, I owe you one as well."

"Oh, surprise? Whatever might this be?" She looks as giddy as a kid on Christmas.

I quickly go to my bag and grab an envelope and hand it to her. "What's this?" she says, looking down at two plane tickets to Florida. "These tickets are to fly out in two weeks. I thought you'd be in South America. How are you going to have time to fly home and do all this?"

I give her a big smile. "Simple, I won't have to fly home."

"You mean, you are done? No South America? No more traveling?" I can see the hope and joy in Tilly's eyes.

Nodding my head, I smile. "I'm done. Greg and I came to an arrangement."

"What's that?" Tilly yells excitedly.

"Well, Greg, our current photo editor, was looking to retire. When I told him why I was leaving, he felt like it was time to pull the trigger. I was offered his position and accepted."

"What does that mean? Won't you need to relocate?"

"That is the greatest part—*I can work remotely, anywhere*. I can stay here, still working with a job I love, without having to leave you all of the time. Greg already had two new photographers lined up, but since I am going to be busy transitioning to his role, another photographer is responsible for any field training with them."

"Oh. My. God. Jax. This is perfect! I am so happy. This is actually happening." Tilly is practically vibrating with excitement.

"It is, and I have one more surprise for you."

"I am not sure I can handle much more. This is already so much."

"One last one. On my way from Japan to the Maldives, I ended up having a day layover in Shanghai. While there, I did a little sightseeing and wandered into a shop. In this shop, a man approached me and started talking to me about being able to see how in love I am. I briefly mentioned to him about us. He began to tell me about an old Chinese folklore—*the Red Thread of Fate*. Basically, the idea is there is an invisible red thread wrapped around my finger that leads to my one true love—*you*. After telling me his story, he showed me some items. And well, when I saw it, I knew it was perfect."

I shift off the bed to kneel on one knee in front of her, presenting a small red box with gold engraving. "I know I have already proposed, but still, you deserve to be presented with the ring properly." I open the box to show her a white gold band. It has a rose gold looking rope wrapped around it, with a diamond sitting center.

"Oh my god, Jax, it is perfect. I absolutely love it. Yes, I still want to marry you."

Chapter 37

Matilda

Finally, Thanksgiving is here and I can't wait. I am dying to wear my ring. We decided to hold off, until we make the official announcements today. Scott has been here all week, pretty much doing a majority of the cooking. Jax has helped as well. He ended up convincing Scott to allow him to brine the turkey, something he saw on one of those cooking shows. Seeing those two in the kitchen yesterday and today has been amusing. They talk like an old married couple.

The doorbell rings. I get up to answer it. "Hey, Scar, come on in." I invited Scarlett to join us for Thanksgiving. We have been talking more and she is really awesome. Also, I felt bad knowing she is new to town with no family. The thought of her sitting alone at her bed and breakfast was too depressing.

"Thanks for having me over. Here, I made a pie. Okay, that is a lie. I bought it." I can tell she is a little nervous.

"Thank you, Scar. Let me go set it on the counter," I say, leading her into the kitchen.

Everyone is here—Jax, my brothers, Letty, and Scarlett. It is weird not having mom and dad here, but we all promised to not let it bring us down. Robbie is sitting at the head of the table this year, on turkey-carving duty. We decided, since he was the oldest, the responsibility has passed to him.

After everyone has dished up their plates, we start a round of saying what we are thankful for, making sure that Jax and I are last. When it finally comes around to us, Jax goes first. "Well, this year what I am most thankful for... is that Tilly agreed to marry me." I quickly slide on my ring and show everyone my hand.

"Oh my god, congratulations!" Letty immediately leans over to give me a big hug.

"Not cool, man," Scott interjects as all of the celebration ceases. Jax raises an eyebrow to him, wondering what his issue is. "I just always figured you would ask my permission, you know? Or at least include me on some elaborate scheme to propose."

The table breaks out in laughter. "Sorry, man. We had the perfect moment and I was not going to pass it up." Everyone resumes their congratulations and I shake with nervousness.

"Well, that is going to be hard to top," I joke, "but this year, I am thankful to become a mother." Now, everyone is silent and staring at me. This is probably a lot to take in, especially since we just announced the engagement. The only one smiling (besides Jax) is Jake, since he already knew. But time to blow his mind. "Well, I guess more accurately, I am thankful to become a mother... *twice*." I hold up the ultrasound photo we got yesterday showing both babies. Now Jake's jaw drops.

Letty is the first one to come back to reality. "Oh my god, I am going to be an aunt! They are going to love me the most."

Jake coughs to interject Letty's comment. "Let's not get ahead of ourselves now, Letty. I am going to be the best uncle and godfather. Not to mention I am the coolest of this lot. They will definitely love me the most."

Scott and Robbie sit there, tense. I give them a pointed look, challenging either of them to make a negative comment. Scott is the first to surrender, throwing his hands up in the air. "Look, I'm not going to say I am not excited to become an uncle—which we already know I will be the godfather, by the way, Jake. But this is a lot, Tilly."

"What we are concerned about is how this is going to work?" Robbie interjects with his poker face; the one that always seems to make me uncomfortable.

"Well, I'm not sure on the specifics of the whole process but I am reading some books. I am sure when the time comes, my body will know what to do naturally."

"No." Robbie shakes his head and shivers in disgust. "What is the plan? You live here with Jake. You run a shop. Jax travels for long periods of time with his job. One baby is enough work, but two... How are you going to manage this?"

Jax takes my hand. "Seriously, Robbie? You really think I wouldn't take care of Tilly or our babies?"

"No, no one is saying that." Scott tries to deescalate the situation. "But Robbie has maybe... a miniscule point. Have you guys figured out how this will work? I mean, obviously we will all help. But it is a lot."

"I will admit we still have some logistics to figure out, but Tilly will not be alone." Jax raises my hand and kisses it. "I guess I have one more thing to be thankful for... *in that case.* I have a new job."

"What, really?" Scott slaps him on the back. "Why didn't you tell me? Dude, seriously, you are sucking as a best friend recently with all this not-telling-me shit."

Jax chuckles. "It is very recent. I am still working for the magazine but I took over as photo editor. It is not only a promotion, which still includes travel vouchers as an employee benefit, but I also get to work remotely. Traveling will be super rare... *if ever.*"

"Holy shit, that is amazing. I am so happy for you." Scott is clearly excited that his best friend is coming home.

We all look to Robbie, who smiles. "Congratulations, man.

Sorry for being a hardass, but you get it, right?"

Jax nods. "I get it, no hard feelings."

"So how far along are you?" Scar inquires, now that the family drama is over. I feel a little bad. That must have been awkward for her.

"Not far. They estimate about ten weeks."

"Oh my god, I am so excited. We need to start planning the baby shower," Letty says, looking at Scarlett before turning back to me. "When is your due date?"

"June 26th. But with twins, it could be earlier from what I read. But then again, because this is my first pregnancy, it could be later. Honestly, the books on the subject are super confusing. There is really no definitive information. It is all speculative."

Everyone chuckles. "Perfect, a spring baby shower will be absolutely splendid. Oh, I need to start making plans. Scar, we need to get together and start organizing everything."

"Oh, we could have it at the bed and breakfast? The garden with the spring blooms will be such a beautiful setting." Scarlett joins in with Letty on preparations.

"Okay, you guys have at it. I give you full control over the event."

"Yes! Are you going to find out the genders?" Letty is practically vibrating from excitement in her seat. "We could even do a gender-reveal party."

Umm, I don't think we are. We were offered to do some sort of early blood test, but declined. Right now, I just kind of want to be surprised, ya know? At the twenty weeks scan, they can tell me... if I want to change my mind though."

Robbie scoffs, "Finding out you are pregnant... *with twins*... seems like a big enough surprise doesn't it? Waiting until they are born seems irresponsible. How are you supposed to buy stuff for the babies?"

"Seriously, mister grumpy-pants? It is fun and exciting to wait. Besides, newborns don't need much right away. I will get more gender-specific items after they are born. What if I have a boy and a girl? I am not going to want to paint the room in pink.

I guess it will be like when Jake and I were born—do something neutral and then accent it as they grow." I counter Robbie's ridiculous argument, which elicits another scoff. Geez, I wonder what is up his butt?

"Dude, not knowing is going to be awesome. We will buy four cigars each, with two wrapped in blue and two wrapped in pink. We can pace the waiting room like the old days and then light the appropriate cigars." Scott beams, finally showing the excitement I had initially expected.

"Or we can do a shot for each baby, get pink and blue bottles?" Jake proposes.

Letty rolls her eyes. "Of course, you would figure out a way to make this a drinking game."

"We will figure something epic out," Scott plots with Jake.

The rest of the day continues with eating and laughing, while the main topics are the wedding and babies. Something is bothering Robbie, but I don't think it is Jax and me. It must be something else... I assume it is the realization that he has to hire someone to help manage his back office. With twins and the shop, he knows I will no longer have time to help him out anymore.

Letty has an obsession with knowing when we plan to get married. Overall, even though the absence of my parents is felt, this is a great Thanksgiving. And next year will be even better, given the fact we will have two new members in the pack. With any luck, this will inspire my brothers to settle down. Granted, I am not sure Jake is capable of that... But my babies are going to need cousins.

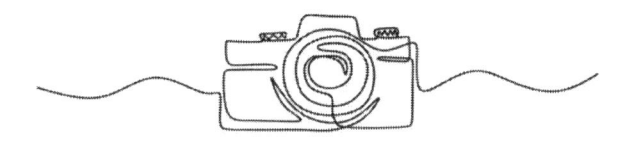

Epilogue

Tilly is admiring how the pinkish sand looks in contrast to the almost turquoise water. I will admit it is one of the coolest sights I have ever seen. Tilly looks absolutely stunning. Her belly has started to get pretty big at twenty-one weeks pregnant. Seeing how quickly these babies are growing, I decided that for Valentine's Day I was finally going to take her on our first big vacation. I was worried if I waited any longer, she might not be as mobile and wouldn't enjoy the experience as much.

Knowing how much she loves Greece, I couldn't pass on the opportunity to whisk her away to Crete. I have never actually been here before myself. But when I was looking at options for Greece and saw the Pink Beach of Balos, I thought it was the perfect destination for a romantic getaway or even a mini honeymoon (we got married last month). It is a little chilly here this time of the year, averaging in the forties. But compared to back home, this feels tropical.

"This is the most beautiful thing I have ever seen," Tilly comments, still admiring the beach. I continue to take images of not only the beach, but her observing it. I used to think she glowed before, but pregnant Tilly is almost blinding. I feel like she is some deity that my human eyes do not deserve to gaze upon. I take in her blonde hair blowing in the wind, while her dress is pushed back against her stomach (showing off how round and perfect it is).

"Oh, come here quick!" Tilly exclaims. I let my camera hang from my neck and approach her. She immediately takes my hand and lays it on her growing belly. "Can you feel it?"

I wait a moment and then there's a little push from her stomach. "Wow, that is amazing." This is the first time I have been able to actually experience them kicking. She has been feeling them for a few weeks now, but I never really could. However, this time it is clear as day. "Does it hurt?"

"Ugh, sometimes... but it is more weird than anything, a lot of pressure. But it is amazing."

After the beach and some lunch, we make it back to the hotel room. Although it has been an amazing day, this pregnancy really takes a toll on Tilly. While she never complains, each week I can see her growing more and more exhausted. The babies put so much pressure on her, that she can't get comfortable enough to sleep more than an hour or two at a time. We unfortunately had to have a hard talk with Robbie a couple of weeks ago about Tilly helping with his books. He understood, but it was hard for Tilly to give up helping her big brother. Tilly was kind enough to find him an office assistant (someone she used to go to school with and could personally vouch for). This seemed to ease some of the apprehension Robbie felt towards letting in an outsider.

Tilly, Scott, and Jake ended up purchasing the space behind their shop and expanding. The McCalesters were more than happy to sell it to them at a steal, given the whole incident. As expected, Keith lost his job and was essentially shipped off. But the actual legal charges were minimal and resulted in nothing more than a fine the family could easily afford.

The best thing about the new space is that there was a giant office I was able to take over. Even though we made an office for me at home, I primarily work at the shop. That way, I can help Tilly out as much as possible. I still assist her with photos and social media, but given her current state, I make sure to also do all the heavy lifting.

Sitting on the bed, I lean against the headboard. Tilly lays on my chest, my hands on her belly trying to find any new movement. Now that I have felt it, I want to touch her belly all the time. "Did you hear back from the Dawsons?" Tilly inquires.

"Yea, they are all set. We will be able to move in at the beginning of the month." After some careful thought and consideration, I approached the Dawson family (they are currently living in my grandpa's home). I discovered that Mr. Dawson was recently offered a new career opportunity, but the commute wouldn't have been feasible. However, they didn't want to break their lease. When I offered them the opportunity to end the lease with no penalties, they were practically in tears. I guess they were planning on having to pay for Mr. Dawson to stay in a hotel during the work week, until the lease was up. It honestly worked out for the best.

We considered staying at Tilly's (well, *our*) house. But Tilly seemed excited to move to a bigger home. She and Jake still haven't done anything to their parents' room, even with Robbie hounding them about "it being time". While the grief is less, there are some things that Tilly has held onto, and that transferred easily to Jake. Honestly, I am just excited about Tilly and I having our own place and not sharing it with her brother anymore. I love the guy, but his critique on my sex life is a little too much.

"I'm so excited. I can't wait to start getting the nursery ready. I think I have officially entered the nesting stage." I can't help but chuckle at her. Even though we decided to still keep the genders a surprise, she has been going hog wild on nursery planning. I showed her Pinterest, and well, now she is a full-blown addict. While Robbie is still frustrated by our decision to be surprised, he is coming around (now that we have a wager on the whole arrangement). Jake and Scott are convinced we will have a boy and a girl. I am certain we are having two girls. Robbie is dead set that we are having two boys. I honestly couldn't care less. We could end up with five girls and I would happily accept being outnumbered. I am just excited to raise a family with Tilly.

"Jake asked me about being a godfather again," Tilly casually mentions. This has been another debate.

"Come on, Scott is my best friend and your brother. He would flip if we picked Jake over him. He is still giving me shit about not going to him about the proposal. Also, hypothetically speaking, if something happens to us… do you really want Jake raising them? Not to mention raising them with Letty? They would kill each other. Scott is the most logical choice."

"I know, but he is very serious about wanting to be their godfather. I have never seen him so excited about something that wasn't sex, booze, or firefighting before."

"Still, I don't think it is a good idea. How about you pick Jake over Letty? They can have two godfathers?"

"Umm, no way, Letty would kill me. She is my best friend."

"See? It's not so easy, is it?"

"Fine, you want to wager on it?"

"Interesting… What do you have in mind?" Tilly is not one to usually wager, so I am a little excited.

"Hmm…" she says, tapping her chin. "How about if I make you come in less than two minutes, then Jake gets to be the godfather?"

I cough. "Are you fucking serious?"

"Yup. Two minutes, I win—Jake gets to be the godfather."

"Okay, well, what do I get if you lose?"

"What would you like?"

"I get to name the babies. You have no veto power." Ha, there is no way she will accept that. We have been arguing about baby names for weeks. We have three lists, depending on what combination we get.

"Fine, deal."

"I knew you... wait, you agree? If you lose, you will seriously allow me to name the babies whatever I want?"

"Yup," she says, popping her 'P'. "But I know I am going to win, so I am not worried," she confirms with a cocky attitude—one that I've never really heard from her before.

"Game on, then, sweetheart."

Tilly gets off the bed and removes her dress. This leaves her in a sexy, sheer lace bra that I can see her pink nipples through, and a matching pair of sheer panties with lace filigree. Damn, she isn't playing around. "Stand up. Get naked. I will start the timer afterwards."

Bossy, I like it. I happily oblige, slowly removing my clothes and giving her a little show. By the way her pupils have dilated, I know she is aroused. Unfortunately for me, she had a little head start. The deal in general gave me a semi. Now, looking at her in her sexy underwear with her pregnant belly on display, I quickly go hard as steel. Standing in front of Tilly, I watch as she peruses my body for one more minute before dropping to her knees. "Google, start timer for two minutes," she yells to her phone. *"Timer set two minutes, starting now,"* her Google assist replies.

Tilly starts by kissing the inside of my thighs, then she continues licking a trail up to my shaft. Working her way from the base of my cock to my tip, she plants wet, sloppy kisses. Glancing down, I see saliva everywhere. At the head, she offers a light kiss before taking me into her hot mouth and rolling her tongue around the top like a lollipop. Her hand starts pumping up and down my shaft, already well lubricated from her foreplay. She gives me a firm squeeze, while twisting her wrist as she works it up and down. Shit, this is good. But I can hold out for two minutes.

She quickly removes her hand from my cock and grips both of my ass cheeks as she pulls me deep into her throat. I can feel my balls tighten immediately, looking for release. "Fuck, Tilly."

But she is not done, and the timer hasn't sounded off yet—*it has to be close, right?* Her left hand releases my ass and reaches to start massaging my balls. I am hanging on by a thread. The stimulation of her holding me so deep, while playing down there, is killer. I'm so focused on her fondling, I don't notice when her fingers make their way between my cheeks. "Tilly..." Before I can even protest, I feel her finger press inside my hole. *Holy Fuck!* I have never had anything there before. *I've never wanted anything there before.* But as she pushes her finger fully inside me and presses against my wall, a wave of euphoria washes over me. There is no stopping my violent orgasm.

After I regain some form of consciousness, Tilly's finger is removed from my rectum. She is in the process of licking me clean. When she comes off my tip, she lets go with a pop, looking up at me with her big amber eyes. Then, her timer goes off. Shit, I didn't make two minutes.

"Where the hell did you learn that?" I stare down at her in disbelief. Tilly has always given awesome blow jobs, but this was phenomenal.

With a smile, she replies, "I have my sources."

"Bullshit, where did you learn that?"

Standing up, she shrugs her shoulders. "Jake."

"Wha-wait Jake? How? Why?" When the hell did Tilly cave into talking about sex with Jake? It is usually a topic she avoids like the plague.

"After the whole Keith debacle, he said he wanted to be the godfather, claiming it would make up for leaving him out of everything. I told him there was no way you would agree to that, and he gave me some tips on how to persuade you." She leans over to grab her dress off the bed. I quickly grab her hips, pulling her back to my front.

"Oh, we are not done yet, babe." I kiss down her neck. "We are just getting started."

The End

Works Cited

[1] Fanaro, Barry, and Mort Nathan. 1996. Kingpin. Directed by Bobby Farrelly Peter Farrelly. Produced by Brad Krevoy, John Bertolli and Jim Burke. Performed by Bill Murray.

TBD Moore Family

Turn the page for a sneak peek at:
Next Moore Family Book

Coming Soon!

(Unedited and subject to change)

Robbie

"Mack, get your ass in here!" Somedays, I really must ask myself why in the hell I put up with his stupidity. The slight pounding in my head is warning me that a migraine is imminent.

"What's up, boss?" Mack enters the back office, pushing his shaggy blonde hair out of his face.

"What the hell is this?" I hold up a work order he recently did for a 2019 Toyota Corolla.

"Umm…" He leans in to inspect. "Looks like a work order for that Corolla I did last week."

"Yea, I see that. What I want to know is what the fuck is this?" I point to the number at the bottom. It reads that the total was only $54.96."

"Yea, she got an oil change," Mack says as though it is super obvious, and I must be some sort of big fucking idiot.

I begin rubbing my temples, trying to alleviate the pressure building up. "You charged her for a conventional oil change. But according to the parts list, you gave her a full synthetic oil change."

"Sorry about that, boss. Must have pressed the wrong button when ringing her up." Mack avoids direct eye contact, picking fake lint from his blue grease-covered jumpsuit.

"Hmm…" I stroke my chin while contemplating just how stupid Mack must genuinely think I am. "I can see that, but what about not chargin' for the wipers and install you did?"

Grabbing the back of his neck, Mack chuckles. "Ha, must have overlooked that. You know how easily I get confused sometimes."

"Seriously, do you think I'm fucking stupid? I can see the discounts you applied right here—" I indicate, pointing at the work order.

Mack drops his arms and shrugs his shoulders, giving up this charade. "Come-on, man, it was Mandy-fuckin-Callaway. You can't charge a chick like that full price for anything." He attempts to reason with me.

Fuck, the sensation that a herd of elephants are stampeding in my skull is a sign that my migraine is almost full-blown now. It isn't that I am not a charitable guy. I have cut deals and given breaks to people who I knew couldn't pay the bill. But the damn Callaways are the last assholes in this county that need a fucking handout. Why do I even keep Mack on staff? Oh yea, right—when it comes to body work, his attention to detail is superior. Well, second to mine that is. "It's coming out of your pay. Don't do it again," I scold Mack.

"Sure thing, boss," Mack replies with a knowing grin.

He knows it will take a lot more for me to fire him than giving discounts to get a piece of ass. This isn't the first time I have had to dock his pay. Honestly, the only reason I am pissed is it just makes more work for me. Normally, Tilly would handle this kind of bullshit; but barely halfway through her pregnancy, she can hardly waddle into the bookshop—I am not going to force her to handle my shit too. "It was worth every penny."
I raise an inquisitive eyebrow to him; Mack holds his hands up in defense. "Seriously, a discount on an oil change and some free wipers gets you laid?"

"Well, it helps. What seals the deal is my good looks and charm." Mack gives me what I am assuming is his panty-melting grin—fortunately, I am immune to that type of shit. No wonder him and Jake are best friends. My baby brother is the biggest manwhore in this town. He can sell a woman in white gloves a red popsicle on a hot and humid day. I am assuming, with that grin, Mack isn't too far behind him. While I have heard some women might find a grease monkey sexy, I am still convinced that is as common as UFO abductions. But Jake being a firefighter gives him the winning advantage over Mack. Women go nuts for the whole 'hot hero' bullshit, and Jake will milk it for every penny it is worth.

After dismissing Mack back to work, I continue going through the damn books. How the hell Tilly manages this shit, I will never understand? My brain is meant for taking crap apart and putting it back together. Whatever, I will figure it out. My pop's ran his junk yard and shop back in the day—practically by himself. If that old coot could figure this out, I know I can. We are cut from the same cloth after all.

"Seriously, Robbie, what have I told you about messing with my system?" I was so caught up in trying to decipher this crap, I didn't notice my baby sister walk in. I glance up from the books, probably looking as distraught as I feel. I have been practically pulling out my hair all day, trying to get everything together to file taxes for last year. Fortunately, I have a guy who actually does them for me, but I can't go in there and toss a box full of papers and tell him to deal with it. Believe me, I've tried, and he nearly kicked my ass for it.

"Well, I got to figure out this shit, don't I?" I calm my features, realizing I am being a dick to Tilly for no damn reason. Glancing at her snow-covered hat then down to her belly pushing the seams of her winter coat, I realize she trekked here in the snow to help me out. And how do I greet her? Yea, that's right, by being an ass.

Tilly gives me a soft smile, probably noticing my change in demeanor. "I told you I would help you with this Robbie. I'm sorry I couldn't make it in the other day. The morning—well, more like all day—sickness wasn't letting me get far from my home."

Yup, I just earned myself the 'biggest asshole in the world achievement'. My very pregnant and exhausted sister dragged her ass out of bed and to my shop. And what does she get for her efforts? Her big brother being a complete and total ass. "I understand. I told you not to worry about it."

Tilly levels her gaze with me, her amber eyes that match mine look right through me. "I told you, I would help you get your taxes together—and I keep my word. But seriously, I had everything organized and you have totally devastated my system." Tilly motions to the stacks of work orders and invoices piled around the office. Picking up the work order I just reamed Mack out for, Tilly sighs, "Seriously, again?"

I can't help but laugh, Tilly has had to have the "talk" with Mack on more than one occasion. "Yea, I already told him to cut the shit, and it is coming out of his pay."

Tilly rolls her eyes at me. "God, he is almost as pathetic as Jake. I still don't understand how he thinks he will be able to handle a video store. That guy lacks any sense of business or responsibility. With his extracurricular activities, he will more than likely end up giving out free movies to every cute chick in town if they promise to..." Tilly adds air quotes. "...'watch it with him'."

After our parents were killed by a dumb-fuck drunk driver four months ago, we all received a chunk of inheritance. Not anything major, but enough to make some improvements in our lives. Jake decided to take his portion and go in with Tilly and Scott on purchasing more space and expanding Moore Books and Coffee. Jake is getting a section of the space to set up a little video rental shop. Although Tilly isn't a fan of the idea, I'm excited. I can't stand the Netflix selection and Redbox doesn't carry the good old shit. I don't get much free time, but when I do, I want to go on a classic 80's action movie marathon.

"Alright, get your ass up. I've got work to do," Tilly demands, gesturing for me to move.

As I stand, Tilly makes her way to my stool. I cringe when I notice her wince and grab her lower back as she takes a seat. Fuck, I don't have an actual office chair. I fabricated a shop stool from an old tractor seat I had laying around at pop's junk yard. My poor pregnant sister, whose belly seems larger than it should, has zero cushion for her bottom and no lumbar support.

"Hey, why don't I take all the stuff to the house, and you can work on it there?" I try to offer. It would make me feel less guilty if she could do this in some form of comfort.

"No, I'm fine... ugh." She groans in discomfort, indicating that she is lying. But that is my baby sister for you. She is selfless to a fault.

"Come-on, that thing hurts my ass. I can't imagine it is pleasant for you in your..." I gesture to her growing stomach. "...condition."

"Robbie, I'm fine. I'm pregnant, not an invalid. Now the quicker you back off, the sooner I will be done." Tilly dismisses me with a wave.

I huff in frustration; she is about damn near stubborn as me. Arguing with her is no use. I concede and decide to let her get to work. "Is there anything I can get you?"

"Some hot cocoa and those sweetheart cookies Scott has been making would be perfect." Tilly looks up with giant eyes, glimmering at the thought of those cookies.

"Sure thing, coming right up." I lean down and give Tilly a quick kiss on the forehead and let her get to work. As I make my way outside, that anger inside me begins to boil over. It is practically a blizzard out here, and she fucking risked her safety to come help my sorry ass. Dammit, I need to figure this shit out. I can't have Tilly hurting herself or the babies for me.

∞∞∞

"What the hell, man?" Scooting out from underneath the Jeep I'm working on, I look up to a pissed off Jackson.

"Can I help you?" I ask my new brother-in-law. It is kind of crazy. This guy has pretty much been my little brother his whole life. But when him and Tilly finally tied the knot the other week at the courthouse, he is now legally my brother.

"Have you seen it outside? It is near whiteout conditions, and Tilly is here sitting in your shitty little office, when she should be home curled up with blankets on the couch sipping tea. Not risking her life and our babies' lives because you are too stubborn to hire someone to manage your books." Jax crosses his arms over his chest, giving me his best "tuff guy" impersonation. I am sure if the situation called for it, Jax could hold his own in a fight. But, at the end of the day, Jax is not as strong as he is making himself out to be.

Getting up, I stand to my full height. Jax might be tall, but I'm taller and bigger. Jax loses his composure a bit, knowing how thoroughly I can kick his ass if he tempts me. "First of all, I didn't ask her to come down here. She showed up on her own. I was trying to handle it, but this is Tilly, and she kicked me out of my office. Secondly, I offered to bring everything to the house, but Tilly refused. She didn't want me messing up her system any more than I already have."

"I know Tilly can be a little headstrong. Just, when I got home from the shop—we closed early because of the storm—she wasn't there, and I panicked. Thinking about her out in this shit. I got worried that she might have slipped and fallen, or worse." I empathize with my new brother-in-law. Tilly does what she wants. It appears that as she becomes more debilitated from the stress the pregnancy is causing her body, the more unyielding her spirit has become. She refuses to back down. "Please, Robbie, you need to fix this."

I cross my arms over my chest and cock my head, looking slightly down at him. "How do you expect me to do that? I may be her brother, but you are her husband," I challenge back.

"Don't be stupid, Robbie. We both know, the only reason Tilly is even here right now is because your stubborn ass refuses to hire the back-office manager that you have desperately needed, long before Tilly was pregnant." Jax attempts to stand tall again, finding a bit of the bravado he lost.

"Look, I don't like strangers involved in my shit. I have told Tilly I will manage it. But she seems to be a little selective on her hearing when it comes to that," I say, stepping into Jax's space. Surprisingly, he doesn't back down from my challenge.

"Because Tilly loves you, and will never abandon you. It is up to you to man up and get over this ridiculous fear you have. Let Tilly find a replacement. I know shit about business, but even I can tell you need the help, a lot more than she can offer."

I am so sick and tired of this fucking conversation. Tilly and I have been arguing about this shit for a couple of years now. When our dad started stepping down at the bookshop and she was taking it over, Tilly had indicated that I needed more help then she could offer. But while it hasn't always been smooth, we never changed our arrangement. I guess in all reality, this time, the issues with Tilly helping aren't temporary problems. If anything, it will get worse as time goes on. Fucking god dammit!

I throw the wrench I was holding to the ground. The loud clunk makes Jax flinch. I storm off towards the back office with Jax on my heels. When I barge into the room, Tilly gasps, startled by my entrance. "Fine!"

"What?" Tilly looks confused. She tries to look back at Jax for some sort of clarification.

"Hire a fucking office manager!" I declare, before rushing back out of the office, roughly bumping shoulders with Jax on my way out. I don't mean to be a dick, but dammit, I hate the idea of letting someone else in my shop, especially after what happened the last time. But I know I need the help. I maybe stubborn but I'm not stupid. I just really hope this doesn't come back to bite me in the ass.

Cassie

"Ouch," I hiss, sucking the blood from my finger. Stupid thorn got me, and not for the first time today. This is flipping pathetic. Here I am, again —back living with my parents, helping at their flower shop, and assisting in making floral arrangements for a bridal shower. White roses, how cliche? I don't mean to be rude. Honestly, the arrangement is beautiful. It is just, right now, the last thing I want to do or look at is anything related to marriage—which is weird coming from me. I love weddings. I had been planning mine for as long as I can remember.

"Níl ach braon beag fola ort." My father chuckles, handing me a cloth to wrap around my finger. While my father and mother immigrated to the US over thirty years ago, he still enjoys teasing me in his native Irish tongue.

"Da, it is more than a little blood." I wave my finger at him. Only small red droplets trickle down, but I can't help but be a little over dramatic. Being the baby of our family and his only daughter, I tend to play it up as much as possible.

"Próseche, you are getting blood on the arrangements, Cassandra." Thanks to my unique heritage, I am fluent in English, Gaelic, and Greek. My mother's Greek ancestry is the only reason I do not have a traditional Irish name like my brothers. Unfortunately, though, my antics do not work as well with my mother. I sometimes think she is harder on me because I am her only daughter.

"Sorry, ma." I rush to clean and wrap my bleeding finger. Turning around, I watch as my mother picks apart my arrangement, undoing all my work. I love her—she is a wonderful mother— but she tends to be extremely nit-picky. But then again, when it comes to floral arrangements, my mother is a true artist. Numbers, math in general, have always been my thing. Burying myself in endless piles of data and spreadsheets calms and centers me. That is what flowers do for my mother.

My mother sighs, pulling blood stained roses from the arrangement and tossing them into the trash. "Why don't you head home and get cleaned up? We will finish up the order and meet you later tonight." She dismisses me, her brow scrunched in frustration as she figures out how to salvage the mess I made.

Yup, I have been politely kicked out of the shop—again. Giving my parents each a brief kiss, I bundle up to face the freezing Minnesota winter. While it is so cold my nostrils stick together when I take in a breath, I wouldn't want to live anywhere else.

∞∞∞

Instead of heading home, I decide to head over to K.O. Murphy, a pub not too far from my parents' house. It is within walking distance, which makes drinking here ideal. Well, that, and the fact my brother Killian owns the bar, so I mostly drink for free. Not that I am a freeloader or anything, he just refuses to accept my money. So, I make sure to always tip everyone well to make up for it. Also, I volunteer to help if he ever needs it. Especially in times like these where I am not working and need something to do to keep myself from going mad.

Taking a seat at the bar, I flag down Sean, my brother's friend who is lead bartender. "Hiya, Cassie, what can I get ya this evening?" Sean asks in a somewhat mischievous tone.

"Really, Sean? I am a little hurt you even need to ask." I feign insult, playing along with his game. Sean already knows what I want to drink. I have been drinking here practically exclusively for five years.

Giving me his token flirty grin, he pours me a Murphy's Irish Stout. Yea, given our family name and heritage, my brother has made sure to coin the Murphy branding as much as possible.

Even if the beer wasn't created by a distant ancestor, it would still be my drink of choice. While Guinness is good, I feel the smooth drink doesn't get the attention it deserves. I take a sip of my beer and enjoy the mild coffee flavor. Glancing around, I notice the place is packed, which isn't surprising for a Friday night. Thankfully, while busy, it doesn't feel overcrowded like other places. Maybe that is because I know almost everyone here?

"What kind of trouble are you planning tonight?" Sean teases while wiping down the bar.

"Just the usual." I toss back before adding, "World domination." I give Sean my most sinister smile.

Sean lifts his chin, gesturing to someone behind me. "I am sure if anyone could do it, you two would."

Before I even have a chance to turn around, I feel two thin arms wrap around me from behind, hugging my waist. "Hey, Cassie." My best friend Moira says as she squeezes me tight. Before taking a seat at the bar stool next to me, Moira gives me a sympathetic smile. Ever since the breakup, she has been walking on eggshells around me. I really wish she would stop. "So, how are you holding up?" Before taking off to help others, Sean slides Moira a Guinness because we haven't been able to convert her yet.

I roll my eyes at her question. "Fine, I guess. I am still looking for work. Hopefully I find something soon. I think ma is going to kill me if I mess up another one of her arrangements."

Moira snort-laughs into her beer. Growing up together, Moira knows my mother well and is aware of how particular she is about her flowers. My ma tried to teach me about flowers and arrangements, but I didn't inherit her green thumb. "I am sure someone will get back to you soon. You have only been looking for a couple of weeks."

"Yea, it's just that I need to get back to work. I miss my numbers and spreadsheets." I pout and then toss a pretzel bite into my mouth.

"Oh, guess who I talked to the other day?" Moira yells excitedly over the music. "Tilly!"

I smile, thinking about my old college roommate and friend. I feel bad for not keeping in touch with her. The past few years, except for Moira, I found myself little time to keep in touch with anyone. Well, outside of Facebook—which Tilly refuses to use. "How is she?"

"Good, I guess." Moira looks down a little sad. "Her parents actually passed away a few months ago."

"Oh, that is awful. I had no idea." I take a swig of my drink, trying to wash away the foul taste of guilt I feel. I can't believe she has been going through such a hardship, and I knew nothing about it. Well, I guess Moira didn't either, although that doesn't stop me from being remorseful for not being there for my friend.

"Yea, it sounds like she is doing better though. Tilly actually got married a couple weeks ago," Moira says, then immediately retreats knowing marriage is a sore subject for me right now.

"It's okay, Moira. I appreciate you looking out for me. But I need to move past this. I am happy to hear that she got married." It isn't a lie. I am happy for her. It pains me a little, and I find myself a little jealous. But I don't want to become one of those people who can't celebrate my friend's happiness, just because things are not so great for me right now.

"I know. I am sorry..." Moira looks a little uncomfortable. "She is pregnant also."

"That is exciting! We should plan on visiting her soon. Or maybe invite her up here and take her out shopping for the baby?" I offer, trying to heal some of the hurt and guilt in my heart.

"Actually, she was calling looking to see if I knew anyone in need of a job," Moira explains.

"Oh yea, what kind of job?" I don't know many people, but still, I would be willing to pass along the word.

"I guess it is helping her brother out. He needs someone at his auto body shop to manage his books and back office." Moira takes a quick drink. "I couldn't really think of anyone looking right now, especially that would be willing to relocate to Tral

Lake. But if you know anyone, you should pass it along. Apparently, her brother is super nervous about letting a stranger come in and manage his books."

"Which brother?"

"Her eldest brother, Robbie."

I nod. "Ah, okay. I never met him. I really only ever met Jake the few times he came to visit campus."

Moira giggles, thinking about Jake. "If Jake needed an office manager, I would quit my job in a heartbeat." We both laugh. Jake was super-hot, and I'm sure he still is. The guy totally seeped sex pheromones from his pores. Tilly had always been so beautiful and elegant. It was crazy seeing those same features personified in her twin Jake.

Goofing off, Moira and I continue to drink our beers and chat at the bar. It is nice getting to hang out with my best friend—it feels like forever since we have been able to do this. Eventually, we hit the drunk state of the evening; the one where we feel the need to pose for selfies at the bar before posting them to Facebook. Scrolling through, we laugh at the comments when something catches my eyes. It seems Moira noticed it as well and tries to take the phone from me.

"Let it go, Cassie," Moira yells, turning her back to me and blocking the phone with her body.

"Moira, give me my darn phone," I say sternly. Moira looks down at the screen with a frown before passing it back to me. As I look at the post, I can't help but feel the broken pieces of my heart shatter more.

"Come-on, Cassie, you are better than him. Don't let this eat you up," Moira pleads, trying to prevent the train wreck that is happening in my head.

"Sorry, Moira. I need to get going." I say, throwing a twenty down for Sean. Getting up, I run smack dab into a firm chest.

"Whoa, Cassie. Where are you heading off to?" Killian asks, his smile quickly turning to a frown as he notices the look of anguish on my face. "Hey, what happened?" Killian prompts, looking between Moira and me. "Did some drunk asshole try something?" Killian cracks his knuckles, prepared to beat up one of his patrons if necessary.

"No, Kill, it's fine. I am just tired. I will catch you both later," I say, walking away quickly while pulling my jacket snug around me. Off in the distance, I can hear Killian asking Moira for details about what happened. I don't stick around to listen to the conversation, because it doesn't matter. I need to get away from here. I love my family—my friends—but right now, everything reminds me of him. I don't even take a second to reconsider, before grabbing my phone and calling my old friend. "Hi, Tilly. It's Cassie."

"Cassie? Oh, hi. How are you? I feel like we haven't spoken in forever." Tilly sounds excited and happy on the phone. That is what I want to be again. I want to be happy, not constantly reminded of my heartbreak. How is it ever supposed to heal when the wound keeps getting picked at?

"I am doing good. I am sorry for calling so late... but I was actually just at the bar with Moira, and she mentioned you were looking for someone to help at your brother's shop?"

Acknowledgement

First off, I would like to give a special thanks to Kat Pagan with Pagan Proofreading https://www.facebook.com/search/top?q=pagan%20proofreading. If it weren't for Kat's time, dedication, and many sleepless nights this book would have never gotten published.

I would also like to give a special thanks to **Daria Loshlin**, a fellow author, for assisting me in coming up with my author brand: **"Saint and Sinner Romance Writer"** and accompanying logo. When you are interested in writing in more than one romance genre, it can be difficult to define yourself. But Daria's brilliant mind was able to say, "Girl, this is you."

Finally, a special shout out to the Beta and ARC readers who took time to read my book and provide feedback. Fellow authors who took the time to answer my many silly questions. My family for supporting me while I decided to pursue writing and publishing my first book.

About The Author

Frankie Page

Frankie Page, Minnesota based new romance writer, Frankie Page. Has been writing and dreaming up stories for as long as she can remember. For the longest time her primary outlet for her stories was screenplay writing and theater. Now, she enjoys writing and reading a vast variety of romance genre. Anything from small town steamy romances, to the dark and depraved — she loves it all. When she isn't plugging away at her computer, Frankie enjoys lounging around her house watching horror movies with her alpha-hole husband, mini-me, and three cats (yes three).

Follow Frankie

Facebook Page:
https://www.facebook.com/FrankiePageAuthor
Let's be Facebook friends:
https://www.facebook.com/authorfrankiepage
Join Frankie's reader group:
https://www.facebook.com/groups/frankiesredhot
Follow Frankie on Instagram:
https://www.instagram.com/frankiepageauthor/
Follow Frankie on Goodreads:
https://www.goodreads.com/author/show/20819203.Frankie_Page

Frankie Page Book List

The Moore Family:
Forever Moore (Tilly and Jax)
TBD Robbie Moore... *Coming Soon 2021*

Vengeance Demon Trilogy
Road to Retribution... *Coming soon 2021*